HADDON TOWNSHIP

m Thu
Thurlo, David, author.
Grave consequences

Grave
Consequences

ALSO BY DAVID AND AIMÉE THURLO

THE CHARLIE HENRY MYSTERIES

The Pawnbroker

THE ELLA CLAH MYSTERIES

THE SISTER AGATHA MYSTERIES

Grave
Consequences

DAVID AND AIMÉE THURLO

MINOTAUR BOOKS

NEW YORK

GRAVE CONSEQUENCES. Copyright © 2015 by David and Aimée Thurlo. All rights reserved. Printed in the United States of America. For information, address St. Martin's Press, 175 Fifth Avenue, New York, N.Y. 10010.

www.minotaurbooks.com

Designed by Omar Chapa

Library of Congress Cataloging-in-Publication Data

Thurlo, David.
    Grave consequences: a Charlie Henry mystery / David and
Aimée Thurlo. — 1st ed.
        p. cm.
    ISBN 978-1-250-02900-3 (hardcover)
    ISBN 978-1-250-02901-0 (e-book)
        I. Thurlo, Aimée.   II. Title.
    PS3570.H825G73 2015
    813'.54—dc23

                                          2014040121

Minotaur books may be purchased for educational, business, or promotional use. For information on bulk purchases, please contact the Macmillan Corporate and Premium Sales Department at 1-800-221-7945, extension 5442, or write to specialmarkets@macmillan.com.

First Edition: April 2015

10 9 8 7 6 5 4 3 2 1

For Aimée, my wife, best friend, and writing partner.
You are with me every hour of every day.

Acknowledgments

I greatly appreciate the expertise, support, and encouragement that our sources, readers, friends, and family have given us over the years. Because of you, our stories will continue.

Grave
Consequences

Chapter One

"Remember the drill, Jake. If anyone ever pulls a gun on you, don't make waves. Just avoid eye contact and hand him what's in the register," Charlie reminded, keeping his voice low.

"And if you or Mr. Sweeney are around I have the option to hit the floor, grab the shotgun, and start yelling," Jake added, his voice a low rumble. There was a retired couple searching for a replacement VCR one aisle over in the pawnshop, and neither he nor Charlie wanted to alarm anyone unnecessarily.

Nothing seemed to faze Jake Salazar, a still tough sixty-five-year-old ex-wrestler with cauliflower ears and a crooked nose. Jake was their most valuable employee and knew more about the business than Charlie or Gordon combined.

"One more thing, boss. I'm always willing to hand over the cash as long as it doesn't come out of my paycheck," Jake added, winking as he looked around the shop, noting that the couple had made their selection and were walking toward the front counter where he and Charlie were standing.

"I've got this transaction, if you want to check back with Ruth and Gordon. In a half hour, we'll be locking up for the day," Jake said, looking past his boss to address the customers. "Did you find what you were looking for, Mr. and Mrs. Goldman?"

Charlie nodded at the couple as Mr. Goldman placed the device on the counter. They were regulars and Jake would have them served and out the door within a few minutes. Charlie excused himself and headed toward the back.

A quick glance at the green light of the surveillance camera across the room came automatically by now, and the feel of the Beretta 92 at his waist beneath his jacket as natural, he supposed, as a person toward their glasses. All those years in the Army working Special Ops now made him feel naked without a firearm within reach.

At the back end of the pawnshop was their office, a short hallway, the alley door, and the entrance to their secure storeroom, which held the pawn—the jewelry, guns, and mostly electronics that provided the collateral for their loans. As Charlie approached the office, Gordon looked up from the desk through the Plexiglas window and stood.

"Really think the punk hoping to retrieve that squash blossom necklace might come back and get ugly? Uglier?" Gordon asked as Charlie came up to the doorway.

Charlie looked down at his old army buddy, who stood five foot five in boots, and shrugged. "He'll need to bring some backup or be packing. I outweigh him by fifty, at least. But my gut says we haven't heard the last of him. The kid gave me that 'hey, we're both Navajos' crap first, then tried to get into my face after I turned down the three hundred cash. Hell, the loan was only for fifty."

"A two-fifty profit would have been nice, but no claim ticket, no turquoise and silver," Gordon replied. "You said it was a young Navajo woman who brought it in, right? Besides, we have to hold on to the piece until APD runs it against their hot sheet," Gordon added. "Someone should have called back by now, I'd think."

They both turned as the sweet scent of lavender swept across the hallway. It was Ruth, their other employee, who, like Jake, had a previous history with the shop. Ruth was either very attractive or extremely charismatic, Charlie could never decide which. His jaw had fallen open and his heart had almost stopped the first time he'd met Ruth. Before that moment, he'd always thought of himself as the person in control.

"Jake was the one who locked away that squash blossom," Ruth explained in her soft, pleasant tone. "I got a good look at it and recognized the silversmith's mark. Unless it's a remarkable forgery, that piece was made by Cordell Buck, the prominent Navajo artist from your hometown of Shiprock, Charlie. Buck was killed last month and now that necklace is probably worth three times as much," Ruth emphasized.

Gordon looked over at Charlie. "Interesting. Suppose there's a story attached to that particular necklace?"

Charlie shrugged. "Could be why the guy wanted it so badly. But until we know, everyone needs to stay alert. And Ruth, if anyone comes into the shop looking for trouble, duck into the storeroom, lock the door, hit the floor, and call APD."

Gordon looked over at the monitor on the office wall, then reached out and picked up his handgun from the desk. "Looks like we've got company coming up the sidewalk."

Charlie recognized the young Navajo troublemaker from earlier. "He's brought two of his pals with him, partner," he observed, "both wearing gloves and stocking caps with that pull-down ski-mask look. One is wearing a long Windbreaker, but I think I caught a glimpse of an assault-style rifle beneath it." He glanced over at Ruth. "Lock yourself in and call APD."

"I will. You two be careful," she whispered, reaching out and touching Charlie's arm briefly.

Charlie nodded, following Gordon out into the display area.

"Bad company coming, Jake," Gordon said, taking a flanking position across the room from the counter in the front corner, behind a heavy oak display case. His position would allow him to cover the entrance in such a way that no one coming inside could use the door as a shield.

"I always liked that song," Jake responded, then nodded as he glanced down below the counter, which stood out from the wall to Charlie's left. On either side of the cash register, which was centered along that wall, was a row of glass display shelves that paralleled the rest of the room's shelves. Charlie knew the counter below the cash register held five filled sandbags, emergency holdovers from days of monsoon rains when it was necessary to prevent seepage entering beneath the front door from sudden downpours. Today, however, they might just stop a bullet. Atop the sandbags and near Jake's hands was a short-barreled semiauto shotgun for a different kind of storm. Charlie had left the choice of using it up to his employees.

"Nobody inside but us," Jake added, checking the security mirrors.

"Good to know," Charlie responded from his current position at the end of the first row of shelves. That section blocked him from view by anyone entering the shop, but one step forward would give him a clear line of sight toward the entrance twenty feet away. The shelves of stacked merchandise offered him cover and some protection as well. It was also one of the few nearly blind spots in the mirror coverage.

The front door itself was concrete-laden steel with a small window, and when it opened a bell sounded. The first person to enter was the same young Navajo man who'd come by a few hours ago. He was about five nine, shorter than Charlie by five-plus inches, and barely twenty-one years old. This time he was wearing thin leather gloves, dark glasses, and a black baseball cap low over his face.

The two thugs following him in had pulled down their ski masks at the door, covering every feature except their eyes and mouths. Charlie leaned out, his Beretta already up, safety off, and placed his sights on the dude pulling out the AR-15 clone rifle.

Jake ducked, and Gordon yelled, "Police! Put down your weapons and raise your hands!"

One of the guys in the caps jumped half out of his skin, but the warning didn't seem to make any impression on the guy with the heavy firepower. He whirled around to his left, bringing up his weapon, and was already squeezing the trigger when his head exploded from two intersecting 9 mm hollow points striking his skull at virtually the same second.

Gordon ducked back as the errant .223 rounds dug into the floor and lower shelves close to where he'd been, but Charlie barely noticed, stepping back behind the row as pistol rounds from the other two punks flew past him.

"Get that big mother," one of them yelled. Charlie took a quick look, but was already back when one of the shooters snapped off three quick rounds.

Charlie lunged out into the aisle in a crouch, relying on his straight out-of-the-manual point-shoot training and firing twice at one of the moving figures. He heard a grunt. "I'm hit!" the guy yelled, then slipped out of view at the end of the aisle.

Charlie stepped back and jumped to his feet, spotting Gordon, who'd circled toward the rear and was now two rows closer to the center of the room, beside the fishing gear. Charlie gave him a nod toward the front, signaling that he'd cover Gordo's advance.

Suddenly a spray of bullets ricocheted around the shop and they were forced to flatten. One of the remaining shooters had grabbed the fallen semiauto rifle.

The shots stopped for a second and Charlie heard the bell of the front door. Their attackers were making a run for it.

"Cover me!" Charlie shouted, leaning out to take a look. The door was half closed already. He advanced down the aisle toward the door, hugging the shelves in case it was a trap.

As he reached the door, Jake popped up over the counter, leading with the shotgun barrel, and looked toward the entrance. "They took off. The one on the floor isn't moving."

Gordon came up the aisle to the front, stepping around the body and spreading pool of blood, then slipped on a shell casing and nearly fell. "Damn. It's a mess up here," he said. "Let's get the other bastards," he added, reaching for the door handle.

Gordon pushed it open and poked his head out. "They grabbed a woman hostage," he said. "Jake, let APD know."

Charlie joined him at the door. "Careful, pal. Let's not get anyone shot who doesn't deserve it."

They stepped out onto the sidewalk. A few feet away lay a torn grocery bag, a squashed loaf of bread, fresh peaches, and various vegetables strewn along the curb. A hundred feet down the sidewalk a slender Asian woman was screaming, trying to pull away from the man with the ball cap. He was holding her with one hand while trying to aim his pistol with the other. Several vehicles were parked along the curb, but the men with the hostage didn't attempt to move toward any of them.

"Gun!" Charlie shouted, spotting the second shooter as the man raised the rifle to his shoulder. The man cursed, manipulated the charging handle, then dropped the weapon to the sidewalk and grabbed a handgun from his belt. Re-armed, he hurried after the other, who was still struggling with the woman.

"He's jammed or out of ammo. I'll hug the wall, you get an angle on them," Charlie said, his voice low.

Gordon had anticipated the tactic and was already moving out onto the street. He advanced toward the fleeing shooters, using the parked vehicles along the curb to screen his moves.

"Give it up!" Charlie yelled, jogging toward the men. He passed Frank and Linda's grocery store and glanced inside, hoping nobody would come out for a look.

He was ready to dodge if either shooter raised their weapons. The guy wearing the cap was still struggling to hold on to the hostage and hadn't tried to fire. The other punk was bleeding, judging from the trail of blood that had pooled beside the abandoned rifle, a Bushmaster carbine with a thirty-round magazine.

"Shoot them," the man yelled. His wounded partner raised his pistol and fired at Charlie. He missed, exploding a basket of apples on the produce display beneath the store awning instead.

Gordon fired into the sidewalk in front of the man and the guy shifted his aim, choosing to shoot at Gordon next. Gordon ducked down and the shooter's bullet struck the windshield of the parked car behind him.

Suddenly the woman broke free and fell to the sidewalk in front of the laundry. The two shooters, now out in the open and vulnerable, ran inside the cleaners.

"Circle and cover the back!" Charlie yelled, sprinting for the entrance. Gordon raced down the street, waving at an approaching pickup to ward it away.

Charlie rushed the door, knowing every second counted if the shooters were looking for more hostages. He burst in, noticed two shocked-looking Hispanic women beside a dryer and big laundry basket, then spotted a set of slacks and black loafers disappearing up the stairs.

"Two guys with guns, Charlie!" Melissa, the sixtyish ex-hippie yelled, poking her head up from behind a long counter containing piles of sorted clothes and linens.

"What's up there?" he yelled back, heading for the stairs.

"Storage. Boxes, unclaimed laundry in bags."

"Any windows?"

"Yeah," Melissa replied. "And a balcony with a fire escape."

"Mel, get everyone out and run for the grocery in case they decide to come back down," Charlie yelled, taking a position to cover the stairs.

Just then, he heard shots from somewhere outside.

"Guess not," he muttered, running up the stairs with his pistol in the lead, aware he was stepping on drops of blood.

He shoved open the door and came in low, but except for cardboard boxes and clear plastic bags of clothes and stuff, the room appeared empty. He ran to the high, open window and stepped out onto the balcony. The fire escape ladder, which was weaving slowly back and forth with a faint squeak, led down into a small alcove, then into the alley. Gordon was standing in the street, cursing as he watched a dark blue van race through the next intersection, then disappear around the corner.

"That them?" he yelled.

"Yeah, the bastards were parked in the alley."

"Anyone else hit? You?"

"No, but one of those dudes will be needing a medic," Gordon added.

"Then it's out of our hands now. Check on the hostage, okay?" Charlie added, then stepped back to avoid contact with the smeared blood on the balcony railing. There wouldn't be any fingerprints from the guy he'd shot, but at least his DNA was everywhere.

"Right. I'll meet you on the sidewalk," Gordon yelled back, then turned and walked up the street toward the corner.

Chapter Two

The Albuquerque Police Department had two police cruisers parked at the curb when Charlie and Gordon approached FOB Pawn, their own business for the past year now.

Except for APD Sergeant Nancy Medina, a good friend and the partner of Charlie's old high school classmate, Gina Sinclair, there hadn't been any uniforms in the shop recently other than a few army jackets and trousers hung on the clothes racks in the miscellaneous merchandise. Now, months after a previous incident, the police had reason to come calling again.

"Is that Detective DuPree talking to Jake and Ruth?" Gordon asked as they advanced up the sidewalk. He'd picked up the discarded .223 rifle along the way and was carrying it by the trigger guard.

"Think so. I recognize that dopey expression all the way from here," Charlie said, also noting that the APD detective was wearing the same tired-looking sports jacket as before, but had shed a few pounds around the gut.

"At least he knows us, kinda. Is that a good or bad thing?"

"Considering our history with him and the dead guy inside, I'm not going to make the call right now," Charlie said, his eyes shifting to the two APD officers in blue uniforms flanking DuPree. They'd already noted the Bushmaster rifle and semiautos at his and Gordon's waists, and were probably on edge, especially if they'd had a look inside. He raised his empty hands to chest height, indicating he was no threat.

"What happened to the other two perps, Henry?" DuPree asked.

"One of them took a hit, but they both got away. Our bad," Charlie responded. "At least they no longer have a hostage."

"Yeah, I heard about that from Dispatch. Is the lady okay?"

"Seemed that way," Gordon added. "You'll have to ask the officers down at the laundry," he said, nodding in that direction. "They pulled up just after we left."

"Any details on the perp's vehicle?"

Gordon nodded. "Dark blue Chevy van, not sure of the model, but the paint was faded and it had one of those chrome ladders in the back."

"Get the . . . ?"

"Tag number. Yeah, New Mexico plates, yellow, XLF-499. Or maybe XLP," Gordon added.

"Got that?" DuPree said to the uniformed officer beside him.

"Yessir," Officer Blaine, according to his name tag, responded, then stepped away and spoke into his handheld.

"What's with the rifle? That yours?" DuPree asked Gordon, looking at the civilian assault-style weapon.

"Nope. Abandoned by the perps after it jammed near the mom-and-pop grocery. We didn't think it should be left on the sidewalk where anyone could just pick it up." Gordon eased it down onto the sidewalk. "I marked an X on the sidewalk with a Sharpie where it was dropped."

DuPree looked over at Officer Blaine, who'd just finished putting on latex gloves. Blaine nodded and took the rifle.

"Did any of the assailants here gain access to your office or the storeroom?" DuPree asked, familiar with the layout. He looked from Jake to Ruth, who was staring at her hands, then turned to Charlie.

"Not even close, Detective. You want to go into our office for the interviews?" Charlie guessed.

DuPree nodded. "But let's all enter through the back." He turned to the other officers. "Block off the sidewalk from here to there," he said, pointing, "keep civilians from picking up shell casings as souvenirs, and don't step in the blood trail," he added. "And warn the crime team to watch their step before they enter."

A few minutes later, Detective DuPree gestured to Ruth and Jake, who were standing in the doorway of the secure storeroom. "I'll interview each of you, but individually, so please don't talk back and forth about this until I'm done. I need your personal responses, not something colored by conversation. I'll start with Charlie. You three"—he gestured from Jake and Ruth to Gordon—"wait in the storeroom until it's your turn.

"Let's go, Charlie." DuPree nodded toward the office door.

Charlie led the way in, DuPree closing the door behind them. Charlie reached for his coffee mug, an almost automatic response whenever he entered the work space.

"Pour me a cup too, if you don't mind," DuPree said, grabbing a foam cup from a small stack on the windowsill and handing it to Charlie before sitting down on Gordon's desk chair.

Charlie poured the coffee, taking his time to avoid spilling the hot brew. His hand was shaking. Grinning weakly, he handed the detective the coffee before taking his own seat at the other desk.

"Good to see that you're bothered by all this," DuPree said, taking a sip.

"Why is that?" Charlie asked, looking down at his hand, consciously trying to steady the mug, and finally succeeding.

"To me, that shake in your hand suggests acts of defense, not aggression, which may help toward clearing you from possible criminal charges. Not that I expect any. But just in case I'm wrong, have you ever had any PTSD symptoms that generate anger or hostility or interfere with your ability to deal with people, or yourself?"

"I've gone through some guilt and anxiety in the past, more so in the first year stateside, but never any unjustified anger or aggression. I'm not depressed, and I pretty much get along with my friends and family. Lately, it's just a bad dream once in a while. I'm good." Charlie shrugged.

"Okay, so now I'm going to record your interview." DuPree reached into his pocket and brought out a digital recorder the size of a pack of cigarettes. "First interview with Charles Henry, owner of the FOB Pawn shop," the detective announced, then gave the date and time. "Start from the beginning, Charlie."

Charlie nodded. "Yesterday, a Navajo woman in her mid-twenties came in and pawned an expensive squash blossom necklace. I handled the transaction and obtained a copy of the woman's driver's license. After the customer left I took a photo of the necklace and faxed a copy to the APD stolen property division, then put the paperwork on file. It's standard practice here. Then Jake, one of my employees, locked away the necklace."

"I'll need a copy of those records, and her name. Go on."

"This morning, a Navajo man in his late teens or early twenties came in and asked for the necklace, offering to pay interest and whatever Lola—the woman—owed," Charlie continued. "The guy said Lola was his girlfriend and she needed the necklace back, but couldn't come in herself. He didn't have the claim ticket so I told him I couldn't hand it over. That's our policy."

DuPree nodded. "Then what?"

"He got pissed, backed down when I gave him the look, then took off."

"What happened this afternoon?"

"The same man came back with two armed men about his age. They were wearing ski masks and packing handguns and that Bushmaster. We saw what was coming via the outside camera. By then, Gordon and I were armed."

"They walked into an ambush?"

"It didn't have to turn out that way. When the man with the rifle brought it out, his finger on the trigger, Gordon yelled for them to put down their weapons. That's when the guy started shooting. We immediately returned fire and the rifleman went down. Shots were exchanged and I hit one of the other shooters. One of them picked up the rifle and pinned us down long enough for them to make it back outside. They fled down the sidewalk toward the grocery, grabbing a woman hostage who just happened to be in their path. We followed. The woman managed to break free and the two fled into the laundry at the end of the street. I pursued and Gordon covered the outside, but they managed to get away."

"Okay, now that I have the framework, let's get to the details," DuPree said, leaning back in his chair.

DuPree was a competent detective, and over an hour had passed since Charlie had been interviewed the first time. Through the clear partition of the office, Charlie could see the crime scene people and the medical investigator going through their routine. Ruth and Jake had already been allowed to leave for the day, and Gordon was in the storage room, nearby but out of the way.

"So, Charlie, now that I've got a clear view from everyone regarding the sequence of events after the three men entered the shop, tell me again about their first visit. The Navajo guy, the one you saw face-to-face, was alone, right?" DuPree reminded.

"At least he came into the shop alone. We never checked back at the outside camera feed, though you'll want to verify that when you survey the surveillance coverage. I was working the front counter alone when he stepped inside, looked around for a moment, then came over. He gave me a name, Lola Tso, and said the young lady was his girlfriend. Said she'd pawned a turquoise squash blossom yesterday and that she'd asked him to come over, pay the loan fee and interest, and get the necklace back."

"Then what happened?"

Charlie was tired now, the adrenaline had faded after the shooting and chase, but he wanted to be clear and accurate, so he concentrated on every detail.

"Like I said before, I asked him for the claim ticket, stating that normally we only settled pawn agreements with the original client. However, if he had the legitimate claim ticket and some form of acceptable identification, I could legally complete the transaction."

"But he didn't have the ticket?"

"No, he said she'd misplaced it. He insisted that his girlfriend had to have it back because it was a family heirloom and she'd catch hell if her mother found out she'd pawned it," Charlie explained.

"Then what?"

"When I refused to hand it over he got pissed. After a moment he calmed down and suggested that because he and I were both Navajos, we understood about family and clans and that things like the squash blossom had special meaning to us—things Anglos didn't understand."

"But no claim check, no squash blossom necklace? That's what you told him."

"Yeah, but then I explained that if he brought in his girlfriend, and she was the same person who pawned the piece, I could deal with her. My hands were tied, I had my business reputation at stake. It's important to honor the pawn agreement with the original client. Besides, according to Jake and Ruth, the squash blossom was the work of one of the most famous Navajo silversmiths, a guy named Cordell Buck. He was killed outside a tribal casino just last month. The necklace has increased in value now."

DuPree nodded. "Your people verified that in their statements. Tell me again how the alleged boyfriend reacted."

"For a second I think he considered taking a swing at me. Then he turned around and cussed his way out the door."

"According to the others, you later warned them that the guy would probably be back, either with the girl or looking for a fight. That's the way it went down?" DuPree asked.

"Yeah, pretty much. I told Ruth that she could go home early today, but she said this was her job and she'd stand with us," Charlie said.

"Yeah, that woman's got a lot of character—and brave as hell after all she's gone through," DuPree added.

Charlie nodded. Everyone on the staff, and especially Detective DuPree, knew about Ruth's past, and respected her for what she'd accomplished. He was also one of the few who knew who she really was, and the secrets she was still keeping.

"I asked the same question to everyone, so now I'm asking you. You've never had any dealings with the deceased shooter, Mario Savaadra?"

"No," Charlie replied. He didn't enjoy hearing the name of the man he and Gordon had killed inside the shop. He was no traditionalist, but there was a Navajo taboo that cautioned against naming the dead. During his military service he'd seen way too many bodies and he lived with that every day and night. But today it had again become all too personal.

"Well, at least everyone on the staff is in agreement there. Jake ran through your computer records and we didn't get any hits on the deceased there either," DuPree admitted.

"The copies of the surveillance feed given to the crime scene unit go back six months. If your people find any faces that match that of the dead man, so be it, but we never recall doing business with him, at least since Gordon and I bought the place."

"Your staff has a good memory for faces, so I'm not going in that direction, at least not yet."

"Then are we about done here?" Charlie asked, seeing DuPree closing up his notebook.

"I'm done," the detective said, standing and looking out through the Plexiglas office window at the three techs in white lab coats still in the shop. "And it looks like they're stowing away their gear. But before you start cleaning up tonight, Charlie, you'll need to take a lot of photos of the damage," he said, looking over at the splintered wood frame where a bullet had passed through the office. "It doesn't look like this room suffered any damage beyond the bullet strikes. They missed your electronics and the Plexiglas partitions, too. I could use your luck. How do you do it?"

Charlie recalled that old line about "luck favoring the prepared mind." *If he and Gordon were so damned lucky, how come people had been shooting at them for the last ten years? When was it ever going to stop?*

"Just clean living, Detective DuPree," Charlie said, standing and reaching over for his camera. He always took photos of expensive or interesting looking pawn, so he kept it handy, but his insurance agent would need the details. The next few hours he and Gordon were going to be busy.

"Also, you and Sweeney can expect a visit from the D.A.'s office with more questions about today, especially after your past history with the department. I'm betting you'll both be cleared on the shooting, especially once their people view the video, but they may have some questions about your pursuit of the shooters and the hostage situation. On your side, however, is the fact that you rescued Mrs. Tamura and she was unharmed. With your military records and the favorable outcomes of the incidents last year, I doubt you'll have any trouble."

Charlie's phone vibrated just then, and he pulled it out of his pocket to look at the display. "How the hell did he find out about this so soon?" Charlie muttered, reading the text message.

DuPree, at the door, turned, the question on his lips.

"It's my brother, Alfred, a tribal cop. He's on his way here now," Charlie pointed out. "Al says *he's* on the case."

"Oh, shit. There's *two* of you?" DuPree responded. Then he looked down at Charlie's phone. "What the hell? This is *my* case."

Charlie's brother, Al, an officer in the tribal police for nearly a decade, appeared at the back door of the pawnshop a half hour later. DuPree had left, headed downtown to raise hell with his captain.

"What's with the retired gangbanger look, Al?" Charlie asked, barely recognizing his shaven-headed older brother. Alfred was clad in a baggy, long-sleeved T-shirt with some indiscernible words scrawled across the chest. His pants were dark brown, baggy as well, and his shoes were almost normal—for a working man in the 1950s.

"Like your boots, Al. Get them at the thrift store?"

"Yeah. Engineer boots are hard to find these days. I'm working to fit in with a rougher crowd, which is why I had to approach from the alley, Chuckie."

Charlie resisted the urge to react to his brother's favorite means of antagonism. They'd teased each other with nicknames all the way through high school. "Then don't be standing around outside. Come on in, bro."

"Hey, Gordon," Al said, stepping inside and reaching out his hand to shake, something traditional Navajos still did only reluctantly. Al, like Charlie, was anything but traditional. Gordon had met Charlie's brother a few years ago.

"Good to see you again, Al," Gordon said, a smile on his face. "Shiny skull, huh? You working undercover?"

Al closed the door behind him, then ran his big hand across his bald head. "Yeah. After I heard what happened here today, I thought there might be a connection with my own investigation."

"The Cordell Buck murder?" Charlie asked, waving his brother toward their small office. "The APD detective assigned to today's incident was concerned about jurisdictional issues."

"Yeah, there are several agencies involved in all this. When the silversmith's name came up as the maker of the jewelry connected to this crime, I caught wind of it," Al explained.

"So the necklace was taken when Buck was killed over by the tribal casino?" Gordon asked, taking a seat in one of the four chairs.

"No, and here's where it gets creepy. When I got a look at the photo of the necklace you'd sent to APD on a stolen property query, I realized it matched another image I'd seen from the dead man's own records. Mind if I have a look at the jewelry?" Al asked.

Charlie nodded to Gordon, who reached for a big manila envelope atop the in-basket of the double desk. "Detective DuPree also took a look, considering it was what the wannabe robbers had come for."

Al opened the envelope, then brought out the airtight plastic zip-lock bag that contained the turquoise and silver necklace. It was a classic Southwest design—with Cordell's custom look and personal mark stamped into the silver. Most silver jewelry of this type was kept in air- and moisture-sealed containers to reduce oxidation, often with a packet of silica gel.

He looked at it closely, not opening the bag, then brought a photo out of his shirt pocket and checked it as well. "This is the one. The spider matrix of the turquoise is a perfect match on every stone."

"So is this squash blossom creepy 'cause it belonged to a guy who's dead now?" Gordon asked.

Al shook his head. "No, and this is the detail that never made the news. This particular piece of jewelry was one of the dead man's favorite works. He didn't have it with him when he was killed— he had it on him when he was buried."

Charlie looked over at Gordon, who whistled softly. "We're talking grave robbing here, brother?"

Al nodded. "About the worst thing a Navajo can do," he answered softly.

•   •   •

It was close to ten at night when the three of them arrived at the remote graveyard on a section of the Eastern Navajo Nation twenty miles west of Albuquerque and south of the To'hajiilee Chapter House.

Charlie was driving his dark-purple Charger, his most valued possession, while Gordon and Al chatted mostly about his and Charlie's years growing up in Shiprock. As usual, most of the stories were about when Al had bested Charlie at baseball, basketball, or football. The fact that Al was bigger, stronger, and older never seemed to come up, Charlie observed, but he joined in with the laughter.

As he drove, Charlie stayed out of the conversation, recalling his and Al's more recent history. The last time he and Al had been together for more than an hour they'd almost come to blows. Al had just been demoted from sergeant down to patrol officer. He'd been suspended for drinking and was having family problems. Al's wife, Nedra, had been forced to go back to work as an office temp and Al was becoming borderline abusive. Even their two boys were avoiding him at home.

Charlie had tried to talk some sense into Al, but his efforts had backfired. Charlie walked away after that and they'd rarely spoken since. Now Al was acting like nothing had ever happened, and Charlie wondered if his brother was finally coming out of his downward slide.

Suddenly Gordon said something that brought Charlie back into the present.

"So, are we checking for evidence that this grave robbing was the work of thieves, not skin . . . you-know-whats?" Gordon said, avoiding the mention of "skinwalkers," Navajo witches.

He'd learned a lot from Charlie over the years about things like this. Mentioning skinwalkers—real people who were either evil or crazy—was said to attract them. Having grown up in a poor neighborhood in Denver, Gordon was highly respectful around other cultures—that was, unless they disrespected him. In those situations, he showed no mercy whatsoever.

"From what I've gathered, gossip mostly, the locals out here think the dead silversmith was robbed by the evil ones," Al said softly. "Personal items belonging to the dead are valuable to the Navajo witches. But I want to take a look myself. I checked with a *hataalii*, a medicine man, and he says it was more likely a greedy Anglo. But he wouldn't say why. It turns out that at least one of the men who came looking for that squash blossom at your shop is linked to a group of carjackers. Some smart-ass cop calls them the Alone Arrangers. I had to look for myself."

"Wait until the TV stations hear that name."

Al continued. "Which is why officers actually involved in the investigation have renamed them the Night Crew. They've been carjacking individuals mostly in the Four Corners area, targeting people caught out alone after dark driving newer model SUVs and such. They rough up and rob their victims, then leave them along the highway. I've been trying to worm my way into that gang ever since I was assigned to track down Buck's killer. The man who died in your shop today—I had some beers with him two days ago."

"Think the guy we shot was the one who actually robbed and

killed the silversmith?" Charlie asked as they climbed out of the Charger.

"Or he knew who did. Before the man buried here was killed, the Night Crew just carried out strong-arm robberies and carjackings, never inflicting serious injuries on their victims. But after they murdered a prominent silversmith, they got everyone's attention, including the tribal president. I'm now working with APD, two county sheriff's departments, and my own tribal unit on this investigation. My focus is on the killer, but putting a stop to the carjackings would be a real bonus. I can't wait to bring these animals in," Al added.

They walked over to the run-down fence that bordered the graveyard and took a look around. The cemetery wasn't much— basically desert, wild grasses, tumbleweeds, sagebrush, sand, and a dozen or more aluminum markers enclosing paper notices under glass with the names of the deceased. A few also had wooden crosses—these were Navajo Christians—but mostly the place looked abandoned.

"Think we can use a flashlight," Gordon suggested, bringing out a small LED light that emitted a bright, narrow beam.

"Don't wave it around too much, Gordon," Al warned. "We're not supposed to be here, I'm not supposed to be a cop, and graveyards make most Navajos nervous."

"Especially those where bodies have been dug up. I see some mounded dirt to our left, up the fence line. Didn't the smith get reburied?" Charlie asked.

"Don't really know," Al replied. "Nobody really wanted to talk to the tribal officers about it and I'm not in a position to go asking. Not if I want to remain undercover. Let's look around. There's an opening in the fence just to your right."

"Besides graves, anything I should be on the lookout for?" Gordon asked. "If this wasn't an ordinary crime, I mean?"

Charlie knew what he meant. "Markings on the ground with charcoal, mutilated animals, stuff like that."

"Twisted, perverted stuff," Al added. "Who knows?"

A minute later they approached the mounded dirt. "The grave is still open," Gordon whispered, bringing out his flashlight. "Oh shit."

Charlie looked down. "I thought you said they just robbed the grave. This guy was fried to a crisp."

The three of them stood beside the hole in the ground, staring down at the burned remains of a wooden casket. The smell was pungent and all too familiar to Charlie.

"Put your hands in the air!" a woman ordered from somewhere behind them. "I'm a police officer."

Chapter Three

"*Yáátééh*, Officer," Charlie greeted, putting his hands in the air, as did Al and Gordon. "We're just looking around. We heard about the grave robbing of the silversmith. And we're not armed except for a couple of pocketknives," he added, hoping that Al wasn't strapped while working undercover.

Remaining as still as possible, he slowly turned his head and noted the outline of a slender woman wearing a tan tribal department uniform. She'd assumed an aggressive stance. One hand held a flashlight, the other a handgun, and both were aimed in their direction. The light shifted back and forth, but the glare was enough to keep him from making out any other details, like her face. She sounded young.

"Two of you look Navajo, but this is Navajo tribal land and I need to see some ID. You, the one who's been doing the talking. You're first." She aimed the beam directly into Charlie's face, then moved it down his body, probably checking for weapons. "Take out your wallet, slowly, with your left hand, and toss it over to me," the officer ordered.

"Of course, Officer." Charlie followed her instructions slowly and carefully, not taking his eyes off her. He'd seen people shot, justly or unjustly, when the soldier with the weapon was nervous or had misinterpreted a gesture.

"Okay, hands back up until I say you can lower them again." She crouched down carefully, feeling for the wallet with her flashlight hand without taking her eyes off him. "Thank you, Mr. Henry," she added a few seconds later, taking a look at his ID.

"You're welcome, ma'am."

"You own a business in Albuquerque?"

"Yes, FOB Pawn, like it says on the business card."

"You also have a concealed carry permit. Where's the weapon?"

"Under the driver's seat of my vehicle over there," Charlie confirmed.

"You're carrying an old military ID card. You related to that Diné soldier they held a parade for a couple of years ago in Shiprock? The army war hero?" the officer added, her tone still unchanged.

"I don't know about the hero part, but I'm the guy," Charlie admitted. "The parade was a bit embarrassing, actually."

"You deserved to be thanked for your service, soldier. Is there any reason why I can't trust your companions, Sergeant Henry?"

"No, ma'am."

"Okay, then. You three can put down your hands and turn around. I'm Officer Nakai with the tribal police. I hope you understand my caution. I've been keeping an eye on this cemetery since the incident, hoping those bastards will return."

The woman officer was as short as Gordon and probably weighed less than one twenty-five. She had shiny, long black hair in a ponytail extending from her cap. Officer Nakai looked nineteen, but had to be at least twenty-one, Charlie guessed. She was also working alone and was probably miles from backup.

"Do you think this grave robbing was more than just theft?" Al asked. "Just curious."

"If it hadn't been for the desecration of the body, I would have said it was just vandalism and theft," Officer Nakai replied.

"What did they use to start the fire?" Gordon asked.

"I was the first officer on the scene. I found an empty gas can beside the remains," the officer replied. "But I wouldn't carry stories if I were you, it'll just confuse the investigation. There are several agencies working to catch the people who killed the silversmith. That's what's important."

"I hope they get their man," Al said. "Well, guys, we'd better get going. You've still got that inventory work at the pawnshop to finish tonight, Charlie."

They walked out through the gate, followed by the officer. Charlie brought out his keys and the doors to his Charger chirped open with a double beep. As Gordon and Al climbed in, Charlie turned to the officer. "Sorry if we caused any problems, ma'am. I guess the lack of excitement in my life has made me extra curious when a well-known member of our tribe is murdered."

"My pop served in Kuwait. I've seen how war can change your perspective, Sergeant Henry. I hope you can get back to the routine of normal civilian life before too long."

"That's my plan," Charlie responded. "Stay safe, Officer Nakai."

"You stay safe too, Mr. Henry. By the way, I read the reports about the shooting at the pawnshop today. Helluva way to unwind after all that—going to check out a graveyard. Better to stay away from cemeteries, don't you think?"

Charlie shrugged. There wasn't much he could say. Nodding to the tribal officer, he climbed into the Charger and headed back for the interstate.

Several minutes went by before anyone spoke. "Thanks for protecting my cover, Charlie. Must be tough being a war hero, having to fight off all that attention from the women. Bet you've seen a lot of horizontal action since you've been home," Al suggested, wiggling his eyebrows.

Charlie kept his eyes on the road. They'd always been competitive, and Al often worked overtime trying to get him distracted or defensive, either with trash talk, or in this case sarcasm and false praise. He'd heard some of this crap the last time he'd been around Al, who, out of envy or jealousy from the attention he'd received, had begun to belittle his military service whenever they were alone. Charlie knew that his brother was falling apart on the job and had his own problems, so he'd ignored the comments. Striking out was Al's defense mechanism, an unfortunate trait for a police officer who often had to deal with people who were already upset. Because Al was trying to provoke a reaction, Charlie chose, whenever possible, to just let it slide.

Another five minutes went by in silence. "The grave robbers dug up the casket, took the necklace and whatever else they could find, then set fire to the body," Gordon said. "I thought the people we were trying to rule out usually stole the corpse, then cut it up to make ceremonial displays—or whatever they're called. Tokens of power for rituals," Gordon added, looking over at Charlie.

Charlie nodded. "From what I remember hearing while growing up, showing off mutilated bodies and stealing body parts for medicine was something these Navajo witches did to stimulate fear. Violating taboos is their thing. That the way you remember it, Al?" Charlie replied, not looking back at his brother in the backseat.

"People didn't talk much about these things, but yeah, that's what I recall. Training and experience tells me that whoever burned the body did it for other reasons—anger, hate, revenge," Al concluded.

"For major league payback, to mess them up real good. That what you're saying?" Gordon replied.

"Pretty much," Al admitted.

"Okay. So, the theory is that whoever confronted the silversmith after he left the casino planned on doing more than just robbing him, they wanted him dead. And when he was buried with his most valued possessions, they dug him up and stole the stuff," Charlie said.

"Then killed him one more time, symbolically, by setting him ablaze," Gordon concluded.

"But they didn't want to be identified, so when the necklace got into the girlfriend's hands and she decided to hock it, they had to get it back because it could tie the killers to these crimes," Al added. "Works for me."

"This Lola woman can't be that bright, guys, if she was willing to connect herself with stolen property linked to a murder," Gordon pointed out.

"Which suggests she wasn't the killer. I'm thinking she didn't know it was stolen, or at least when and how it was taken," Al replied. "Not that it's going to save her ass. The guys who got away are going to be pissed at her now. I kind of feel sorry for Lola Tso."

"Okay, but let's get back to the original crime, which doesn't make sense to me either. If these carjackers are responsible for all the prior robberies, why kill the silversmith and bring on the extra heat? Why not just rob their victim and steal his car like they usually do?" Charlie asked. "We're missing the motive. Why would they kill the guy, then rob his grave and burn up the body, what, three or four days later?"

"Maybe they hadn't planned on killing him in the first place, but when he fought back they had to take him out. The desecration and grave robbing later on, who knows? That's why I'm trying to get connected with the Night Crew," Al said. "Once we're back at the pawnshop, I'm going to go bar hopping. My contact is dead, but maybe I can meet up with some of the others."

"They'll probably be going to ground for a while, don't you think?" Gordon asked. "Besides, one of them got shot."

"APD and county are checking hospitals, ERs, and clinics. Unfortunately, there's no way of identifying the guys who got away except through their associates," Al explained. "I'll check back with the rest of the team and see what they've learned so far. You're right, Gordon. No sense in wasting my time hitting the bars tonight."

"You should arrange a meeting with Detective DuPree and get his take on this, Al. By now, he's been over the surveillance images a dozen times, and there might be enough to make an ID from when they were still outside—before they put on their masks. The detective sometimes comes across as a bully, but he's got good cop instincts, and he'll listen to other theories if they fit the facts," Charlie suggested. Now that they'd reached Albuquerque, he took the freeway exit and headed north up Second Street.

"I really want to catch these guys, bro," Al confessed. "The murder was big news on the Rez, and Window Rock would like a tribal cop to be in on the takedown. I'm the only tribal cop actually on the team in the field. Making an arrest would put me back in solid with the department."

"God's ears," Gordon said.

"Huh?" Al asked.

"From your lips to God's ears," Charlie clarified.

"Oh, yeah," Al replied. "After today, I'm going to need all the help I can get to crack this murder investigation. This carjacking crew may sit back for a while, and if things go stagnant, I could get pulled off the case and back onto patrol duty."

"You're a good cop, you'll think of something," Charlie reminded him.

"Thought you'd given up on me," Al said softly.

An awkward silence followed until Charlie's cell phone rang. "Get that for me, Gordo," Charlie asked, motioning toward the center console where he'd parked the device.

Despite the state ordinance against cell phone use while driving, Charlie would normally have taken the call, but he was still a little pumped up on adrenaline and didn't want to lose focus behind the wheel now that they were driving into the city.

"It's Gina," Gordon announced. "Putting you on speaker," he added, placing the phone back on the console beside the stick.

"Charlie, I heard you and your friends had a rough time today. Everyone okay? You okay?" came the sweet, soft voice of Gina Sinclair, Charlie's old high school girlfriend. She'd been demoted to best friend after she'd come out. Gina was now APS Sergeant Nancy Medina's life partner. She was also his and Gordon's attorney.

"What did Nancy tell you?" Charlie asked.

"That there was a robbery attempt, that one of the robbers was dead, and that you and Gordon rescued a hostage the perps had grabbed. Oh, and that one of the escapees was probably wounded. That about it?"

Charlie looked over at Gordon, who shrugged. "Yeah. Did Nancy happen to find out anything else?" Charlie asked.

"The woman who pawned the target of the robbery, Lola Tso, has a connection with Nancy," Gina replied.

"What kind of connection?" Gordon asked.

"Nancy asked me to hold off on that until she got the chance to talk face-to-face. You up for a late-night cup of coffee after she gets off duty?"

"Sure. Who needs sleep?" Charlie responded, glancing over at Gordon, who nodded. "Besides, we have some work to do at the shop."

"Shot up the place pretty bad, huh?" Gina asked.

"Nothing a mop can't handle," Gordon said.

"Gross. You'd better use Clorox and get the splatter and smell taken care of before we arrive. We'll give you a call when we're on our way. Okay?"

"Sounds good. See you then," Charlie added, nodding to Gordon, who ended the call with a touch to the screen.

"Gina? Is she the same Gina Sinclair who broke your heart by switching teams your senior year?" Al asked from the backseat. "Woman on woman. What a waste."

Gordon turned around and looked Al straight in the eye. "Charlie didn't tell me you could be a real dick. Brothers don't fight brothers, and if they did, you'd get your ass whipped. You two have a history, I get that, but next time you disrespect Gina or Nancy in front of me I'll drop you, cop or not."

Chapter Four

Al sat up straight, anger in his expression, took a deep breath, and eased back into his seat. "Okay, I may have worded that badly. It's been a long day and it's not over yet. It won't happen again, Gordon."

Gordon shrugged. "Good." He turned around and looked down the street. They were approaching FOB Pawn, and there were no cars parked along the street this time of the night. There were security lights on in the laundry, the grocery, and the shop, but everything seemed dead quiet.

Charlie turned the corner, then, halfway down the block he pulled into the alley behind FOB Pawn. Al's sporty little Honda sedan was sitting there in a slot beside the loading dock, apparently untouched.

As they climbed out of the low-slung Dodge, Al thumbed a key fob, unlocking his car door. "Charlie, will you give me a call tomorrow on this Lola Tso? I'll be checking with the team, but maybe you'll have something extra I can use."

"Sure, Al. Watch your back around these people," Charlie added.

Al nodded to Gordon, who returned the gesture, then climbed into his vehicle as Charlie unlocked the rear entrance to the pawnshop.

Gordon stepped in first, flipped on the hall light, and quickly entered the alarm code on the pad a few feet away. "It smells beyond funky. Looks like we've got a lot to do before Nancy and Gina show up."

Charlie and Gordon were rearranging the shelf displays containing the merchandise that had escaped damage, when Charlie's cell phone started ringing.

He sat down the microwave oven he was holding and reached over to read the display. "The ladies are pulling into the alley."

Gordon stepped back to look down the aisle. "Well, we're ready to open tomorrow, at least. I'll let them in."

Seconds later, Gina Sinclair, a tiny, delicately featured woman with short brown hair came into the back hall, wearing jeans and a fleece pullover. She was accompanied by Sergeant Nancy Medina, a slender, five-foot-nine blonde still in her dark blue APD uniform.

Gina rushed over and gave Charlie a bear hug, followed by a kiss on the cheek. "I'm so glad you're not hurt, Charles, and you too, Gordon. Nancy showed me the video of what happened in the shop on the way over here. It all went down so quickly."

Charlie looked over at Nancy, who gave him a sheepish expression. "DuPree e-mailed the video to me after he found out I knew Lola Tso," she said.

"That's what Gina mentioned earlier. What can you tell us about her?"

"I'll give you what I can, then you and Gordon fill me in on the details of what went down before and after the incident. Maybe you know something I can pass along to the unit working the case."

"We've got chairs in the office and instant Starbucks Italian Roast—decaf if you want," Gordon said, motioning toward the small office at the front end of the hall, past the door to the storage room. "Ladies."

Charlie and Gordon brought them up to date on the pawning of the squash blossom, the attempt to buy it back, and all the rest, including the graveyard encounter outside To'hajiilee. Nancy whistled softly, then sat back. She looked over at Gina, then shook her head slowly before taking a sip of decaf from a foam cup. "How do you guys get into shit like this, time after time?"

"I met a Navy A-4 pilot when I was working in a homeless kitchen in Denver. He'd served during Vietnam, and he'd been shot down twice by SAMs. He told me they started calling him magnet ass. Guess we're kind of like that," Gordon said.

"Yeah. Trouble just seems to find us," Charlie added.

"At least we manage to come out on top," Gordon said with a grin.

"So far," Gina replied, rolling her eyes.

"Enough about us, what about Lola Tso? There was an address on her driver's license and in our transaction records, so officers should have paid her a visit hours ago. She got that necklace from someone, maybe the silversmith's killer, and that makes her a liability," Charlie concluded.

"DuPree sent officers to that address, but she wasn't at home and they couldn't find a neighbor who admitted to knowing her or recognizing a photo. They left someone to watch the place and DuPree is trying to track down the landlord," Nancy said.

"She may have moved out months ago. People are always changing apartments without updating MVD," Gina pointed out. "And with cell phones, it's harder to find out what carrier someone has. DuPree has someone checking state databases, right?"

Nancy nodded. "Unfortunately, everything points back to that apartment. He's going to get a warrant tomorrow morning and enter the place one way or the other if she doesn't show up."

"Any chance Lola left town?" Gordon asked.

"Not by commercial carriers. DuPree is thorough," Nancy replied. "There's an ATL, attempt to locate, out on her black Ford Focus, but she could be two states away by now if she headed out of the city after pawning that necklace."

"So, Nancy. How do you know Lola?" Charlie asked, looking over to see Gina's reaction.

Gina just grinned.

"Lola and I were hookers back then."

"Whoa. I thought you were on the vice squad, not the mattress," Gordon said, trying but failing to look shocked.

"Yeah, I *posed* as a hooker, dumbass, busting the johns. Lola was the real deal, though I was never around when she was doing the nasty or getting busted. We worked the sidewalks and bars on East Central and got to know each other a little," Nancy explained. "She was eighteen then, but had already been hooking for about a year when we met."

"Was she still working when you left vice?" Charlie asked.

"No, we got to be almost friends. I managed to help her get a job at one of those call centers and she enrolled in some community college classes. Wanted to get into retail management and sell something besides her body."

"Think maybe she slipped back out onto the streets?" Gina asked.

"I hope not, but perhaps CNM has a phone number or address that'll help track her down," Nancy said.

Charlie nodded, having taken a business seminar at the College of New Mexico once he and Gordon bought the pawnshop. "Did Lola have a boyfriend back then?" Charlie asked.

"Some of the girls did, but not Lola. At least if she did, she never mentioned anyone. She usually shared more of her personal life than the others," Nancy said. "I think I would have known about it."

"DuPree should be close to getting an ID on this guy claiming to be her boyfriend. The police department has an image from our surveillance, both days, plus our own descriptions and what was recorded on the sidewalk. And 'boyfriend' wasn't the one who got shot," Charlie pointed out.

"When DuPree gets a name, he said he'd text me," Nancy replied.

"And?" Gordon asked with raised eyebrows.

"Yeah, and I'll pass that along to you two. You don't plan on getting involved in this, do you?" Nancy asked, looking from face to face.

Charlie nodded toward the front of the store. "I'd say we're already involved. Someone tried to rob and kill us, and if they're the kind of guys who take things personal—we're on their to-do-in list. We hurt them more than they hurt us."

"From what they did to the dead silversmith, if they were actually the ones who offed the guy, I'd say these boys have issues. Charlie's right," Gina added, speaking to Nancy. "Not that I want him or Gordon to put themselves in any more danger. But they need to be ready to defend themselves."

"I'm willing to help out Al, who seems to be getting his career back in order, but it looks like there are already a lot of officers on this and we're not cops. Once things are back in shape here and I know Jake and Ruth will be safe, maybe I can do more without getting in the way," Charlie said.

Gordon stood and reached for the coffeepot. "I'm not that concerned about your brother, Charlie, but I don't like being a target. I've got your back," he said.

"A word of advice, guys," Nancy said, holding her cup out for Gordon to refill. "Stay in touch with Detective DuPree. He's given you two a lot of slack, so don't go all vigilante against these . . . killers."

Neither of them said a word, but Gina sighed loudly, shaking her head. She knew they weren't going to let this go.

"So, Nancy, if we wanted to help out, where do you think we

should start? Find Lola?" Charlie asked. "That leads back to who-ever she got the necklace from—the killer or someone who dealt with him."

"Not a bad idea. You don't look and act like cops, and I cer-tainly can't approach her outright. She found out what I do for a living," Nancy replied.

"Her last known apartment is under surveillance. Any place else you recall she used to hang out?" Gordon asked.

"When she was hooking, her favorite hangout was the Fire-house Tavern on East Central. She had a pimp for a while who was part owner of the place—Mike something. You might want to try there first. Lola used to show up early, maybe five thirty, trying to catch men just off work, hoping they'd choose sex over beer. She hated working late at night, I recall. Too dangerous."

"So, if she was working the streets again, she wouldn't be look-ing to hook up this time of day," Charlie asked. "No sense in us going out tonight."

"My guess is that if she's heard the news on radio or TV, she's made the connection with FOB Pawn and is lying low—no pun intended," Nancy said, rolling her eyes.

"Sometimes, if your life gets turned around, you go back to old habits," Gordon said softly, staring across the room blankly.

Gina looked at Charlie, who shrugged. Gordon was like still waters sometimes.

"Yeah, or maybe just old neighborhoods. You might want to try tomorrow afternoon, guys, and try to catch the clientele when they've stopped off for a beer after work," Nancy added.

"Yeah, by then, we might have a name on the boyfriend," Charlie said, yawning.

Gina stood. "You guys look beat, and I've got to meet with a client in the morning, so maybe we'd better take off."

Hugs were exchanged, and a few minutes later Gordon was closing up the office while Charlie checked the locks. As he passed by the spot where he'd been standing when the shooting first started, he noticed a bullet hole in the shelf chest high. He stopped, turned around, then got back into the firing position he'd assumed and looked down. The bullet coming in his direction had passed under his arm, only a few inches from his side. That was close.

"About done up there?" Gordon called from the other end of the shop.

Charlie looked down, saw his hand was shaking, and jammed it into his pants pocket. "Almost, Gordo. Almost."

The next business day was hectic. The first people walking into the shop were local TV reporters with perfect makeup and beautiful, styled hair—and that was just the two young men from the networks. But the routine was pretty much the same for all the coverage. Once the reporters got a few sound bites from Charlie and Gordon, with references to Detective DuPree and the police department, they were allowed to film some of the bullet holes before being told to leave.

Hours went by before anyone wanting to do actual business stopped in—everyone else was just curious. Fortunately, the physical damage still visible was limited to the bullet holes. The damaged and destroyed merchandise was in the Dumpster or the store room and the blood and gore had been cleaned up.

Jake took care of the front register and Ruth handled the insurance photos and paperwork on their losses and assisted customers and clients. Whenever anyone came to her with questions about yesterday, she referred them to Charlie or Gordon, who were doing all they could to stay focused on the job.

A half hour before quitting time, six o'clock on weekdays, Jake and Ruth clocked out and left. Charlie and Gordon locked up, filled the bullet holes with wood putty, then drove toward the interior of the city, looking for Lola.

"We should have heard something by now. You think DuPree will be able to ID the alleged boyfriend?" Gordon asked, looking over at Charlie, who was behind the wheel of the Charger.

"When Nancy called she said APD officers were going through old area high school yearbooks. They tried a facial recognition program on DMV records but got so many hits it'll take awhile to run them down."

"A dark-skinned Indian or Hispanic, black-haired, black-eyed guy about five nine, medium build, short hair, and about twenty-five fits a lot of locals," Gordon added. "Not including a hoard of guys from Arizona, Texas, Colorado—and Mexico. Utah, home of the blue-eyed blonde, I'd probably put at the bottom of the list."

"Supposedly they'll be running the photo from our shop on the local news. That could also help," Charlie added.

"What's the plan tonight? Driving around looking for Lola, or tracking down Mike the pimp?" Gordon asked, placing his Beretta and holster beneath the seat. They were still illegal in bars, even with concealed carry.

"Mike sounds like our best bet. There's a chance that he knows where Lola is or was, or maybe he can connect us with a working girl who can provide us with some new information on her location," Charlie suggested.

"Either way, the pimp will expect to get paid," Gordon pointed out. "Count on having to fork over some twenties. Hate to think of giving a hooker money and not getting entertained."

"When was the last time you had to pay for sex?" Charlie knew Gordon had no problem attracting women.

"There was that night in Ramstein, 2010, around Thanksgiving, when we were on layover."

"Those girls were U.S. Air Force, not prostitutes, and we didn't pay for anything except dinner, the movie, and the hotel rooms," Charlie recalled. "That's what we call a date."

"You remember just how much we paid for dinner? I do. Over a hundred euros."

"Less than a hundred and fifty bucks at the time, and it never was about money. You and that girl wrote back and forth for months, didn't you?"

"Yeah, Molly. Too bad she got married. Okay, maybe you have a point. We split the costs tonight, though."

"Deal." Charlie chuckled.

Traffic was heavy, and they pulled into the parking lot of the East Central tavern—a former firehouse—at about six thirty. Charlie noted that half the vehicles were pickups or big SUVs, and there was one Caddy. This was a working man and lower management clientele, so they'd fit right in.

The main entrance was actually at the side, and once they were in the bar Charlie noted that the big overhead doors for the fire department engines had been walled over on the interior, replaced with a big mural of the neighborhood during the sixties, judging from the vehicles in the painting.

The tables were heavy wood and metal trim, bolted to the floor, and the padded chairs looked comfortable. At the rear of the big room, formerly the firehouse garage, was the bar. It was divided in the middle by the traditional shiny brass pole used to slide down from upstairs. It was surrounded by a railing now, probably to discourage patrons from giving it a trial run.

The opening to the floor above was still there in the ceiling, and stairs along the back wall led up to what the signs listed as a private lounge.

A pleasant-looking freckle-faced redhead dressed in blue slacks and a red blouse met them within seconds of their arrival. She led them to an empty table at the side of the room opposite the stairs. The woman smiled automatically, then took their order of draft beer, nachos, and salsa.

"Not too dark to make out faces, that's a good sign," Charlie commented, looking around but not seeing any Native Americans. "According to Nancy, Mike is supposed to be tall and slender, with yellow hair and a disarming, delicately handsome face, like an angel."

"Maybe he's up there?" Gordon pointed toward the ceiling. "With Jesus?"

"No, moron, in the private lounge." Gordon laughed for the first time in a couple of days, and Charlie joined in. Humor had kept them sane more than once during the past decade.

"Just us uglies down here," Charlie said just as the barmaid showed up with their drinks, nachos, and pungent salsa.

"Hey, I resent that," the redhead said, grinning for real as they paid for the beers. Charlie looked at her closely for the first time and saw pale, blue eyes and a broad, attractive face. Unlike some redheads, who overused the makeup to hide their freckles, she accented her complexion with bright lipstick and a hint of color in her cheeks.

"I was talking about me and my wingman, Meg," he said, glancing only briefly at the name tag on her chest.

"Just trying to liven up my day, boys," she said, winking at Gordon. "Never seen you two in here before. You from out of town?"

"More like across town. We heard about this place and wanted to check it out," Charlie answered.

"He means we're two bachelors on the prowl, Meg," Gordon said. "Would you say this is a good place for guys to meet women?"

Meg shrugged. "I've only worked here for a few months, and I usually get off at eight, but the few times I've filled in for one of the girls on the late shift I've noticed there are a few ladies who come and go on pretty much an hourly basis. You guys aren't cops, are you?"

"Naw, we're ex-military. We have a business over in the north valley, and despite what Gordon here says, we aren't really looking for anything besides conversation and a few drinks," Charlie added. "By the way, a friend of a friend recommended this place, but she gave us a wicked grin when she mentioned one of the owners. She had a thing for him," he lied.

"The guy's first name is something like Mike—supposed to be a real ladies' man," Gordon joined in.

"Mike Schultz," Meg said, a trace of a scowl on her face. "He runs the place and shares ownership with a family up in Raton who inherited half from their grandfather. The old guy was a fireman for the county for a really long time."

"So Mike must know about the girls working out of his establishment," Charlie concluded.

Meg's expression changed quickly. "You never heard anything like that from me, guys. I need the job and the pay is good. At least with Mike around, the patrons don't give the staff any shit. I worked at a downtown bar for a while and every night I got propositioned a half-dozen times. Even when wearing a wedding ring."

"Not wearing one now," Gordon pointed out.

"Don't need one here. Mike's got a couple of heavy hitters that'll throw their sorry butts out to the curb."

A cowboy at another table waved at Meg, and she looked over and smiled. "Be right there, sugar. Gotta go, guys. If you need anything, just give me a nod."

"Don't forget your tip," Gordon said, sliding over a twenty.

"Thank you, Gordon," she said, crinkling up her nose with an even bigger smile. She whirled around and hurried over to the cowboy, who was raising an empty glass.

"So Mike is either still a pimp or he's being paid to look the other way," Charlie commented, taking a swallow of his beer. He looked down at the nearly full glass and thought of Al, who'd been the drinker of the two back in high school despite their father's heavy hand.

Seeing how booze had turned his older brother into an ass had pretty much limited his own drinking, even later when Charlie enlisted. He'd been an Indian in a white world, then an American soldier in a Muslim world, and being drunk and out of control in either place was an idiotic thing to do. He'd never allowed alcohol to slow him down.

Gordon was much the same. Growing up in the inner city, he had been on the streets around drunks and derelicts and seen how they were treated. Gordon had explained that being the runt of the litter, he had enough trouble staying alive even when he was sober. Both of them were survivors, though their roots had grown in different soil.

Now they drank only to be social and to blend in, like tonight. If they needed to react quickly, alcohol wouldn't impair their skills.

"No sign of Lola. I'm thinking that if she's still hustling for Mike, she'll be sticking close for a few days. If he's got muscle here, she'll want the extra protection. Unless Mike is the real boyfriend— but that doesn't seem likely," Charlie admitted.

"Well, if you're going to talk yourself in circles, at least we arrived at the same place, Charles. If Mike knows anything about Lola, he's got to be our next contact tonight," Gordon said, sliding his half-empty beer away. "Shall we take a climb?"

"Why not?"

Chapter Five

They stood, pushed their chairs in, then walked toward the stairs against the far wall. "No security?" Gordon asked as they neared the steps.

"Probably at the top. Uninvited guests are easier to control when they have so far to fall," Charlie commented.

"Makes sense." Gordon nodded. "So I'll go first—lower center of gravity."

There was a chest-high wall instead of a railing on the outside of the stairs, which meant anyone below would hear, but not necessarily see anyone falling down the flight.

Charlie was several steps behind Gordon. When Gordon reached the top, a buzz-cut goon in a tropical guayabera and tan slacks saw the little guy. The goon yawned and strolled over. Gordon was forever underestimated, which gave him the advantage in a hand-to-hand situation.

The guy looked at Charlie coming up behind Gordon and

stopped, realizing he'd not only lost the height advantage, but the numerical one as well.

"Gentlemen," came a surprisingly soft voice, "this is a private lounge. Who is your host tonight?"

Charlie could see into the room, illuminated by recessed ceiling lights and a large-screen TV playing what looked like soft porn. Seated on comfortable looking leather-look sofas were a half-dozen or so men and women, paired up and snuggling seriously.

"At least they still have their clothes on," Gordon commented matter-of-factly, a big grin on his face. "Hi, Guido, we're here to talk to Mike about a mutual client."

Charlie, who'd been watching three people clustered together across the room, saw two of them stand up—one of them a tall blond that fit Mike Schultz's description.

"Mike, can we have a word? Up here, or maybe outside, if you prefer?" Charlie asked, loud enough to be heard above the gasps and groans coming from the video.

If it came to a fight he didn't want any hookers or horndogs injured, and by giving Mike a choice it was a concession, of sorts. It also reduced the number of potential witnesses or participants.

"Keep your voice down, please?" Guido's expression making it clear he wasn't really asking. He moved his hand to his front pants pocket, where the outline of a big folding knife bulged.

"Like anyone else up here is interested in the dialogue," Gordon muttered.

Mike was tall, lean, and clearly fit, with an overly pretty face, but he had the eyes and expression of a predator. The goon who'd accompanied him was a little shorter, about Charlie's height of six one, but outweighing him by maybe fifty pounds. His low forehead suggested the guy was all muscle and no brains, but Charlie knew that believing in stereotypes could be dangerous. The worst ass-kicking could come from the least likely direction, and, at the moment, Charlie was grateful for his own training and experience. Then there was Gordon, who was worth two superheros, maybe two and a half.

"What can I do you for, friends? If you think we might have business to discuss, the parking lot is just fine with me. More privacy," Mike offered, sounding amused.

The two goons exchanged glances, something Charlie knew Gordon had caught as well. There was going to be trouble, and Mike was going to watch. He'd probably already seen the movie.

Charlie gestured toward the stairs. "After you," he said to Mike, thinking there was no way the guy would put his back to them. He and Gordo would have to precede him.

"Fernando—" Mike glanced over at the guy who'd first greeted them—the one in the Cuban shirt. "The back lot, please. *Mátalos afuera.*"

Fernando took a step down, turned, and motioned toward them. "*Bueno.* Follow me, gentlemen."

Charlie spoke three languages, Navajo, English, and Pashto from his years in 'stan, so he couldn't understand what Mike was telling the goons. Gordon, however, despite his blue eyes and Irish blood, had grown up in a Denver neighborhood full of Latino families.

"Charles, this reminds me of our first night in Honolulu. Those three lady Marines?" Gordon added, following right behind Fernando, who'd reached the bottom of the stairs.

"Yeah, it took us an hour to get them down to the beach," Charlie replied. "Then there was that awkward moment when one of the girls realized she was the fifth wheel."

"You ever have one woman too many on a date?" Charlie turned to look at Mike's bodyguard. The Neanderthal guy packed fists the size of boxing gloves.

"One can never have too many women," the guy answered with a grin.

"Amen," Mike added, following at the rear of the column.

Charlie focused on his first move, trying not to tense up. Gordon had just reminded him of a night they'd both been set up for a beat down.

Fernando turned left instead of right, then stepped behind the bar and led the way through the kitchen area, which was empty at the moment except for Meg and another waitress. They were ladling salsa into serving bowls.

Charlie winked at her as they passed by, and he heard a faint "oh, shit" escape from her lips. "Out front, ladies," Mike instructed firmly as Fernando reached the exit.

Fernando unlocked the door with the turn of a lever and stepped out, Gordon right behind him. Charlie followed, watching Fernando's hands. His fists clenched and he whirled around, throwing a punch at Gordon, who blocked it effortlessly.

Charlie had noted the move out of the corner of his eye. He

was already into his own turn, halfway around and sweeping his right leg into the door. The heavy metal door slammed into the side of Neanderthal's skull as the guy lunged at him.

Ignoring the thuds and grunts coming from behind him, Charlie grabbed the door handle and slammed the door into Neanderthal's shoulder as the stunned goon tried to block the blow with his forearm. Then Charlie jumped back, careful not to bump into Gordon, who was hammering Fernando with left and right body punches.

Blocked by his own man, Mike pushed the guy forward, slamming the door behind him. "Take that Indian down, Cesar," Mike urged. The guy rushed Charlie like a blitzing linebacker, arms extended to make the tackle.

It only took a couple of seconds. Charlie faked a knee kick, then pulled his right leg back, letting Cesar grab his left knee. Extending both arms, Charlie brought his hands together and slapped the heels of both hands against the man's head, pivoting sideways as the man brushed past him. They both fell to the pavement, Charlie's attacker still clinging to him.

Cesar tried to wrap his arms around Charlie and save himself, but Charlie struck him on the right clavicle with a shuto strike, a chop with the edge of his hand.

The man groaned, let go, then rolled away, trying to sit up. Charlie stood, noting in his peripheral vision that Gordon had his opponent on the asphalt facedown with an arm-shoulder pin that suggested aikido.

"Enough!" Mike yelled, pulling back his silk jacket to reveal a small Ruger pistol at his belt. "Stop with this shit, guys. Clearly, you have some skills. You want to talk to me, okay, you've earned it. Let's all cool down, I don't want anyone calling the cops."

"You okay with this?" Charlie asked Gordon, who didn't appear to even be breathing hard.

"Sure, as long as everyone keeps their knives in their pockets and their guns away," he replied, nodding at Mike's weapon. Gordon released Fernando's arm, but watched him carefully as the man struggled to stand. It took a few seconds because the guy was still wobbly and doubled over slightly.

Charlie held his palms up, showing the fight had ended, then took a step back, now nearly shoulder to chin with Gordon.

"Go inside and clean yourselves up," Mike ordered, and the two damaged bouncers both reached for the handle. It was locked.

Mike chuckled, reached into his pocket, then brought out a ring of keys. "Leave it unlocked for me," he said, tossing the keys. Fernando made the grab, and a few seconds later, Mike, Charlie, and Gordon were alone, facing the alley.

"Something tells me you two aren't here looking for a job, and I've never run into you before, I'd have remembered. What do you want?" Mike asked, keeping his hand near the butt of his pistol.

"We're looking for a young woman you'd worked with in the past, a gal in the same profession as the ladies getting your upstairs clients in the mood."

"A good-looking Indian girl, maybe?" Mike asked, looking at Charlie closely. "Hey, the girls who work here come and go on their own. If your sister or girlfriend . . ."

"Naw, I'm not here to rescue anyone from their sinful ways, I'm just trying to locate Lola Tso. Have you seen her lately?"

"Ah, Lola, good-looking, young, and a hard worker. We parted company about two and a half years ago, maybe three. Said she had enough money saved up to enroll in community college. Hated to see her go, but I had a big enough stable at the time to keep the money coming in. Why are you looking for her?"

"She's got some people on her trail, violent people, and we need to find her first. She's keeping a low profile right now, but she's made a couple of costly mistakes. We were thinking she might have come around here looking for protection."

"How do I know you're not the ones out to hurt Lola?"

"If we were, your goons would be dead or dying and we'd be conducting whatever painful act was necessary to make you talk," Gordon said. "You're lucky we're the good guys, trust me."

"Unfortunately, you're going to have to take me at my word. I haven't seen Lola for almost two years, and if she's still a hooker, it isn't for me or anyone I know. And I'd know."

Charlie brought out his pocket notebook and a pen and wrote a number down on a piece of paper. He tore it out and handed it to Mike.

"If you hear from Lola, or get some intel, either call this number or have her do it. This is important. The police are looking for Lola too. The quicker they find her, the easier it'll be for any of her former employers to remain anonymous," Charlie explained. "Assuming she's still alive."

"I get that," Mike replied. "I like Lola and I'll do what I can to keep her safe. I take care of my people."

"Then we're done." Charlie nodded to Gordon, and they walked away, into the parking lot. There was no more reason to stay and chat with the pimp.

"Think he was lying?" Gordon asked as they reached the front of the building and walked toward Charlie's Dodge.

"Nah, Mike's a tool, but he seems smart enough not to make any enemies who could come back and cause trouble. Meg didn't particularly like the guy, but she respects that he takes care of his own. That's a good thing."

"Whose phone number did you give to Slick?" Gordon asked.

"The one for my old burner phone. Remind me to take it out of the drawer and recharge it. I doubt we'll hear from Mike again, but who knows? Instead of helping out he might decide to retaliate, and right now, we can't afford any more trouble for FOB Pawn."

"So what's next?"

Charlie thought about it as they climbed into his car. "If we go by Lola's apartment, the officer watching the place might see us. And if she had shown up, we'd have already received a call, probably, from Nancy."

"But if Lola is smart, she might be in her neighborhood right now, watching to see if her apartment is clear," Gordon surmised. "She might be keeping a low profile, disguising her looks and waiting for an opportunity to get at her stuff."

"What about her car—it's a black Ford Focus, right?"

Charlie nodded. "How about we cruise her neighborhood and see if any of the coffee shops, restaurants, or places have one of those cars in the lot? If we find one, we'll ask Nancy to run the plates."

"Lola's place is in an apartment complex near Wyoming and Montgomery. Do you remember the name?" Gordon asked.

"Village Apartments, Village Square, something like that." Charlie brought out his notebook and handed it to Gordon. "I took notes."

"Schoolboy."

"You're the one with the college degree, Gordon."

"It was either that or start knocking over convenience stores. That was a real career path in my 'hood. What about you?"

"My dad wanted me to get a degree and become a lawyer—my mom thought I'd make a good Navajo shepherd. So I joined the Army," Charlie replied. They'd talked about their backgrounds a lot, but never their goals. In the beginning, when they'd first met in the service, their pasts were the only thing to share besides their gripes.

"Good compromise. In all three careers you'd be surrounded by coyotes and encouraged to carry a gun. And the Army has the best guns," Gordon responded.

Fifteen minutes later they cruised through the parking lots of the multi-unit apartment complex, searching for a black Focus. Finding a total of two, they went to a coffee shop on the corner within sight of the apartments. They had coffee while Charlie called Nancy to see if either plate was for Lola's car.

Gordon, sipping his Italian brew, had already checked out every customer. Lola wasn't there.

Charlie ended the call, shook his head, then drank some coffee. "We struck out. So much for that idea."

"Wanna check the lots up and down the neighborhood, just in case?" Gordon suggested. "She could be sleeping in her car."

"Or in a motel in the area. There's one at the west end of Montgomery, just off I-25."

"Let's work our way west, then. And if that doesn't play out, maybe we should call it a night," Gordon said, yawning.

Two hours later they gave up and headed west, back into the valley. Gordon had walked to work—he lived just a half mile from the shop—so Charlie dropped him off in front of his apartment, then reversed course and headed back east, to home.

He was just pulling into the driveway of his two-bedroom rental home when his cell phone rang. It was Nancy Medina's private cell.

"What's up, Nancy?" Charlie asked. He and Gina's significant other had been through hell last year after Gina had been shot, but their friendship was solid now and Charlie really liked the tall, slender blonde with knockout looks. She was a good cop too.

"Detective DuPree got a hit on the guy who tried to redeem the squash blossom from a tribal database. He's Steve Martinez—the half brother of the guy Lola's been dating, Jerry Benally. Once DuPree got the ID on Steve, he tracked down photos of his siblings and came up with Jerry. The neighbors confirmed that Jerry had been seeing Lola."

"You figure Jerry may have been the one who got shot?" Charlie asked.

"Fifty-fifty chance. DuPree's got an ATL on those brothers underway. The photos are already going out to area clinics and other medical facilities, on and off the Rez," Nancy said. "You two have any luck tracking down Lola Tso?"

Charlie described the incident with Mike Schultz and his goons, then his follow-up.

"You guys better take care of yourselves," Nancy said. "Hang on, I'm getting another call." There was a brief pause, then she spoke again. "Time to go earn my paycheck."

"Bye," Charlie replied, then saw she'd already disconnected. Nancy supervised several patrol officers on the evening shift, so he knew she might be busy for a while. Tucking the phone into his shirt pocket, he reached under his seat for his weapon and extra magazine, pulled the key from the ignition, and climbed out of the Charger. The sky was clear, and despite the glow of the city, he could see several constellations, enough with which to navigate out on the open desert. Or he could just follow the road signs. This was urban New Mexico, not Tangi Valley.

Chapter Six

The phone woke Charlie up with a start and he groped for the receiver on the nightstand. "Yeah, what?" he mumbled, trying to suppress a yawn.

"Hey, brother, now that you're awake, can you help me burglarize somebody's house? I need to build some street cred if I'm going to get in tight with these people."

Charlie paused a moment, half asleep, wondering what the hell Al was talking about. Then the gray cells began to kick in. "You're undercover, Al, I get that, but I'm no cop. If we get caught, even if that's part of your plan, how would I stay out of jail?"

"Not to worry, this is just a setup and it should be an easy-in, easy-out operation. It's going to make the news, and I'll be stealing something that'll prove to the right people I did the deed," Al said, excited despite the early hour.

Charlie looked over at the clock on the nightstand—it was six fifteen in the morning and the sun wasn't even up yet. He was a civilian now and didn't need to put up with this crack-of-dawn crap anymore.

·   "You're talking about today, right?"

"Yeah, yeah, this morning around nine thirty, after the neighborhood has gone to work. The early thief gets the jewelry, guns, and laptops," Al replied. "People at home are settling in or doing laundry and the day shift of cops are working on a cup of coffee after their first call. Trust me, I know."

"Let me tell Gordon I'm coming in late, then we'll meet—where?"

"Your place? The target residence is only a few miles from there and I want to go over the details once or twice. That work for you?" Al asked.

"Yeah, okay, but don't show up before seven thirty unless you're bringing breakfast. You're supplying the burglary tools, right?"

"Of course, and a disguise or two. See you in a while," Al said, ending the call.

Charlie reached for his cell phone, but changed his mind. Might as well let Gordon sleep in 'til seven. Groaning, he stretched his long legs and rolled out of bed.

Charlie was used to kicking in doors of all shapes and sizes, but that was supposed to be part of his past. He and Gordon had spent many months together as a snatch-and-grab team, first in Iraq, then Afghanistan. They'd target and kidnap enemy combatants or suspected insurgents, then deliver them to intelligence units for interrogation. That usually involved infiltrating neighborhoods and conducting covert break-ins, ambushes, or whatever else was necessary to snatch informants, leaders, or anyone else who might have access to useful intel. They often accompanied units conducting sweeps in hope of capturing enemy leaders or their communications people, so they'd also had their share of firefights.

Today, though, he was just going to help his cop brother steal something—hopefully. If it would help Al or someone else bring in Cordell Buck's killer, it was worth it.

Charlie pushed up his annoying fake glasses and fiddled with the itchy, heavily starched collar on the white uniform shirt Al had provided. Both the shirt and the dark blue pants he wore were used, faded, and stained. Today he was "Martinez," according to the name tag above the pocket, an employee of a well-known local home heating-and-cooling outfit. Al had on a similar uniform. They were now approaching the target residence in a rented white van with one of those magnetic signs on each door.

The northeast Albuquerque neighborhood of mostly earth-tone stucco homes was upper-middle class, with houses Charlie judged would sell for 300K or more. There were only a few cars in the matching concrete driveways and they were all recent models. In his experience, the fewer cars on a residential street, the more prosperous the neighborhood.

"Whose house are we busting into, anyway?" Charlie asked as they came to a halt at a stop sign. He adjusted the white cap with the company logo so the bill was lower over his forehead.

"It belongs to some university professor who's on sabbatical in Latin America, a friend of Detective DuPree. The house sitter is going to be away all day. I'm taking a couple of expensive watches, a Bose system, and an antique Colt pistol," Al added.

"And the next-door neighbors are at work?"

"They're supposed to be," Al said.

"Our cover is that we're changing filters, checking out the systems, stuff like that—right?" Charlie asked.

Al nodded as he pulled up in front of the target house. Next, he brought up a clipboard and filled out a fake work order while they casually checked for witnesses or curious neighbors up and down the street. Residential burglars usually worked fast, so the plan was to take their time to avoid suspicion.

"Looks clear to me, no faces visible at windows, nobody outside at the moment," Charlie announced. "We need to stay casual. We're supposed to be here."

"Let's go for it. You get the box of filters, I'll get the tools," Al said, climbing out. "We should be here at least fifteen or twenty minutes to make it look legit." He brought out an overhead garage door control, pushed the button, and it opened as they unloaded their stuff.

Five minutes later, Charlie was replacing the furnace air filter while Al was in the house, tracking down the items they were "stealing" and placing them in the empty filter box. Out of the corner of his eye, Charlie saw a bald-headed Anglo man in tan shorts and T-shirt, about sixty years old at the end of the driveway, look toward him, and then back at the truck.

The man walked halfway up the drive, looked at the sign on the truck, then called out. "Where's D.J.? His car's gone."

"Excuse me?" Charlie replied. "There's just me and my supervisor here today. Scheduled maintenance, changing filters, checking out the system."

"Can I help you, sir?" Al said, coming out of the garage door leading into the house, carrying the filter box.

"I'm with the neighborhood watch. Jorge asked me to keep an eye on the place while he was away. There's supposed to be a house sitter, but I don't see his car."

"That's not it?" Charlie nodded toward the burgundy Mercedes in the garage.

"D.J. drives an old Acura," the man said, turning to look down the street.

Al sat down the box and took a small notebook out of his pocket. "This is Professor Wheeler's house, isn't it? San Ignacio Road, Number 2088." Al turned to check the house number running along the trim of the porch. "All we got was a key and a work order. This job was scheduled months ago."

"Right address, right name," the man replied. "I guess D.J. is in class."

"We're about done here," Charlie said, picking up the toolbox. "Maybe you should stick around until we leave, if that's a problem."

The man looked at the box on the concrete driveway, seeing only a dirty air filter on top, then glanced around the garage. "No, just trying to do my part. There have been a few break-ins in the neighborhood so we watch out for each other."

"You can't be too careful," Charlie said, looking back at Al. "We ready to load up and get going? We've got another job before lunch."

"Right. Thank you for your diligence, sir. You're an asset to the neighborhood," Al said to the man, then turned and went back into the house.

Charlie carried the box, which was a lot heavier than it looked, and loaded it into the van. The neighbor had wandered over to the sidewalk, and stood there watching as Al came out of the garage, the door closing behind him.

A minute later, they drove off.

"Suppose he'll check up on us? He wrote down something onto that notebook of his," Al asked as they pulled out into a major street and headed south.

"I was just hoping he wouldn't take out a cell phone and start taking photos," Charlie said.

"Didn't think of that. Glad I'm not a burglar. Even when it's all laid out, it can get complicated," Al said.

"At least we didn't have to shoot him," Charlie mumbled.

"Huh?"

"Just kidding. Let's stop once we're clear of the neighborhood, take off that damn sign, and change out of these uniforms. Then you can drop me off at home before you get rid of this van and continue on with your criminal career."

Charlie came in through the back and walked into the office an hour later in his business clothes—a cotton-blend short-sleeved shirt, brown slacks, and a thin, microfiber jacket that mostly concealed his backup Beretta. His matching 9mm model 92 was still in the APD forensic lab and it wasn't the first time. The shooting had been declared righteous, however, according to DuPree, and he should be getting the weapon back in a few days.

Ruth, who'd just come out of the storeroom across the hall,

poked her head into the office just as he sat down. He stood as she entered. He'd been raised in a home where respect for women was not only a tradition—it was required.

"Good morning, Charlie. How'd the breakfast go with your brother? You two get a chance to catch up?" she asked, smiling with that little crinkle with her nose he found so endearing.

Gordon knew the truth and had already suggested a cover story. There was no need to spread the deception to Ruth or Jake. If something went wrong they wouldn't be involved.

"Yeah, he's working undercover on a case and needed someone to talk to. I'm not supposed to talk about it, though." Charlie had discussed his family with Ruth from time to time and they'd gotten to know each other pretty well. There was a level of attraction between them that went unspoken and hadn't been acted upon, and neither was ready to cross that line.

Ruth was a single mother with a son, Renée, in kindergarten, and was living below the radar as much as possible. Ruth Adams wasn't even her real name. She'd been in the witness protection program since the arrest and conviction of her ex-husband. Everyone at FOB Pawn knew the truth and they all did what they could to make sure Ruth and her son were safe.

"My lips are sealed, boss," she said, then reached for her coffee cup. "I'm pouring, if you're ready for another coffee," she added, picking up the carafe.

"Sure, why not?" he said, grabbing his mug from atop the desk.

Ruth and he finished their coffee while discussing yesterday's transactions, then they went out to relieve Jake and Gordon, who were due for a break.

At lunchtime, Jake walked Ruth down to the grocery to pick up shrimp salads—his and her favorite noon meals at the moment, so Gordon and Charlie got a chance to discuss the morning's events while tending the front counter. There were three people looking at the for-sale inventory, so they kept their voices low.

"So this college student who'd been house sitting is going to report the burglary?" Gordon asked.

"Yeah. Al opened drawers and disturbed the interior enough so it'll be obvious. And once the police show up, that neighborhood watch guy will probably be right there with a description of the van—and us."

"What if the man had decided to take photos? Even my neighbor's cat has a cell phone," Gordon commented. "You guys got lucky."

"The glasses and cap will throw them off, hopefully. Al offered me a fake mustache but that was too weird," Charlie confessed. "We wore gloves. No prints."

"Al going to show his take to his potential pals, right?"

"Yeah. If he's really unlucky he's trying to join the wrong crew and they'll rat him out," Charlie said. "There's always the outside chance that these people didn't kill Cordell Buck."

"Or maybe he'll get really, really unlucky, and they'll turn on him and steal his stuff," Gordon teased. "How much was it worth, anyway?"

"We'd try to sell the same items here for maybe seven hundred or so total—unless that Colt is a real collector's item. I never saw what he brought out, actually."

"Hey, that provides you plausible deniability in case anyone ever knocks on your door."

"As long as it's a real cop I wouldn't mind. Speaking of cops, did Nancy or Detective DuPree give you anything more on Jerry and Steve, the two shooters who got away?" Charlie asked, speaking in a whisper now. One of their potential customers, a lady in her early sixties, was walking toward them carrying a handmade teddy bear Ruth had set a value on just the other day.

"Nope. All I know is what you told me this morning before you met Al," Gordon said.

He turned toward the woman and gave her a big smile as she placed the fuzzy guy wearing a western hat and blue bandana on the counter. "Looks like Cowboy Teddy found a home," Gordon said.

Nd u an grdn 2 hv my bk 2nt at pnyn msa stkhows @9. Stay clr f psble. Mtn w/crw. Cnt use reg bkup r cl. Al.

Charlie looked at the text message again, thought maybe he really did understand it, then answered with "K. Chk."

"Gordon, how are you at reading text message gibberish? I just got something from Al," Charlie asked, looking over at his pal, who was locking the front entrance. Jake and Ruth had left at six fifteen, and they were closed for the day.

"I was pretty good at Army-speak, and Naomi sometimes texts me while she's waiting for a flight. Let's see." He walked over to the counter where Charlie was standing, cash box in hand, and

Charlie handed him the phone. He'd met Naomi Buchanan once before. She was a flight attendant for Southwest and went out with Gordon whenever she had a layover in Albuquerque.

"Let's see," Gordon said. "'Need you and garden to have my back tonight at Piñon Mesa Stickhouse. At nine. Stay clear if possible. Meeting with crew. Can't use regular backup or call. Al.' How's that?"

"Garden is Gordon, wiseass, and stickhouse has got to be steakhouse. Let me look it up." Charlie took the phone back. "Yeah, it's a restaurant off Central Avenue, near Old Town."

"Guess Al's already made contact with the crew he's trying to infiltrate," Gordon said.

"And he can't talk at the moment, which means he's with them."

"Suppose he texted you from the can?"

"Thanks for the image. But yeah, that's about the only time someone undercover is able to communicate with the outside unless they're wired. So, Garden, you with me on this?"

"Yeah, there's nothing good on TV tonight anyway, and I haven't been in a brawl outside a restaurant since, well, last night. But let's have a burger or so before we go. I'm not starving until nine and if I'm hungry when I get into a fight I might get carried away and really hurt somebody."

Chapter Seven

The Piñon Mesa Steakhouse was a family-owned restaurant with old, thick adobe walls, kiva fireplaces, a corrugated metal roof, and brick floors worn by decades of foot traffic. Reservations were suggested, but Charlie and Gordon were able to get seated in the long, narrow dining room after a short wait. During that break they each had a rum and cola in a small bar nestled in what was probably at one time the front porch.

It was after nine by then, so Marco, their greeter, had no problem allowing them to choose between three tables, one with a good view of a private alcove off the kitchen. Charlie had already spotted Al seated with several other diners in that section, one woman among men. They chose seats where Charlie could watch his brother's back.

Gordon sat across from him, his eyes checking the entrance whenever there was activity, as was their custom. No spot was outside their field of view.

They'd elected to switch to small handguns tonight, easily concealed. Charlie kept his in his right pocket and Gordon wore his .380 on his ankle inside his pant leg. They'd planned to do nothing more than watch and dine, remaining as anonymous as possible. For Gordon, Charlie knew that would be a challenge. He loved to flirt.

The two prettiest women in the place appeared to be the waitresses, but Charlie sighed a breath of relief when a waiter approached instead, a guy with a name tag that read Lane.

Lane was efficient, and within fifteen minutes they were dining on fork-tender twelve-ounce sirloins and some of the best-tasting summer squash and asparagus tips Charlie had ever had. The mashed potatoes were just a little chunky, cooked with enough sour cream and butter to make him consider a second round.

Gordon was deeply engrossed in his own steak, and it wasn't until Charlie heard a subtle "oh, shit, Steve" that he looked over.

Charlie didn't turn his head—he'd learned to watch people with his eyes when around strangers and possible insurgents, so he reached down and took a sip of iced tea and looked near the figure at the front entrance talking with Marco, the greeter.

"Steve Martinez, the boyfriend's brother—the guy I looked at eye-to-eye across the counter. If he sees my face . . ." Charlie said quite casually, now looking back at his plate.

"At least Al seems to have found the right guys," Gordon said, keeping his voice low.

Charlie set down his fork, brought out his cell phone, and made a point of appearing occupied. His elbow was on the table and he was resting his forehead in his fingertips as he looked down at the cell phone display. "Let me know when I can look up."

"He's checking out the customers, table by table. There he goes, already looking past us at one of those beautiful waitresses. Wonder if they date customers?"

"Eye on the target, bro," Charlie mumbled. "Where's he going?"

"Over to the long table with Al's new best friends. I'd like to get a photo."

"Too risky and too dark in here for a cell phone camera at this distance," Charlie said, checking out of the corner of his eye. Al was being introduced, it appeared, but there was no hand shaking. No surprise.

"Good thing you and Al don't share a family resemblance," Gordon said.

"Be careful who you say that to. My father almost kicked a guy's ass at a tribal powwow one time when he suggested Al and I must have different fathers. The guy had been fired from a tribal job and was looking for trouble. And his comment was a lot more graphic."

"I'd have dropped him myself. How'd that end?"

"Al punched the guy in the balls. Caught him off guard. I pulled Al—who was barely fifteen—off the guy, and Mom hustled Dad away. I never looked back, but from the retching it sounded like the guy, well, don't let me ruin your dinner."

"Thanks. You and your sister look a lot alike, though. Those bright eyes, full lips, and high cheek bones. She's pretty and it works on her."

"Mom says I'm good-looking."

"Moms always say that."

Charlie looked up at him briefly, but Gordon was watching the table in the alcove, fork dangling above his plate in a rock-steady hand. Gordon had only mentioned his own mother a few times. She was, in Gordon's words, a lady with bad judgment when it came to men. Charlie didn't have to ask to know Gordon hated his father.

"The man coming out of the kitchen in the black jacket—he's come and gone from that back table twice now, each time speaking to the dark-haired woman with the silver streak. Think the guy is management?" Gordon asked.

"Yeah, and I think that the woman is important. Maybe she's the owner."

"Now the black jacket is talking to Steve. Looks like they're having words. Wish I could hear," Gordon said. "They're too far away to lip read."

"No worry, Al will know what was said."

Charlie watched as Steve Martinez stood. His stride suggested Steve was angry, and he left the restaurant in a hurry, never looking back.

"Think we should follow Steve?" Gordon asked, finishing his iced tea and pushing away his empty plate.

"Somebody's already on that," Charlie pointed out, watching as two more men from Al's table rose, nodded to the woman and the guy in the black jacket, then quickly left the restaurant.

Lane came over to ask if they wanted dessert.

Gordon ordered pecan pie, and Charlie the flan. Then Charlie complimented Lane on the excellent meal. "I don't know how I've missed out on this place until now. I'm coming back again soon, and will recommend your food to my friends. Is this a family business?"

"Thanks for the compliment, and yes, this restaurant has been owned and operated by the Fasthorse family for three generations now. My family has been with Piñon Mesa for two of those generations, and my father was head chef until he retired."

"Fasthorse. That's a Navajo family. Doesn't Mrs. Sheila Mae Fasthorse manage a tribal casino?" Charlie asked.

"The former Mrs. Fasthorse did, but she now owns a business consulting firm. Her son, Mr. Clarence Fasthorse, runs the restaurant," Lane answered. "And he's here right now, so excuse me, I need to stay busy. I'll clear the table and bring your dessert."

Less than five minutes later, they were eating their desserts when Al stood, placed some money on the table, then turned and walked across the room. He glanced in their direction casually, without any signal or sign of recognition, before continuing on to the exit. As soon as he left the restaurant, one of those men who'd been at Al's table went into the kitchen.

"Follow Al?"

Charlie shook his head. "No, I think this was just a meet and greet to size him up. If these hoods are smart they're going to be extra careful for a while. Al will be followed to make sure he doesn't stop and meet anyone on the way home."

"They got rid of Steve in a hurry. He's still hot, and probably pissed them off by showing up, basically in public, and going directly to their table like that," Gordon surmised. "So we wait for Al to contact the task force he's working with—and us."

"Yeah, assuming he wasn't made and is going to turn up tomorrow on the West Mesa, burned to a crisp," Charlie said softly as he enjoyed his last spoonful of flan.

"Hey, Al's a smart cop, right?"

"He used to be, but recently he's been sliding. Hopefully he's got his shit together."

"Guess we'll see," Gordon said, catching the eye of Lane, their waiter. "Ready to go?"

Charlie nodded, watching the man in the black suit, Clarence Fasthorse probably, talking to the woman with the streak in her hair. Was that his wife, girlfriend, sister, or mom? Either way, she was seated with a dangerous crowd.

Charlie drove east down Mountain Road past the museums and a small urban park. The street was narrow here so close to Old Town, passing through a mixed neighborhood of last-century homes and businesses. Many of the old houses were now smoke shops, law offices, or the site of bail bondsmen conveniently located within walking distance of the county jail. The grocery stores, delis, and pharmacies, like most of the homeowners, had largely fled north up the valley or east toward the Sandia Mountains.

Having grown up in a part of New Mexico where there were few multistory buildings at all, and one could see open desert for miles in any direction, cities bigger than fifty or sixty thousand were an eyeful for Charlie and he enjoyed the streets, sidewalks, and even the stoplights.

He made the turn north at Fourth Street, then glanced over at Gordon, who had been silent since they'd left the restaurant.

"What's on your mind?" Charlie asked.

"I was wondering how Al hooked up with these guys. Did he meet them while dealing with a fence? A guy who sells stolen crap on Craigslist? An ex-con?"

Charlie shrugged. "Hadn't thought about it. An informant? Another undercover cop? I can ask, maybe he'll tell. You and I are a little more direct when we want information."

Gordon nodded. "Why don't you take the next right, circle the block, then come back onto Fourth?"

Charlie automatically checked the rearview mirror. "You think we picked up a tail?"

"Maybe. That black Impala pulled onto the street behind us a little past that park on Mountain, then followed us onto Fourth. He's been inching up slowly ever since."

Charlie took another look. "Two, no, three guys?"

"Maybe Steve and the two who left just after he did." Gordon reached down and brought out his .380, holding it in his right hand beside his pant leg. "If he recognized us, we're being played."

"Wish I had the 92 now." Charlie said, placing his small handgun in his right-hand jacket pocket. "Next right."

"Easy or hard?" Gordon said, grabbing the door handle.

"Hard!" Charlie said, whipping the Charger into a sliding right-hand turn, then accelerating.

"He's sticking with us!" Gordon said, hanging on.

"Next left!" Charlie said, just making the light as it turned yellow. The Impala followed, barely missing a car at the intersection. Charlie raced down Second Street, here a wide, four-lane road.

The guy must have floored the Impala. It came up even with them all of a sudden. Charlie looked over, saw guns, and hit the brakes, fighting the wheel to track straight and true. "Duck!"

The squeal of tires was so loud the gunshots were mere thuds ricocheting off the windshield, which spiderwebbed instantly.

Charlie closed his eyes and looked down as the glass collapsed and a shower of glass cubes flew into him. Fighting the urge to touch his face, he continued to pump the brakes and keep the wheel steady as he shook his head back and forth. The roaring wind through the disintegrating windshield buffeted his face and he took a chance, opening his eyes. No glass!

Looking up, he heard an angry auto horn and reacted instantly, whipping the Charger back into his lane just as an oncoming car shot past him. The Impala was far ahead now, and he watched helplessly as the car made a left on a green arrow and raced west down an intersecting street. He slowed to a stop at the upcoming red light and finally looked over at Gordon.

His pal was hunkered down below the dashboard, shaking his head vigorously and throwing out cubes of glass from his hair. "Are we there yet?" he asked, then inched up to full height, looked down and opened his eyes.

A half hour later, Charlie still had to fight the urge to rub his eyes. The EMT had flushed them out with saline twice, but each time had cautioned him to avoid touching his face or hair until he'd gone home and showered. Same with Gordon.

Now the rescue people were gone and all they had to worry about was APD. Fortunately, Sergeant Nancy Medina was working this neighborhood tonight and had been the third officer on scene.

"You should have called this in the moment you spotted Steve Martinez. People could have been injured or killed , including you two," Nancy whispered harshly, not wanting the patrol officer to hear. "Officers could have made an arrest."

"He didn't hang around long enough for anyone to arrive. Here's the deal, Nancy. We were backing up Al, my brother, who's trying to get in with the people probably involved in the Buck murder, those carjackings, and the incident at FOB," Charlie answered.

Nancy looked over at Gordon, who had a tiny cut on his cheek. "True," he confirmed. "Charlie's brother didn't want to risk blowing the cover of the others on his team if he got ID'd, so he asked us to stay close, just in case."

"I get it, but now Martinez thinks you were after him. Why else make a move on you like that? Do you think the people with him at that table also consider you a risk?"

"Which would keep us and FOB Pawn in the crosshairs?" Gordon asked. "Is that what you're saying?"

"Steve's got to be worried about more than just us. Every law enforcement agency in the area knows his face since he was ID'd. I'm just hoping he'll have enough sense to go to ground now. I doubt he's the leader of this crew, and I'm sure they don't want officers coming to Piñon Mesa Steakhouse, asking around," Charlie said.

"By letting you guys get away, Martinez is putting them all at risk," Nancy said.

"So, unless Steve is really stupid, he'll stay well away from us, is that what you're suggesting?" Gordon asked, shaking cubes of glass out of the pant cuff of his chinos.

"Maybe, maybe not," Nancy said. "Either way, you two have to keep looking over your shoulders until he and the others are put away. I'm keeping the details out of my report, but I hope this still doesn't come down on your brother, somehow," she added, looking at Charlie. "If he gets made . . ."

"As long as they don't find out we're brothers we have a chance this will slide by them," Charlie said.

"Any news from Al?" Gordon asked.

Nancy and Gordon looked on as Charlie checked his phone. "Nothing but e-mail spam."

"Al ever e-mail you?" Nancy asked.

"No. Talk or text, that's it," Charlie answered. "Do you have any connections with the agency team Al's working with, Nancy?"

"Sorry. DuPree is my contact, and for you, I guess it's your brother. We'll just have to wait this one out," she said.

"Yeah, well," Charlie said, looking over at Gordon, who shrugged. "Can we go now?"

Nancy looked over at the officer, who looked up. "We good here?" she asked.

The officer nodded. "You fellows might be getting a visit from a detective tomorrow or the next day. And get that windshield fixed ASAP. I'll give you a copy of the report for your insurance company. Okay to e-mail it to your business address?"

"Sure. And thanks. Let's take care of the glass on the seats, Gordon, then go home. Speak to you soon, Sergeant Medina," he added.

"Yeah. You guys make it home safe, okay?" she added softly. "Gina's going to throw a fit when she hears about this, you know."

Charlie had a brush and dustpan in the trunk, and they were able to get most of the glass off the seats before driving to an all-night car wash, where they vacuumed out the rest.

Finally Charlie pulled up in front of Gordon's apartment. "I'll be in a little early tomorrow," Charlie said as Gordon climbed out. "I'll get some work done, then see about getting the windshield replaced."

"Good idea. I'll drive to work instead of hoofing it in case we need to go somewhere and the Charger isn't ready yet," Gordon answered, stepping onto the sidewalk.

"Yeah. Sleep lightly, partner. Somebody tried to kill us tonight," Charlie reminded.

"We can't let that slide, you know."

Charlie nodded. "Ready to make them starting looking over *their* shoulders?"

"I was hoping you'd say that. Let's take the fight to them," Gordon suggested.

"Even if it means getting a little badass?"

"Exactly," Gordon said. "Tomorrow, we come up with a plan to nail these punks."

"Tomorrow," Charlie agreed. He nodded to Gordon and pulled away from the curb as his pal walked up the sidewalk to his apartment.

The drive home was cool, almost cold with no windshield, but it helped keep him awake and alert. His pistol rested on the console within the reach of his right hand, and the cell phone in his shirt pocket where he could feel the vibration of a call above the stiff breeze. Charlie kept his eyes on the move as he tried to think more about tomorrow and less about tonight.

Chapter Eight

Charlie heard a car door slam somewhere outside. He reached under his pillow and brought out his .380 as he glanced at the clock. It was four AM and dark as hell. Sitting up, he listened, hearing the sound of a vehicle driving away from close by.

It was probably nothing, but he'd learned not to ignore his instincts so it wouldn't hurt to check it out. As usual he'd parked the Charger in the garage, and the rumble of the ancient overhead door going up would have woken him. He knew the Dodge was still there.

He slept in pajama bottoms, no shirt, so all he had to do was slip on his loafers from beside the bed. For a second, as he fumbled for the small flashlight on the nightstand, he considered grabbing the bigger handgun from inside the drawer. The 9 mm offered more firepower and accuracy with the tritium night sights.

"Probably nothing," he said aloud, then stood and walked quietly out into the hall, listening for anything, the sound of breathing, vehicles, footsteps . . . anything. All he heard was the humming of the refrigerator in the kitchen.

Continuing down the hall, he stopped at the entrance to the small living room and listened again. Nothing. Inching over to the living room window, he stood beside the curtain and peered outside through the small gap, checking the street, then the driveway. Turning his head, he saw something big on the porch.

"Crap, that's one frickin' big dog," he muttered. He undid the lock, opened the door, and looked down. Instantly he realized it was a man, scrunched up in a fetal position, lying on his side. Flipping on the flashlight, he aimed the bright beam at the face. It was Steve Martinez, glazed eyes open and extremely dead. A pistol—a Beretta like his model 92, was on the concrete porch beside the man's bloody chest.

Charlie looked out into the yard—then the street. Everything appeared normal and the only vehicles were those of his neighbors, all in their driveways. Not touching a thing outside, he stepped back, closed the door, and returned to the bedroom. Placing the .380 back underneath his pillow, he opened the nightstand drawer. His backup Beretta 92 was still inside.

If this was a setup, it was a hasty, sloppy one. Picking up his cell phone from the nightstand, he dialed 911 as he walked back into the living room. He wasn't going to get any more sleep tonight, that was clear. Hopefully, he'd also stay out of jail.

His second call was to Gordon, then he texted Gina, not wanting to wake her but to make sure she knew what had happened as soon as she woke in the morning. He didn't know if he was going to need a lawyer tonight, tomorrow, or ever. That depended on the D.A., the detective on scene, the medical investigator, and ultimately the investigation into what was obviously a murder committed elsewhere—then the dumping of Martinez's body at his doorstep.

Gordon beat the crime scene unit to the house, but by then Charlie was being interviewed by an APD sergeant. At least nothing had happened at Gordon's apartment—apparently.

Gordon and Charlie were finally catching up when Detective DuPree arrived, yawning and bleary eyed. "Now what the hell did you do, Charlie?" the middle-aged APD cop asked, absently tucking in his shirt tail beneath his sports jacket as he looked down at the plastic tarp covering the body.

"No, don't say it. You shot an intruder and dragged his body *outside* your house just to mess with me," DuPree commented, stepping over and lifting up one corner of the tarp. There were floodlights around the yard and the porch light was on, so it was easy to see the face. Gordon looked over and took a look as well, then shrugged. "Not much blood on the porch. Wasn't killed here, was he, Detective?" Gordon commented.

DuPree shook his head, then glanced up as a lab tech came out Charlie's front door, which had been propped open. Moths circled around the porch light and the tech brushed them away from his face.

"Good morning, Detective," the tech declared. "In response to the question, no, there is no sign of any blood or disturbance inside the home or garage. There are, however, drag marks and blood spots leading up from the street." He motioned toward the numbered markers on the lawn, then the sidewalk.

"This is—was—Steve Martinez. We agree on that?" DuPree said, covering the body again.

"Yes, sir, the same guy who tried to buy the squash blossom, then hold us up, which led to the shooting incident," Charlie replied, nodding.

"And how did he end up here, dead?"

"I'm no cop, but I'm guessing he was shot somewhere else, hauled to this spot, and dumped," Charlie said.

"We know that, smart . . . never mind," DuPree grumbled. "Will you excuse us for a minute, Carl?"

"Kevin. I'm Kevin, Detective. No problem." The tech stepped back inside the house.

DuPree motioned for them to follow him across the lawn, away from the porch. "Quit messing with me, guys. Sergeant Medina sent me a copy of her last report, about you two being shot at last night while in your vehicle."

"Oh, yeah, that," Gordon said.

"Not funny. Fill me in on what went down from your arrival at the Piñon Mesa Steakhouse to Charlie finding Martinez's body on his front porch."

For the next ten minutes they went back and forth, describing everything they remembered, up to the present.

"Damn, you guys are right out of a *Die Hard* movie, aren't you?" Dupree announced.

Charlie didn't have anything to add to that, and neither did Gordon, so DuPree kept talking.

"How do you read what happened with Martinez? If neither one of you did this, who did?"

"Steve must have recognized us when he came into the restaurant. Then he pissed off the guy at the table we think might be Clarence Fasthorse, possibly his boss and maybe head of the Night Crew. From where we were sitting, it looked like Steve got reamed out," Gordon replied, looking over at Charlie.

"Martinez left in a hurry and a few seconds later two guys at the same table followed," Charlie added.

"After *we* left, Steve and these two guys tried to take us out in that drive-by," Gordon said. "It was Steve who fired the shots, right?"

Charlie nodded.

"So did Steve get popped because he tried to make the hit, or because he failed?" DuPree asked.

Charlie and Gordon exchanged glances. "I think it was because he failed," Charlie suggested.

Gordon nodded. "He showed up at the restaurant instead of lying low, got recognized by us, then had to take us out before we talked and made the connection between him and the people at the table. But that didn't turn out as expected."

"I know about Al being there. You think those people will figure out you weren't really following Steve? Especially because you arrived before him?" DuPree asked.

"Good question, one they can reason out eventually if they ask the right person or get a bump up in their IQs. Whether or not that'll point back at Al, I don't know. They've got to know we're shop owners, not cops," Charlie said. "I'm hoping they'll think it was just a coincidence."

"But if they check into your background, and family . . ." Gordon began.

"They'll find out your father is a retired judge, and that Alfred Henry is a tribal cop," DuPree jumped in. "If they find a photo of him somewhere . . ."

"We've got to get word to Al," Charlie said. "I haven't heard from him since he asked us to watch his back, and we don't know if he's aware of what happened to us after he left. Has he made contact with the undercover team since dining at the restaurant?"

"I'll check with my captain. He knows how to contact the team," DuPree said, bringing out his phone.

Gordon motioned Charlie aside. "You want to text Al?"

Charlie nodded. "Yeah, but I don't think it's a good idea right now. The bad guys are trying to decide if they trust him, and with all this going on"—he nodded toward the body—"it's going to take awhile longer. I can't risk anyone else seeing the message."

"I see your point. And even if you two had a code, that would still create some suspicion. At least it would for me."

"Yeah, Gordon, but you're naturally paranoid."

"With good reason. So, assuming you and I are cleared in this shooting, what's the plan? We're still going after them, right? Bring down the Night Crew, catch Cordell Buck's killer, and make New Mexico safe for innocent motorists once again."

"Damn straight," Charlie said, suppressing a smile. He looked over at Detective DuPree, who'd just ended his call. "To be continued," Charlie added softly.

"Your brother hasn't called in, which suggests he might still be with someone in that crew. He never made it to his apartment either," DuPree explained. "They have a location for him, though. He's currently at an apartment not far from that steakhouse."

"How is the undercover unit keeping track of him?" Charlie asked. "Following him closely enough to know exactly where he is can be risky unless they have a big team."

"The team leader didn't say, but I'm guessing there's a GPS on him or they're tracking his cell phone," DuPree said. "As long as they let him keep it, we'll know where he is."

"More precisely, his cell phone," Gordon corrected.

DuPree shrugged.

"Any way we can get a read on his GPS?" Charlie asked.

"Afraid not, at least not from APD," DuPree replied, looking at Charlie. "Well, unless you can think of anything you can add to what you've already stated tonight—this morning—I'm done here."

"What does Charlie do now?" Gordon asked.

"Wait until everyone leaves, then go back to bed. That's if they don't consider the interior of your home a crime scene," DuPree added.

"Welcome to sleep on my couch," Gordon offered.

Charlie looked around the yard and into the street. The crime scene team were taking down the lights and putting away their gear, and the few sleepy, curious neighbors had already gone home. "Thanks, Gordon, but I'll be sticking around. Forget about me going to work earlier, like I planned. The auto glass people will be here at eight, and I want to get back on the road in my own car."

"Okay. I'm outta here. Give me a call when you're on your way to work, Charlie, or if another body shows up," Gordon said, giving DuPree a glance.

DuPree walked away, shaking his head slowly.

"Talk to you later, bud," Gordon said. "And keep some firepower handy."

"You too," Charlie answered, watching until his friend drove away in his big pickup, then went back inside. He walked through every room, locked the back door, then checked the garage. Grateful that only the windshield had been shattered, he locked the garage door as well and stepped back out onto the front porch. The body had been taken away and blood samples collected. All he'd need to do would be to wash off what remained. The crime scene team was still putting away their gear, so he might as well do what he could before going inside a final time.

A big flower pot was over against the house wall, containing nothing but dirt and the stub of a long-dead plant. Digging into the potting soil, he brought out two large handfuls of dirt, then sprinkled it into the blood, effectively covering it up. Later he could sweep up whatever soaked into the dry soil, then hose down the porch.

Kevin, the same lab tech that DuPree had spoken to earlier, came up, left his card, then walked back to the large mobile unit. Charlie was inside, washing his hands, when he heard the vehicle leave. Five minutes later he was in bed, asleep.

Chapter Nine

"Jake, Ruth, if either of you feel uncomfortable sticking around here today, just say the word," Charlie announced once they'd all gathered in the office. He'd made it to the pawnshop only a half hour after opening, and when he arrived it appeared to be business as usual. At the moment the shop was empty of customers so he'd called them in for coffee and a quick meeting.

"Just how dangerous do you think this place is, guys?" Jake asked, looking from Charlie to Gordon. "I'm not one to run the other way, but this involves all of us and we have family members to consider."

"As long as we're careful and stick to our safety procedures, I don't think we face any real risk, at least not you or Ruth," Charlie added. "Gordon and I have just really gotten somebody ticked off."

"So, does that mean you and Gordon are going to back away and let the police handle the murder investigation and find the missing witness?" Ruth asked, her eyes narrowing.

"For the record, we're saying yes to the question," Charlie answered, not looking at Gordon. They'd already settled on a plan. "But we may be gone from time to time during the working day, and officially, we're out conducting business."

"So if the police ask us what you two are up to . . ." Ruth said. "We don't really know."

"Well, whatever you two won't be doing, good luck, and stay safe," Jake replied, looking through the Plexiglas office panel as a man in his fifties entered the pawnshop carrying a cardboard box. "We've got a customer, so I guess this never-happened meeting is over." He stepped out into the shop area and walked up to greet the man.

"And you, Ruth?" Charlie asked.

She touched him on the arm briefly. "Stay safe. Renée would miss you terribly if something happened. And you too, Gordon." She grabbed her coffee and walked back into the storeroom, where she'd been checking inventory.

Gordon looked over at Charlie. "Ruth would miss you more."

Charlie laughed, grabbed his own mug, and stepped out into the hall as the bell went off at the front entrance. Two college-aged kids walked in carrying a game console and a clear plastic box containing a big stack of games.

His cell phone chimed. He stopped, set down his coffee, and read the text message. "It's Al. He wants to meet me at the Subway inside the Cottonwood Walmart at one PM."

"That could work. It's public, and the bad guys won't want to be caught on surveillance, which is everywhere in those stores,"

Gordon replied. "While you're talking I can pick up some groceries and watch for hostiles."

"I like that," Charlie said, answering the text with a single letter—k. "I wonder what Al's got on his mind. You'd think his team would prefer that he avoid me."

"He might be doing this without their knowledge. Maybe Al has trust issues," Gordon said.

"Only one way to find out. Let me tell Ruth and Jake about our lunch plans so they can take their breaks early," Charlie said, putting away his cell phone.

Al was already at a small table in the back of the Walmart Subway section, alone and eating when Charlie arrived, taking his place in the line waiting to order a sandwich.

The tables were almost full. Charlie turned and casually surveyed the grocery customers, paying close attention to a young, slender, dark-haired woman in road crew orange short shorts and a tight sleeveless crop top with a half-full cart. She was leaning over, sorting through the juice section. He wanted to seem like an ordinary guy eyeing the ladies while on lunch break—something that required little effort at the moment.

"Can I help you?" the woman behind the counter said, interrupting his ogling with a sarcastic tone.

He turned around and grinned at the bleached blonde, closer to his age, pleasant enough looking and with meat on her bones, probably more his speed. "Caught me. Umm, I'll have a foot-long turkey on Italian, double mozzarella, not roasted."

She grinned back. "Sure, honey. Anything else?"

"One can only hope, but, no, just a large Coke."

This time she laughed.

Two minutes later, Charlie put his wallet back in his pocket, looked around at the mostly occupied chairs, then over at Al. "Got room, buddy?"

Al nodded. "Sure."

Charlie came over and sat, brought the sandwich out of the bag, took a bite, then a sip of Coke. "I'm Dave," he announced loud enough to be heard from the next table if anyone cared.

"Justin," Al replied. "Like the boots."

Charlie kept chewing for a while, giving Al a chance to talk.

"You and Gordon caused a stir last night. That guy Steve recognized you as soon as he came into the restaurant."

"Yeah, after what happened later, we kind of figured that out. We were hoping his quick glance around the room had passed over us," Charlie replied. "What did he say?"

"He held back at first, not knowing who I was when he came to the table," Al answered, then took a bite of his sandwich before continuing. "After I was introduced as a new 'employee,' he announced that you two were the pawnshop shooters."

"Okay."

"Then Steve added that his brother Jerry had taken a bullet and was feeling a lot of pain. He wanted payback—to take you guys out."

"Almost did, Al. What about the guy in the black suit? The boss? How did he react to this news?"

"That's Clarence, the owner of the place. He was pissed. Clarence told Steve he was a dumb-ass for showing his face in public and putting them all in the spotlight. He needed to get the hell out of there and take care of the problem. He was told not to come back until the job was done—and this time, done right."

"That's when Steve took off?" Charlie asked, taking another bite of sandwich.

Al nodded.

"How did his mother, Sheila Ben, react to all this?" Charlie asked.

"No reaction at all, from what I could tell, but by then I was focusing on Clarence, trying to cinch my acceptance into the group. Once I'd heard them discussing the pawnshop screwup, I knew I was either going to be ranked in or killed." Al looked down one of the grocery aisles, then focused back on Charlie. "See you brought protection."

"Don't say it quite like that."

Al smiled. "Okay. Yeah, once Steve left, Clarence told two of the others, Ronnie and some other guy whose name I never heard, to go with Steve and make sure he didn't screw this up too."

"When did you find out what went down later?"

"I returned to the steakhouse after you left, then, just before the place closed, the two guys came back alone. Ronnie whispered something to Clarence I couldn't hear, then Clarence whispered something back," Al said. "I didn't know if you were alive or what until I was able to leave Ronnie's place this morning. Said I needed some sack time and a change of clothes. Once I was clear, I sent the text. When you answered I knew you were okay. Later I heard on the news about a body turning up in your neighborhood. Was that Steve?"

Charlie nodded. "Shot twice, dumped on my front porch. Some kind of warning, I guess."

"Well, at least you and Gordon are okay."

"How much of what happened does your team know?" Charlie asked.

"Everything Detective DuPree told them after talking to you this morning," Al replied, sipping on the last of his soft drink.

"So, you think the Night Crew is going to find out we're related?" Charlie asked.

"Hope not. I thought of that, but it's worth the risk if I can track down whoever killed the silversmith. I don't know any of these people. I don't know who I can trust, not yet. Which brings up the obvious. You and Gordon are taking these attempts on your lives personally, aren't you?" Al asked. "Obviously he's backing you up right now."

"We don't want to do anything that'll threaten your safety, Al," Charlie said, glancing around. Everyone was busy eating and talking, and nobody had even looked their way.

"That sounds more like a yes than a no, so let's try not to get into each other's way. What do you have in mind?"

"Okay, Al, but keep as much of this to yourself as you can without getting into trouble." Charlie had kept his voice low, but now it was even lower. "We're going to do our best to disrupt these people's operations and basically screw with their lives in every way we can. Once we thin out the Night Crew they'll need someone like you to fill in. Hopefully, you'll be able to get in a position to hear or see something that'll lead you to identifying whoever killed Buck."

"What if you hassle someone who's not part of the crew?"

"We'll be careful. Just count on us pissing them off," Charlie added. "If all you can do is discover who's trying to find Lola Tso, and where she got the squash blossom necklace, that might be enough to make the case."

"Sounds interesting, but I have to follow the law and procedures," Al said. "Don't do anything that'll hurt our case, suppress evidence, or get you arrested, bro."

"Do your best to have your team look the other way."

Al sighed. "And here I am, working with crazies, trying to salvage my career."

Charlie suspected it was more than that, but what could he say about Al's loss of pride, of his reputation, that would help right now? "You'll do just fine, brother. We're both on the same team, we're just running different plays."

"I'm leaving now," Al said, putting his wrappers inside his empty drink cup. "Contact me through DuPree if the need arises."

Charlie nodded. "Have a good one," he said in a normal voice as Al stood.

"You too," Al said, then walked away, throwing his wrapper in a trash can as he left the table area.

Charlie finished his sandwich, then left the Walmart and walked over to a building materials warehouse on the same block. He went into the store, waited a few minutes looking at some paint chips, then exited out into the parking lot. Gordon pulled up and Charlie jumped inside the pickup.

"Didn't pick up on any surveillance, Charlie. How'd it go with Al?"

"He didn't know for sure who'd died until this morning, though he knew Steve was in a tight spot. Clarence Fasthorse had told Steve to take care of us. Al also saw Steve's companions after the attack on us—without Steve. They traded secrets with Clarence, so it confirms that Mr. Fasthorse *is* connected with the Night Crew," Charlie concluded as he drove them east across the Corrales Bridge.

"You tell him what we plan to do?"

"Yeah, he doesn't like the idea, but didn't offer any alternatives. He's worried we'll hurt the undercover operation."

Gordon shrugged. "Your brother's a cop, so I wouldn't expect DuPree or even Nancy to look at it any other way either. Closing these people down and catching a killer puts us on the same path as the cops, but we have to make sure we don't do anything that'll endanger any of the undercover people. We want it to look like a blend of personal and business rivalries. The one thing we don't want to do is show any knowledge or interest in the Buck murder."

"Exactly. Let's get back to work now and think about our first move."

It was easy finding Clarence Fasthorse's address through an Internet search. Next, they had to find out if he really lived there. The structure was a large, modern, flat-roofed two-story stucco and brick building that appeared to be the newest house on the block. It blended in well with the high-end homes in this old, affluent, near-downtown neighborhood.

A dark blue SUV was parked along the curb and a red Mustang in the narrow driveway, visible just inside a metal remote-operated power gate. All this Charlie noted and photographed with a small digital camera as they passed by in Gordon's pickup.

"Okay, we've already got photos and vehicle tags for all the vehicles in the restaurant parking lot—which should include the employees currently at work. And we have these vehicles as well, now," Charlie added. "Once we find out which vehicle Clarence drives and he leaves for the restaurant, we can check out his home more closely."

Gordon stopped at a red light and looked over. "That sexy little Mustang looked more like a chick car to me."

"Could be a girlfriend. If she's living with him it might present a problem," Charlie said. "We'll have to find a time when nobody's home. What if he has a housekeeper?"

"All part of a good recon, Charlie. We may have to take a few days before the time is right—except for the GPS on his car. I'm betting he doesn't travel alone, either, not with a crew at his disposal. He'll have a bodyguard, maybe?"

"Someone to help keep his people in line," Charlie suggested. "Once we see him leave, we'll look for the best time to place the tracker."

"Now we stake out the place and watch for activity. Where to park?" Gordon asked.

"How about the home with the For Sale sign on the lawn? If anyone comes out, we'll be interested, if not, we'll stick around like we're waiting for a Realtor."

"Yeah, and we can look up the place on a cell phone to get the right names and details."

They'd been there less than ten minutes when a man and a

leggy, buxom, black-haired woman came out the front entrance, stopping by the gate for a quick kiss. The woman walked over to the Mustang, climbed in, and backed out as soon as the automatic gate opened. The man, dressed in slacks and a dress shirt, went back inside.

"That was Clarence?" Gordon asked.

"Yeah," Charlie replied, lowering the small telescope, then collapsing it to the size of a pen before placing it into his pocket. "The woman looked to be a few years older than Fasthorse, but is good-looking and probably not the housekeeper."

"Maybe she's a married girlfriend? It would explain the afternoon weekday visit," Gordon suggested.

"We'll have a friend of ours look up the license plate and get us a name. If Mustang Sally doesn't live here, we'll have more opportunities to get inside."

"Once we get past his surveillance cameras," Gordon pointed out.

"One step at a time, Gordo. Here comes Clarence and his backup, bodyguard, or whatever," Charlie said, glancing up into the passenger-side mirror of the pickup. He brought out his pocket telescope again and turned around for a look.

"Tall, athletic black guy about thirty, short hair, shades, with the build of a basketball player, or end," Charlie described. "Light sports jacket, probably to conceal a sidearm. Yeah, caught a glimpse of a holster."

"What's Clarence carrying? A laptop?"

"More like a tablet. Probably uses it at work, assuming he actually does run the restaurant," Charlie added.

"Let's leave before he does. Based on the time of day and the suit jacket, he's probably going to work the evening shift," Gordon suggested, starting the engine. He had to wait a second for a passing vehicle before pulling out into the street.

Five minutes later they were parked across the street from the Piñon Mesa Steakhouse, watching as the blue SUV pulled into the restaurant lot and parked in a space marked "staff."

The driver climbed out the same time as Clarence and the two met in front of the vehicle. Then they walked around the corner of the building to the rear, disappearing from sight.

"There are cameras covering most of the lot, including that SUV. We're going to have to do some sneaky crawly work to place that bug," Gordon observed, "and approach from the blind side, using the SUV itself as a screen from the cameras."

"Flip you for it?" Charlie said, grinning.

"Yeah, like a guy your size can fit underneath that SUV," Gordon said, then sighed. "You're gonna owe me a prime rib dinner, you know that?"

Charlie laughed. "You're on. Now let's round up what we need. We'll want to get this done after dark, during their busy dinnertime when there's going to be a lot more noise and activity."

"It'll be a lot more fun if you let me place a bomb as well," Gordon said, watching in the mirror for an opening in traffic so he could pull out into the street.

"Maybe next time."

It was seven thirty at night, and Gordon had been gone for ten minutes. Another five, maybe less, and he should be done, barring any unforeseen problems. Charlie had parked in the restaurant's lot as close as he could this time, using a rental car they'd picked up across the city. They couldn't risk bringing the pickup again, or his Charger, which was back in service again but recognizable by the two guys who'd accompanied Steve Martinez—and maybe killed him later.

Charlie had been making his pretend cell phone call, watching the restaurant's corners in case Clarence or his bodyguard came out. So far he'd seen nothing but customers entering and leaving.

"Three more minutes," came Gordon's voice over Charlie's Bluetooth earpiece. "I'm waiting for the superglue to set up on the body pan."

"Still clear," Charlie replied. They'd learned to place bugs, bombs, GPS trackers, and other devices years ago, creating ways to disguise their work with fake, weathered covers that appeared to be part of the normal vehicle undercarriage when examined by anyone manning a roadblock.

If done right, their work would pass a casual visual inspection by mirror. Hidden by this particular cover was a tiny microphone placed beneath the front seat of the SUV, via a hole drilled from below. They'd learned where to drill these holes so they'd be difficult to spot from the rear seat. The microphone was purchased locally from a friend of a friend who owned an electronics store. There was also a GPS tracker similar to those used on fancy dog collars.

Charlie, watching the corner of the restaurant, suddenly saw two figures coming around the corner. The lot was well lit and he recognized Fasthorse and his black companion instantly.

"They're coming your way. Time to get out of there!" Charlie ordered, then climbed out of the car. He was wearing a western hat, glasses, and an enhanced belly disguise that added fifty pounds to his frame. He thumbed the panic button on his key fob and suddenly the rental car's horn started beeping and the lights flashing.

He started cussing, then played the fool for about ten seconds fiddling with his key before turning it off. "Dammit to hell," he cussed, then walked toward the restaurant entrance, glancing at Clarence and the other man out of the corner of his eye.

They'd stopped in their tracks and were laughing aloud.

Chapter Ten

Unable to stop now, he continued to the entrance, hoping he'd given Gordon enough time. Just outside the door he paused to tie his shoe. He heard the SUV back up, turn, then drive away toward the street.

Turning, he watched out of the corner of his eye until it disappeared.

A shape rose up from the asphalt behind the concrete parking barrier, picked up a backpack, then walked away from the restaurant toward the sidewalk that paralleled the street.

Charlie walked back to the rental car, and a few minutes later, pulled up beside the curb. Gordon, looking like a street person in a dark hoodie, sneakers, and jeans, climbed in. He was covered with metal shavings and oily dust.

"It's been a long time since I've worked this hard to become invisible. If they hadn't had to back up out of that parking slot I'd have been spotted for sure," Gordon added. "That eight-inch-high barrier was the only cover I had."

"But you got the job done," Charlie replied. "Way to go."

"Let's see for ourselves, fat boy." Gordon reached into the backpack, pulled out a small receiver, and turned up the volume. A voice came out loud and clear. "Yes. I know. I know. At least he can't screw up again. I'm working on it, give me some time. Wait until I get there, okay? We'll talk then. Yes, I had dinner—the Rancher's Special. I've got to go now. Bye."

There was silence for a moment before the person spoke again. "This could take awhile, Leroy. After you drop me off go back to the restaurant and keep an eye on things. If either of those assholes show up again, give me a call."

"Will do, C.J.," came another voice.

After several seconds, Charlie spoke. "The first person is Clarence, the second, his bodyguard—Leroy."

"Did anything strike you about Clarence's tone when he was talking on his cell? What did it sound like to you?"

"Like . . . like he was talking to a nagging wife, or, no, even better, to his mom," Charlie concluded.

"Exactly. I'm betting Clarence is going to talk to his mommy right now. And the way it sounds to me, he's a momma's boy."

"Or under her thumb. She's probably the one who controls the money in the family. She's got a CPA or MBA and used to manage the tribal casino over by Farmington. Sheila Mae Ben's her name now," Charlie recalled.

"We should check into her background as well. Maybe Sheila finances the Night Crew—or manages their ill-gotten gains."

"Ill-gotten gains?" Charlie asked. "You sound like a cop in a forties movie."

"*Excuuuse* me. How about I call it loot?"

"Same movie, but yeah. One syllable, our speed," Charlie joked.

"Are we going to follow Clarence to mommy's house?" Gordon asked, reaching into the glove compartment where he'd kept his smartphone during the bugging operation.

"Yeah, and assuming the GPS also works, we can stay far enough away to avoid being spotted," Charlie said, checking in his rearview mirror.

"I wonder where Al is right now?" Charlie asked. "In the restaurant with the Night Crew?"

"Shoulda bugged *him*," Gordon pointed out, checking the GPS tracking app. "Hey, Clarence is heading toward his home," Gordon noticed. "How many strong-arm crooks still live with their mothers?"

"I keep telling you, this generation has no self-respect," Charlie said. "But if he does, at least he's saving on house payments. It must work for him, he's obviously a lot richer than us."

"Where did we go wrong?" Gordon replied and checked the device. "The SUV stopped a few houses down, so maybe he doesn't live in the same house after all. Still creepy, though, his age and living just down the street from your mom."

"Switch on that mike again," Charlie suggested, holding up his hand.

Gordon nodded, grabbed the device, and turned up the volume.

They heard country-western music, then Clarence spoke. "I'll call you later, Leroy. And keep an eye on this new guy, Biggs. We're pushing our luck right now, so make sure he's kept in the dark as much as possible until we see him in action and know he can do something besides breaking into houses. He already knows way too much to let him get away."

Gordon looked over at Charlie. "Al is Biggs?"

Charlie nodded. They heard an "Okay, boss," then the slam of a car door. The country-western music continued for another thirty seconds, then they heard rap lyrics and a rhythmic *boom boom* of heavy bass.

"Leroy's playing your second most favorite music." Gordon looked over at Charlie with a grin.

Charlie nodded, then repeated one of their favorite phrases. "Everything else tied for first."

A few minutes later they passed the residence where the SUV had been briefly parked. A green Mercedes was in the driveway of this older building, just three homes down from Clarence's place. This home was larger than Fasthorse's, with tile roofs and a Spanish Colonial look. The walls were topped with decorative wrought iron railing topped with sharp points, and the twin metal gates were massive.

"That looks like a tougher nut to crack than C.J.'s house," Gordon commented as they continued down the street.

"When we bug his place, how about using a small drone, going through an open window, then dropping the mike, concealed in some everyday object, or hidden behind something, or in a vase?" Charlie speculated, driving out of the area in the direction of his home.

He checked the rearview mirror, noting a dark van about a block behind them. In a few minutes, he'd change directions and see if they'd picked up a tail.

"Sounds tricky and maybe a little too expensive. Think simple," Gordon said, not noticing Charlie's concern.

"Okay. Get one of their waitstaff pens—the ones with Piñon Mesa Steakhouse on them—hide the mike inside, then slip it into Clarence's coat pocket."

"I like that idea, but who's going to get that close except the babe in the Mustang?"

Charlie shrugged. "Yeah, let's think about it a little longer. You about ready to call it a night?" He turned left at the last second and the van behind them continued down the street.

"Yeah. Drop me off at my place. Call me in the morning when you're ready to return the car and I'll pick you up at the rental lot," Gordon offered.

Charlie nodded, fiddled with the seat adjustment, then grumbled to himself. He was so comfortable in his Charger now that no other ride seemed to fit his frame.

Five minutes later he decided to stop checking the rearview mirror. No van, no tail, and no reason to worry. Maybe it was one of the undercover cops backing up Al—Mr. Biggs. They had the resources to check up on the rental car, which meant they'd found out who was driving by now. He'd rented the sedan in his own name.

Charlie yawned and Gordon laughed. "Get me home before you doze off, Chuck, and try to keep the dead guys off your porch. This keeps up and you're going to get a reputation."

•   •   •

Charlie woke up to the faint tone of his cell phone—a text message was coming in. He reached over blindly, groped across the top of the nightstand, and grabbed the cell. Pulling the charging cord loose, he looked at the display. It was Al.

Deciphering the text language, he learned that Al was going with a crew tomorrow night to "jack some guy" they'd targeted. He hoped to learn how they chose their targets, and what happened to the stolen money—and particularly the vehicles, which, apparently, were usually pickups. It made sense; stolen pickups were hot in Mexico for transportation and parts.

He acknowledged the message and reminded Al to be careful. The text conversation ended quickly and Charlie hooked up the charger again. He lay there for several minutes, thinking about the bug he wanted to place in Clarence's home.

Planting one on the man himself would be risky and short-lived because it usually involved placing it on clothing, which was subject to laundering and discovery. The more he thought about it, though, the better the pen idea seemed, and they had a few small bugs salvaged from their experiences last year that could be put to good use. His mind made up, Charlie cleared his thoughts, listened to his deep breaths, and quickly went to sleep again.

The next two days passed quickly, and, after watching Clarence's habits, they'd come up with a plan to bug the man's residence. Now, all it had to do was work.

Charlie, parked in his Charger down the street, watched as Gordon walked up the sidewalk, walked over to the locked driveway gate, then stuck a rolled-up piece of yellow paper in the gap between the doors.

"Clear," Charlie said into his cell phone, noting that no cars were coming down the street. Gordon brought out a pen and tossed it over the wall. It landed on the grass inside the yard. He turned, walked back out to the sidewalk, and proceeded to the next house, placing a rolled-up flyer at the gate.

Charlie picked up Gordon around the corner, and Gordon set the flyers advertising a legitimate landscaping service down on the floor. They'd made copies of one left on the pawnshop's customer-shared bulletin board.

"Perfect shot. The pen landed about a foot from the flagstone walk. All he has to do is see it on the way to the front door, pick it up, and put it in his pocket," Gordon said. "Hopefully, my throw didn't get picked up on any surveillance camera he may have."

"Yeah, if he reviews every camera every day, it might get noticed, but even then, it's such a small detail. We just have to hope he keeps it with him, or, because he's probably already carrying a nicer pen, set this down someplace inside as a spare," Charlie said.

Gordon looked at his watch. "He should be coming home about now if he keeps his after-lunch schedule."

Charlie nodded, making the turn along a parallel street. He parked and Gordon turned on the receiver. The sound of a vehicle came through clearly on the device. "It works. Now let's just hope he falls for it."

Five minutes later, they switched on the bug, instantly picking up some classical music that sounded familiar. Charlie looked over at Gordon. "It worked, the pen is in the house. Clarence is playing mood music. I bet he's expecting the chick in the Mustang."

"Maybe. What do you say we circle the block and verify the chick is part of his schedule?"

"And if she isn't—gross. I'm turning off the mike," Charlie said. "And, no, if she shows up and they start getting it on, we don't listen."

"Rats," Gordon said. "You're no fun."

Once they verified that Clarence was going to be busy on noncriminal matters for a while—Mustang Sally had arrived—they decided to get a late lunch. When the girlfriend left they might be able to learn something important, especially when Leroy arrived to pick him up.

It was mid-afternoon when they saw Leroy leave the restaurant and climb into the blue SUV. They'd switched vehicles now, to Gordon's truck, and changed their appearance with hats, glasses, and different shirts. As they neared the neighborhood where Clarence lived, Charlie switched on the bug.

It only took a few seconds to realize Clarence was on the phone with his mother, Sheila.

"The timing was off and the target left early, Mom. That pickup will get a great price, so it's worth waiting for our next opportunity. The new guy, Biggs, will be there and we'll see how he does. McCrystal and Atcitty will handle the details, and after the grab Biggs will stick with Atcitty. There's no reason for Biggs to see the garage until we've vetted him out just a little more. I know. I know. Don't worry, Mom. Yeah. My ride is coming up the street. See you after dinner. Love you too."

Gordon looked over at Charlie, and rolled his eyes. "C.J. really needs to grow a pair."

"Based upon how long Mustang Sally stayed, he might still have some. But until he cuts those strings I doubt any chick is going to move in. He's probably buying her lots of stuff, though, like that car, and keeping the girl away from Mom. I bet Sheila's the mother-in-law from hell," Charlie added.

"Wouldn't know about that, thank God."

"Think you'll ever get married, Gordon, seriously?"

"Ask me again in ten years."

Charlie knew just enough about Gordon's mom and pop to understand Gordon's hesitation with a long-term relationship.

"How about you?"

Charlie shrugged. "My mom and dad made it work, my brother not so much, though he's sticking it out so far. And Jayne, she goes from one loser to another. At least she hasn't married one yet."

"Ruth is available. And you know she likes you," Gordon said. "If you don't start making a move she'll think you're not interested. A woman like that, smart, beautiful, and maybe rich someday . . . is quite a catch."

"She's outta my league, bro."

"Don't sell yourself short, Charlie."

Charlie shrugged. "I need more to offer. She deserves the best."

"The best isn't always something that can be measured in numbers. Remember her ex-husband? Character—it really does count."

Charlie nodded, then, hearing voices coming in from the bug, was grateful he didn't have to respond. Ruth *was* out of his league.

Chapter Eleven

That afternoon Al had managed to text Charlie the license number of the vehicle scheduled to be highjacked—a crime Al was going to commit along with some of the Night Crew. A call to Nancy and the promise to keep her informed resulted in the name of the owner and his vehicle—a 2011 silver Ford F-250 pickup.

Charlie and Gordon decided that this offered them an opportunity to upset the Night Crew's plans in a way that would gain instant attention—and maybe motivate Clarence into making a mistake that would bring the killer or killers among the group into focus.

They learned that the owner—the crew's target—was a man who taught conversational Navajo at an evening CNM class at an Albuquerque campus. He lived a half hour away north near Algodones, a rural community between Bernalillo and Santa Fe. Charlie and Gordon had quickly driven the route during the day and

decided upon the best location for a highjacking on a truly iso-
lated section of highway.

There was only one practical route for the carjackers to take
as they made their escape from that location, so all Charlie and
Gordon had to do was sit and wait. They'd already learned when
the class was supposed to end and could make a good estimate
of travel time.

They'd rented a big old Suburban at a "rent-a-wreck" place in
the south valley, and the heavy vehicle, dents and scrapes at no
extra charge, was ideal for their plans. They stuck a fake paint company sign on the door and mounted a ladder on top.

Within a few minutes of their scheduled time, 9:30 PM, they
saw headlights, then the Ford pickup approaching. Following several car lengths behind the pickup was a white van.

Gordon, in the backseat, was crouched down low, the rifle with
the nightscope on the bench seat beside him. It was up to Charlie, pretending to be using his cell phone, to keep track of the
vehicles.

"Okay, there goes the target," Charlie announced, getting a
quick look at the rear tag as the big pickup cruised by at a leisurely
pace. It was very dark this far north from the city lights, the speed
limit was 45 mph, and the part-time instructor was driving con-
servatively. "And here's the chase vehicle, an old, dirty Chevy van,
nice and heavy."

The van slowed as it passed him and Gordon, and Charlie,
wearing a painter's cap, turned his head away to avoid a good
profile in case anyone knew his face. "Giving me a good look, I'm
guessing. These guys are careful."

The van accelerated on. Charlie waited a moment before making a three-point turn, facing in the direction of the two vehicles but keeping his lights off.

Gordon sat up. "They should be making their move right around the next curve, if we guessed right. According to what DuPree's told us regarding victim accounts, they follow a regular routine—signal to pass, then cutting off the victim and forcing him or her to stop to avoid a collision."

"And they jump out and wave around their guns." Charlie checked the rearview mirror, just in case. "Nothing behind us but Bernalillo."

They had their windows down and only a few more seconds passed before they heard the squeal of tires in the distance. Ahead, he could see the two vehicles that had passed blocking most of the road, which was narrow here, with irrigation ditches on either side.

"It's going down," Gordon announced. "We missed picking the spot by less than a quarter mile. Let's do this." He pulled the ski mask down over his face.

Charlie drove slowly toward the site of the carjacking, lights still off, then stopped, blocking the narrow road at a forty-five-degree angle. Gordon jumped out with the assault rifle. He ran over to the irrigation ditch, dropped to the ground, then found a suitable firing position, hidden by tall grasses. Charlie pulled down his own mask, climbed out, ran around and raised the hood, placing an old skillet atop the radiator.

Whipping out a lighter, he watched the carjacking in the distance, waiting for the right moment to light the fuse of the smoke bomb he'd placed in the skillet.

Once the two vehicles down the road began to move, Charlie lit the smoke bomb and stepped away, moving from side to side in mock panic but keeping his back to the approaching headlights. It took less than fifteen seconds for them to arrive, the pickup leading the way.

The just-carjacked F-250 skidded to a stop and the driver jumped out of the cab, still wearing a black ski mask and waving a pistol. "Get that piece of shit off the road!" the guy yelled. The following van stopped just behind the pickup. As Charlie turned to face them, he could see two masked men inside.

Gordon shot out the driver's side front tire of the van.

The pickup driver looked toward the ditch and Charlie used the distraction to Taser the man. The carjacker's pistol went off before it fell out of his hand, the bullet striking the pavement. The driver fell to the asphalt, thrashing around like a trout on a hook.

"Out of the van, assholes!" Gordon yelled, walking rapidly toward the vehicle, keeping the dot of the laser sight on the van driver's face mask.

Charlie turned off the Taser, then brought out his Beretta as he advanced toward the dazed pickup driver still twitching on the road. "Make a move and you'll have more blood than piss on your pants," Charlie yelled, yanking the Taser leads away from the man and breaking the circuit.

A few minutes later, all three disarmed carjackers, one of them Al, were facedown on the pavement, bound with plastic ties behind their backs. Charlie took their wallets, and three cell phones, two of them cheap burner phones, plus a high-end one that probably belonged to the owner of the Ford pickup.

While Gordon guarded their prisoners, Charlie put away the Taser, then got rid of his phony smoke diversion before turning the Suburban around, facing it toward Albuquerque.

He joined Gordon, looked down at the 'jackers, then kicked Al in the ribs.

"Listen up. You punks tell Deadhorse or whoever's running your crew that we're going to get a great price for this F-250. We're taking over the jacking business in this state, so you'd better switch to purse snatching old ladies and busting open parking meters. We're smart and you're stupid. Come after us and we'll rat your boss out to the cops."

Gordon laughed. "When I say get up, losers, you're going to walk over to the side of the road and jump down into that irrigation ditch. If you try anything else, I'll shoot you in the balls. Really," Gordon added. "Now, get up!"

The three men scrambled clumsily to their feet, unable to use their hands, then walked over to the side of the road. "You guys are dead!" Al threatened.

"You first!" Gordon replied, then fired a shot into the ditch just beside Al. Immediately, the three stepped into the icy water, which was a disappointing two feet deep.

"Start walking back toward that guy who just lost his pickup," Charlie yelled. "Turn around and I'll Taser you in the water."

"Do it! That'll fry them up good," Gordon responded. The three men, still wearing their masks, picked up the pace, splashing water everywhere.

Charlie backed away, nodding toward the vehicles.

●　　●　　●

They were five minutes down the road, with the lights of Berna-lillo in sight, when Charlie's phone rang. It was Gordon, and he put it on speaker.

"You think the victim—the real one—is okay?" Gordon asked. "We didn't hear shots."

"Hope so. It's only a few miles farther to his home, so I'm guessing the teacher is hot footing it there now. I used my burn phone to call the sheriff's department," Charlie replied.

"What if the Night Crew can't get loose in time?"

Charlie chuckled. "I slipped a pocket knife into Al's pocket while I was searching them, and he had a cell phone I didn't find. They've probably already called for help and are no doubt running back to change that flat before the deputies arrive or the victim can make it home and report the incident. Hopefully the GPS you hid in the van will lead us to where they stash their vehicles."

"At least Al did a good job playing the tough guy in front of the others, considering this was a surprise for him as well. Bet his ribs are gonna hurt," Gordon said.

"I kicked him harder than that when I was back in the sixth grade. The bruise will give him some cred, along with the pocket-knife and cell phone he managed to hide. This incident will make everyone but him look bad. He was just along for the ride."

"So, we'd better pull over so I can attach that fake license plate. I'm driving a hot truck now, Charlie."

"Copy that."

An hour later Charlie and Gordon left the Rio Rancho RV yard after dropping off the Ford F-250 in their newly rented space. Not long after that, they pulled into a parking space at Gina and

Nancy's condo next to Charlie's Dodge and climbed out of the rental Suburban.

"What's Nancy going to say when she comes off shift and finds this beast in one of their two parking slots?" Gordon asked as they walked to the Charger.

"She'll guess, probably correctly, but we couldn't stash it at our places or the shop—in case some of Fasthorse's crew comes looking. They don't know for sure it was us, but count on somebody checking anyway," Charlie said. "The Suburban goes back to the rental place tomorrow morning, which means we'll both have to get away sometime during the AM."

"What do you think Clarence is going to do about this?"

Charlie shrugged. "Hopefully he'll be pissed enough to try something stupid. I'm still trying to figure out how to link him back to the killing of that silversmith—and the incident at our place."

"We can't forget about Lola Tso either. She's the key to all this. I wonder how APD is doing tracking her down," Gordon said as they climbed into the Dodge, Charlie behind the wheel.

"Well, DuPree and Nancy both were supposed to keep us current on that, and sometimes no news is no news. Let's ask tomorrow."

Gordon smiled. "It'll also give us a chance to see their reactions to what we did tonight. That's got to filter up through Al—you think?"

"Yeah, all Al needs to do is get in deep enough to find out who did the hit on Cordell Buck. Once the undercover people get a name everything focuses on the motive—and gathering enough evidence to put the shooter away." Charlie started the engine and pulled out into the street. "Stopping the carjacking crew is just icing on the cake."

"I'm hungry. Wanna stop for a burger?"

Charlie looked at his watch. "They're still open. Five Guys?"

"Nothing about last night's fun and games on the news or in the paper, but I'm sure there is a police report on the missing F-250," Gordon said, looking up from the *Albuquerque Journal*.

He was in their office, waiting to open for the day. Jake and Ruth were already out front getting the register set up and the paperwork out. Every pawned item had to be photographed and cataloged, and since the squash blossom transaction they were being very careful. Each customer was also being recorded digitally by their surveillance system, which included a low-angle camera to catch faces.

Charlie turned away from the keyboard of his computer. "We can ask Nancy to check crime reports for us when we drop by to pick up that Suburban. We'll have to keep the F-250 out of sight for a few days before we think of a way to get it back to the owner."

"How's this? We might just 'find' it by the road with the keys in the ignition and turn it over to the sheriff," Gordon suggested.

"Okay. Let me call Gina and see if Nancy's awake now."

There was news from Nancy, but it wasn't much help. She'd found out that Leroy was Leroy Williams, a former Army MP listed as a Piñon Mesa Steakhouse employee, and that the woman they called Mustang Sally was really Melinda Beth Foy, a divorced and apparently unemployed "entertainer" with a brief prostitution record.

She'd also worked for a local caterer as a server until three months ago.

A few hours later they decided to follow through with the next phase of their plan. They immediately got a hit on the GPS Gordon had planted in the van, a converted gas station close to the downtown area that was now part of a used car dealership called Rex's Quality Rides.

When they drove past in Gordon's pickup, Charlie counted nearly three dozen cars in the lot and spotted two salesmen outside. "I don't see the van, so it must be inside the service bay," Charlie observed.

"Can't think of a better place to stash stolen vehicles until they can be driven south to the border," Gordon said. "The garage windows are painted over, naturally."

"A nice setup. This lot is only a half mile or so from Fasthorse's restaurant. Jack the vehicle, park it at Rex's in the bay, then stop by for a late-night steak. What do you think?" Charlie asked.

"Convenient. Shall we fire up the bugs and see if we can hear any reaction from Clarence? He usually arrives at the restaurant this time of day." Gordon nodded toward the glove compartment.

"Good idea," Charlie said, reaching for the monitor unit. "I wonder what excuses he got from the two regulars—McCrystal and Atcitty? This could backfire, you know, if Clarence ties this incident to the presence of a new guy, Al. It never happened before."

"Well, we don't know how many guys are working the Night Crew, but he's lost two already and has another out of commission—assuming the guy you shot is still alive somewhere," Gordon pointed out. "Clarence might need Al and be willing to take the risk."

Charlie nodded, trying to come up with a reasonable number for Clarence's gang. "There's the three at first, minus two and a half, and I recall seeing five guys, including Al, around Clarence the night we dined at the restaurant—before Steve showed up. Help me here, bro."

"Okay, I get four and a half—the half being the wounded guy, plus Al. Leroy might be one of the others, or just Clarence's security. Either way, according to what victims have said, they hit in teams of three. Clarence had seven people, at least. Maybe more."

"There's whoever he has in the auto theft pipeline, here and around the border. You suppose he hires freelancers to deliver the stolen vehicles?" Charlie asked.

"It's what I'd do. If they get caught, who could they rat out?"

"We're getting close to the restaurant, well within bug range. Hit the horn," Charlie requested, holding his ear to the receiver.

Gordon complied, then looked over at him. "I picked it up on the bug, which means the blue SUV is probably at the restaurant."

"Try the frequency for the home bug, just in case he put the pen back into his pocket."

They tested it again with a honk of the horn, but heard nothing. "Pass by the restaurant, then let's pass by Clarence and Sheila's homes. Maybe we can pick up some chat."

The block containing the two buildings was less than five minutes away. As Gordon passed Clarence's home, Charlie touched the pad to activate the pen bug.

"Nothing." He tried again. "I can't get any signal. It won't turn on. The battery was good. What happened?"

Gordon continued down the block, passing the Ben residence,

and turned the corner. "If it won't activate, either the bug had given up the ghost or Clarence found it."

"Or he threw it away or gave it to someone else, or . . . Well, it doesn't really matter. We're screwed," Charlie admitted.

"We still have the one in his SUV," Gordon pointed out.

"Yeah, but if he found this one, he'll be searching for another."

"And if he didn't, maybe we'll get something new. We know his schedule, well, his old schedule."

"Which he might just change around now that he's feeling some heat," Charlie agreed. "He's got to wonder how we knew about the carjacking, so he's going to be watching all of his crew, not just Al."

"Good point." Gordon nodded.

"Let's come back after lunch and see if he goes home to meet up with his girlfriend—Melinda," Charlie suggested. "He might also have something to say to Leroy during the drive."

"If not, I've got an idea, a way to use the stolen pickup."

"What's the plan?"

Gordon chuckled, turning north along Fourth Street. "If what we did last night has Clarence pissed off, this will probably put him over the top."

Chapter Twelve

Wearing gloves, Charlie drove the stolen F-250 past the Piñon Mesa Steakhouse just after lunch, Gordon following in Charlie's Dodge. The restaurant parking lot was full, and the blue SUV that Clarence Fasthorse used for transportation was in its usual slot.

"The bug in the car still works," Gordon announced via Bluetooth, "and I'm going to see if we can still listen in when we reach the used car lot. With all the high-rise office buildings around, the signal might be blocked."

"Okay. Stand by to make that call to APD. I can see Rex's lot ahead," Charlie replied, stretching out his left leg, appreciating the space. The pickup was nice and the cab enormous. This truck was almost as well appointed as Gordon's.

Charlie took one more look around the cab, making sure there was nothing left behind, then came to a halt, waiting for cars to pass so he could make the turn into Rex's customer parking area. Beyond were four rows of cars plus the business office. In one of the garage bays was the van used in last night's carjacking—or at least the GPS bug Gordon had stuck under the seat.

Nancy had helped him search public records for the owner of Rex's Quality Rides and got a corporate name neither recognized. It was a shell company and would take awhile to backtrack to the actual owner. Charlie's money was on Clarence, his mom, or maybe a relative of theirs.

Charlie parked the truck, climbed out quickly, tossed the key under the vehicle, then waved at a salesperson in a white shirt and tie standing just outside the office. Charlie turned away and took off his gloves as he walked over to the sidewalk. Gordon pulled up in the Charger and Charlie jumped in.

"Cops are on their way?" Charlie said.

"According to dispatch," Gordon said, racing away from the curb, heading back in the direction of the Fasthorse restaurant.

"How did the department employee working dispatch react when you told them where to find the stolen truck—and more?" Charlie asked, listening in on the bug beneath Clarence's SUV.

"She wanted my name. So I repeated Rex's Quality Rides, their address, and asked her to advise officers that there might be other vehicles on site that are connected to crimes. I told her I was an anonymous caller and didn't want to be involved. I added that she should ask Detective DuPree to come to that location as well." Gordon grinned.

"All that?"

"What can I say? I like to talk to women, and they usually listen."

"Huh?"

"Funny man. Anything on that bug?" Gordon said, nodding toward the receiver Charlie was holding.

"Hang on. Better pull over," Charlie said, glancing in the side mirror.

Gordon squeezed to the right, allowing an unmarked sedan with emergency lights to race past. "Hey, is that?"

"DuPree. Looks like he got the message. Better get out of here before he sees us," Charlie advised.

They were heading north, halfway to the pawnshop, when Charlie's phone rang. He looked at the display—the call was unlisted. "Bet that's Detective Dupree," Charlie said, touching the green phone icon.

"If it is, put it on speaker," Gordon whispered.

"Charlie, what are you and that evil dwarf up to now? The salesmen here claim a big Indian dropped off that stolen truck and that they know nothing about it."

"Dwarf? I'm hurt," Gordon said, loud enough to be heard.

"They said it was me?" Charlie asked.

"Not by name, but the description sure fit you," DuPree responded.

"Well," Charlie replied, "it is possible that the people working at Rex's aren't among the same three that took the pickup last night, though they're connected. That site is where the Night Crew parks some of their vehicles—maybe the stolen ones as well. What else did you find besides the van used by the crew when they 'jacked that pickup?"

"How did you . . . never mind, I don't want to know," DuPree said, his voice rising in pitch.

"Breathe deeply, Detective, then count to ten," Gordon suggested.

"Count the number of fingers I'm holding up, Sweeney," DuPree replied. "How did you two end up with a stolen Ford pickup, anyway?"

"Is taking a truck away from someone who just stole it from the owner, stealing?" Gordon asked. "You might want to check with your sources on this case, if you catch my drift. One of them might be able to tell you more about this."

Charlie wondered why Al hadn't passed the events of last night along to his undercover team, but didn't want to ask, knowing DuPree might have someone standing close by who didn't need to hear.

"I'm alone now, speak freely," DuPree responded. "And, no, our inside contact hasn't reported in yet."

"Probably because of the encounter he witnessed. If they were trying to show him how the professionals jack a vehicle, they failed," Charlie added. "And now that their vehicle stash location may have been compromised, they're having to go with plan B."

"You think the subjects under investigation have any idea who's been screwing with them?" DuPree asked. "You two aren't very subtle and you certainly have a motive. They've encountered you two, what, four times now, and tried to take you out at least twice."

"I'm hoping they're going to try one more time and we can finally take them down," Gordon said.

"But with a murder charge, not just strong-arm carjackings and robbery," Charlie added.

"Don't forget felony assault and windshield bashing," Gordon tossed in.

"Droll, Sweeney. Someday, guys, you're going to put yourselves out there in the bull's-eye one too many times," DuPree warned.

"We're whittling them down, though, and this might help your source get what is needed to put them away—a witness, a gun, something . . ." Charlie pointed out.

"Just be careful. You guys create too much paperwork for me as it is."

"Sorry for the inconvenience," Gordon responded, looking over at Charlie, who couldn't help but smile.

"Go home, go back to work. Whatever. Just stay out of trouble," DuPree advised.

"One question first," Charlie replied.

"What?"

"Has anyone found any trace of Lola Tso? She knows where she got the squash blossom necklace, and that makes her a threat to the Night Crew and Mr. Fasthorse."

"We've got officers watching her place, twenty-four seven, and checking the places we think she might visit, but she hasn't turned up anywhere. The tribal cops have been following up with their sources on tribal land and none of them have heard a thing either. Lola Tso has gone to ground."

"Hopefully not literally. Let us know if there are any leads whatsoever, okay?" Charlie asked, deciding to press Nancy again and see if she could come up with a lead on Lola.

"Give me something you've learned about Clarence Fasthorse or his Night Crew. This sharing has got to go both ways, boys."

Charlie looked at Gordon, who nodded. "We've been in a position to overhear a conversation or two, and we've discovered that Sheila Ben, Fasthorse's mother, definitely knows what's going on. She even knew about the move on the Ford F-250, the one that ended up at Rex's," Gordon explained.

"That didn't come from our source," DuPree responded, meaning Al Henry.

"No, but it adds another name to the short list of known Night Crew affiliates. The lady may even be financing the operation. She's got a business background and ran a tribal casino at one time, right?" Gordon said, looking over at Charlie, who nodded.

"I'll pass this along. We knew that Clarence and his mother are close, but this info will open up additional avenues of investigation," DuPree said.

"So what else do you have on Lola Tso?" Charlie asked.

"Like I said, not much. There's been some discussion about pulling the surveillance on her apartment. Three officers are tied up their entire shifts and so far we've got zip. Have to go now, guys. Watch yourselves."

By then they were approaching FOB Pawn. There were several cars parked along the street. "More traffic than usual," Gordon observed. "Is it the curious, or customers?" Gordon added.

"Hopefully the latter. Park this baby and let's see if Jake and Ruth can use some help," Charlie said, making a mental note to call Nancy in the evening after she went on shift. Maybe she could offer something new concerning Lola.

There were a lot of people to serve, as they'd hoped, and Charlie and Gordon ended up doing some heavy lifting, boxing then loading a big screen TV and gas barbecue grill into the van of a wheelchair-bound vet. They offered to help him unload the items when he got home, but the man, a former Marine, said he had friends who'd be off work by then and were coming to help.

There was also paperwork to do, catching up on the cataloging of pawn, then locking the items, which included three guns, into the secure storeroom's metal locker. Around four in the afternoon business tapered off and Charlie and Gordon took over the front room while Ruth and Jake did the bookkeeping, a never-ending process.

After a while, Jake poked his head out of the office. "There's a guy standing out back beside a dark blue SUV that's blocking the alley. Thought you'd like to know."

Gordon glanced over at Charlie. "Young, slender, good-looking Indian, white shirt, a dark suit jacket?"

"Naw, a big black guy in his early thirties wearing a light Windbreaker. Looks like he played football—or wrestled," Jake said. He'd once wrestled in one of the pro circuits.

"Leroy Williams," Charlie replied. "Looks like we're finally getting through to somebody. Guess the man's here to deliver a message."

"Or a threat," Gordon said, reaching into his pocket to make sure his pistol was handy.

"Is this shotgun trouble again?" Jake asked, glancing over at Ruth, who'd come up beside him, concern in her expression.

"No. If he was looking for a fight he wouldn't be the only one out there," Charlie said.

"Maybe he's not," Ruth suggested, turning to look at the other outside camera monitor, which covered the front.

"Anyone?" Gordon asked, walking in that direction.

"Not that I can see," Ruth said.

Jake also took a look, shaking his head.

Charlie checked both monitors again. "Tell you what, guys. I'll go out and talk to the guy. Gordon, keep an eye out but stay inside unless you spot a problem."

"I've got the front door," Jake said, coming out and walking toward the front counter.

"Ruth . . ."

"I'll help keep watch and stand by with the phone, just in case," she said. "I know where the emergency pistol is kept and have no problem using it."

Good girl, Charlie thought. Ruth had kept a revolver handy for years while on the run with her son, Renée. Charlie wished she'd never have to live in fear again, but around him, and this place, things just seemed to happen.

Charlie checked his own handgun before placing it back into the holster, safety off. Leroy probably knew Charlie carried a weapon, and Charlie knew that Leroy did.

Charlie paused for a second, nodded to Gordon, then stepped out onto the loading dock, closing the door behind him.

"Been waiting long?" Charlie asked as he looked at the

fit-looking black man, leaning casually against the side of the blue SUV, a handgun visible in a shoulder rig just inside his Windbreaker.

Leroy shrugged. "Long enough. Don't you watch your security cams?" He nodded toward the surveillance camera along the roof parapet.

Charlie shrugged. "Ask your boss's three stooges, Jerry, Steve, and Mario. You're going to have to speak real loud to the last two."

"You're getting to be a real pain in the ass, Henry," the man replied, taking a step forward.

"Just getting started, Mr. Williams," Charlie said, his hand a little closer to the butt of his weapon.

Leroy looked surprised, for a second, upon hearing his name.

Charlie continued. "We're the new game in town, and we know way more than your boss thinks we do. We're much better thieves than those punks who hang around his restaurant, jacking cars and stealing turquoise jewelry.

"Just so you know, for two guys running a pawnshop, my partner and I bring in a lot of cash off the books," Charlie added, wishing it was actually true. At the moment, they were still learning the business, and if it wasn't for Jake and Ruth's experience they'd barely be breaking even.

"Then why give up that Ford F-250? There's a big market for newer model trucks below the border. Makes you look stupid."

"No, what it does is make your boss, Clarence, look like a car thief. Who owns that car lot anyway, one of his relatives? His mommy?"

Leroy's expression turned ugly, and he took another step closer. Charlie stopped him by placing a hand on his Beretta.

Leroy calmed down visibly, but his voice was cold. "You're disrespecting people I care about. If you and your buddy don't back off, you're going to get more than a beat down. That's a guarantee."

"Okay. Go back to your boss— if he hasn't been arrested and hauled downtown—and tell him you've delivered the message. Warn him not to cross us or get in our way or we're going to do a lot more than embarrass him with the cops. We've kicked bigger butts than his, I guarantee."

Leroy stood there a moment, started to say something, then mumbled a curse and walked back to the SUV. Ten seconds later, he raced down the alley, tires squealing.

Charlie turned toward the camera on the parapet above and made a face.

The door opened and Gordon stuck his head out. "Why'd you let him escape?"

Charlie laughed, climbed the stairs to the loading dock, and stepped inside. "Let me tell you about it."

Chapter Thirteen

"Okay, we've clearly been made, there's no question about it now," Gordon said, taking a sip of beer and leaning back in his office chair. They were closed, Jake and Ruth had gone home, and it was just him and Charlie. "That might have taken some pressure off Al—assuming they don't connect you as his brother," Gordon added.

Charlie shrugged. "There are a lot of Navajos, and, as you pointed out, we don't look related."

"Are we still going to step up our game?" Gordon asked.

"Of course, and the more attention we get, the less Clarence will be looking at Al—I'm hoping. Either way, we've rattled the cage and hopefully put some nervous heat on Fasthorse and the Night Crew. We need to find out more on how they've reacted," Charlie replied. "And really watch our backs."

"Always. But we also need to know where the cops are in this, not just with DuPree's investigation, but also from your brother's undercover team," Gordon pointed out. "For instance, have they found anything solid that links any particular crime directly to Clarence?"

Charlie didn't know. "Maybe we'll have to give them some time for things to unfold. Details from Al come in when they come in. He's probably being closely watched by Clarence and the rest of his crew."

"And Clarence is clearly worried about blowback or he wouldn't have sent his muscle to warn us off. He can't exactly rat us out to the cops without putting himself into the spotlight even more. Maybe we should sit tight for a few days," Gordon suggested.

"We don't sit tight."

"Then what?"

"I'd been thinking about this earlier. How about we meet up with Nancy and see if we can get anything else on Lola? DuPree hasn't been able to come up with anything, but then again, anyone who sees him coming knows he's a cop." Charlie stood, dropping his empty beer bottle into the trash.

"I'll check the locks out front and set the alarm. Wanna take my truck or the Charger?"

"Let's swing by your place and leave the pickup behind. That's the last thing those boys at Rex's saw of us, so let's give them a different look. Of course, they may just be fronting for the crew," Charlie answered.

"You can bet those used-car salesmen described my truck perfectly. Let's keep them guessing. Purple Dodge Charger it is. Who's going to remember something like that?" Gordon said, grinning.

Ten minutes later, they were cruising south across the city, heading toward downtown. Nancy had agreed to meet them for dinner at one of her favorite late-night spots, a sandwich shop near the bus depot.

Charlie's cell phone started to ring. "Put that on speaker, will you?" he asked, since he didn't have his Bluetooth.

"It's Nancy," Gordon said, pushing the speaker icon as he looked at the display.

"Charlie, sorry, I have to cancel dinner. I just got a call," Nancy said, all business at the moment.

"Sure. Contact when you're free," Charlie answered.

"Later," she answered, ending the connection.

Gordon looked over. "You wanna swing by Lola's apartment again, just in case?"

"No, I've got a more interesting idea. We're already headed in that general direction, how about we have another talk with Mike the Pimp at the Firehouse Tavern?"

"Do they serve anything besides beer, chips, and bouncers? I'm hungry," Gordon said.

"I recall some of the patrons were eating sandwiches."

"Good, even cold cuts will hit the spot. I need more than nachos or pretzels. I need to eat my weight every day to stay alive," Gordon joked.

Charlie nodded, having seen Gordon down an entire large combo pizza in a half hour. He signaled at the next intersection, waiting for a green arrow to make a left-hand turn. The Firehouse was several miles from their current location. "If you're starving, we can stop along the way."

"Naw."

Charlie drove down Louisiana Boulevard, knowing it intersected Central Avenue within a half block of the tavern. He checked randomly in the rearview mirror for a tail.

After a while, Gordon spoke. "That Mike Schultz guy—you've kept that burn phone charged so he could call, right?"

Charlie nodded. "Think it was a waste of electricity, asking him to call if he came up with any news on Lola."

"Well, he's probably still pimping. From what we heard from that waitress, though, at least he protects his women."

"Kind of a backhanded compliment."

"That's the most he'll get from me," Gordon admitted.

They pulled into the tavern's parking lot just as the evening crowd was starting to file in, and were lucky enough to find a slot out of sight from the street. Charlie's car was in great shape again and he was very protective.

After placing their handguns in the glove compartment they entered the tavern, which was rowdy in a good way at that hour. There were two tables occupied by a group of firemen apparently having a just off-shift dinner, Charlie guessed from the uniforms.

Charlie looked around, trying to see if Meg, the redheaded waitress they'd spoken to before, was working. Not seeing her, he caught up with Gordon, who'd found an empty table against the wall, looking out into the room.

"Guess we have to break in a new waitress," Charlie announced, sitting down.

"Speaking of breaking, there's one of Mike's heavy lifters coming in the door," Gordon replied, nodding in that direction.

Charlie looked over, saw Fernando, the buzz-cut Latin guy in the guayabera and slacks, followed by Mike Schultz, smartly attired again in a comfortable-looking tan suit, no tie.

"Where's Fred Flintstone?" Gordon whispered, referring to the second bodyguard, the big guy with the small forehead and bushy eyebrows.

Charlie looked up the stairs toward the second-floor private guest locale. "Top of the stairs. He's spotted us. Be polite. Stay cool. Be . . ."

"Icy," Gordon whispered as Mike the Pimp and his slightly smaller bodyguard strolled casually toward their table.

Charlie noted that Mike looked a little less confident than before—almost worried.

Not wanting to send the wrong signals, Charlie and Gordon remained seated, both nodding a greeting. Mike seemed to visibly relax. He whispered something to Fernando, who turned and walked away toward the bar.

"Hey, guys. Mind if I join you?" Mike spoke as if they were all friends.

"Go right ahead." Charlie pushed back the third chair with his foot. "Have a seat, it's your place."

Mike smiled, sitting down and pulling the chair toward the table, revealing a pistol in a shoulder holster beneath his jacket. He looked toward Fernando, who'd taken a seat at the bar, positioned so he could watch the door, before turning back to Charlie and Gordon.

"We're not here to rough up your people or you, Mike," Charlie said softly.

"Yeah, but you're not the only ones looking for Lola now. Just

#31 08-08-2015 3:56PM
Item(s) checked out to EASTWICK,

TITLE: Crimson joy
BARCODE: 05000002429541
DUE DATE: 08-29-15

TITLE: Murder in Little Italy
BARCODE: 05000001934186
DUE DATE: 08-29-15

TITLE: Stay a little longer
BARCODE: 05000004456138
DUE DATE: 08-29-15

TITLE: Death and Mr. Pickwick
BARCODE: 05000008046935
DUE DATE: 08-29-15

TITLE: Grave consequences
BARCODE: 05000007401644
DUE DATE: 08-29-15

what the hell did she get herself into? There are some punks from a downtown neighborhood being paid to track her down, and they've already come by here twice asking if I'd seen her. The last visit was about two hours ago, and this time they brought their boss, some fancy-dressing Indian dude—no offense," he added, looking at Charlie.

Charlie smiled, thinking this slippery pimp in the silk suit, hundred-dollar shirt, and paycheck-busting shoes was calling someone else a fancy dresser. "None taken."

"His last name wouldn't be Fasthorse, would it?" Gordon suggested.

"You've met the bastard?" Mike asked.

Charlie nodded. "He's bad news, especially for Lola. You tell him anything?"

"Less than I told you. Just that she worked for me a couple of years ago, then said good-bye. Hadn't seen her since, didn't know where she was," Mike replied.

"But you've seen her since our last meeting?" Charlie asked.

Mike looked away, across the room, and lowered his voice even more. "Yeah, Lola came by around closing last night, asking to borrow some money. She said her old boyfriend Jerry-something had turned on her. I barely recognized Lola, she'd dyed her hair and cut it real short. I gave her what I had in my wallet—five or six hundred. After she split I tried to find that number you gave me and track you down. No luck. I'm hoping you could help her out. I'm not in a position to get involved with the cops."

"Fasthorse is Jerry Benally's boss. They've got some kind of criminal operation going on. No offense," Charlie added.

Mike thought about it for a moment, then smiled. "I looked up Fasthorse online—he owns an old family restaurant near Old Town. You talking mini-organized crime?"

Charlie shrugged, not wanting to give out any details that might compromise Al or the undercover operations. "They're just thieves," he said.

Gordon spoke. "Fasthorse make some threats? Looks like your boys are keeping an eye on everyone who comes inside."

"The bastard said if I was lying to him or protecting Lola, I'd regret it. He said there was a bounty, though, on Lola, and if I helped him track her down there was a finder's fee," Mike retorted, contempt clear in his tone. "Arrogant shit."

"The guy is getting a little desperate, and desperate people are dangerous, Mike. He's been suffering some losses lately and has several wannabe badasses working for him," Charlie said. "They pack some heavy firepower and won't hesitate to gun you down."

"Which is why we're packing," Mike pointed out.

"Did he give you a number to call if you heard from Lola?" Gordon asked.

"Wrote it on a napkin," Mike said, pulling it from his shirt pocket.

Gordon wrote it down. "Probably a burner, certainly not the Piñon Mesa Steakhouse number," he noted.

Mike looked back and forth between them. "What is your connection to this punk anyway? Just why is he so eager to find Lola?"

Charlie looked over at Gordon, who shrugged. "Lola took something that had come into the possession of Fasthorse, and he wants it back—bad."

"Bad enough to kill for? What is it, drugs?"

"Nothing like that," Charlie said.

"You're still not telling me what it was, or how you're involved," Mike said, then looked up as Fernando came over. The man whispered something to Mike, then walked back to his seat at the bar.

Mike nodded. "You're the guys from the pawnshop shooting. You killed one of the robbers and ran the others off. My man just recognized you from the news," Mike said, a satisfied smile on his face.

"Damned liberal media," Gordon said. "Screw privacy."

"No wonder you kick ass. Special Ops and all that. You the good guys?"

"We'll do until the heroes arrive," Gordon replied.

"I get it. Lola pawned some stuff she stole from Fasthorse—at your shop," Mike said.

Charlie shrugged. "Maybe. Either way, we're out to screw the bastard over and he's starting to feel it now."

"Any way I can help out?"

"If we need something, we know where you work, Mike. Thanks. For now, though, just keep your eyes open and be very careful who you talk to. If Lola contacts you again, text us ASAP. We'll protect her." Charlie wrote his own cell number on a napkin this time. "Don't throw it away."

"And watch your ass," Gordon added.

Mike nodded, sat back, then caught the eye of one of the women waitstaff, waving her over. "Suddenly, my appetite is back. You guys had dinner? I'm buying."

"Thought you'd never ask," Gordon said. "You have anything nonalcoholic to wash down a sandwich or two? I need to keep my edge."

Mike laughed. "Got coffee, ginger ale, mineral water—no milk. But I do keep a case of Mexican Cokes for true connoisseurs."

"Now you're talking," Charlie said, looking up as the waitress arrived with two laminated parchment menus.

They left after an hour of good food—oversized green chile cheeseburgers on locally baked buns, fries with the skins on cooked in peanut oil, and ice-cold Mexican Cokes straight from the bottles. Even the sliced tomatoes on the burgers were locally grown, fresh and tasty.

As Charlie drove west toward I-25, they discussed the few additional details Mike Schultz could provide. "We have the image from her driver's license, and with the mug shots Mike provided of Lola from her hooker days, we have a lot more to work with," Charlie pointed out.

"Yeah, but it would have been a lot easier if she'd have parked her current ride in the Firehouse lot so we could have grabbed an image from his surveillance camera. We'd know what she was driving, and maybe even gotten a look at the plates," Gordon said.

"She's smart, not wanting anyone, not even her old pimp, to know exactly how she arrived. If she has a car at all right now," Charlie answered.

"For all we know, she's a bushy redhead riding a motorcycle at the moment. But at least we have various 'looks' she's chosen in the past to work from."

"You know what I think?" Charlie asked.

"That the money she borrowed was getting out-of-town cash?" Gordon responded. "If you want to truly get lost, you go someplace you've never been and avoid contacting anyone you've ever been around. You also work at something you've never done, and always pay in cash."

"But she doesn't have the money to go far, either, so let's come up with some possibilities," Charlie said.

"Lola won't go among local Navajos, who might have connections with the Night Crew. Maybe she's living near or among another tribe, so she wouldn't stand out to any non-Indians. How's that?"

"Okay. We make it an Indian community, but not too small. A large pueblo, like around Taos," Charlie said. "That's far enough away."

"Okay, but she needs work," Gordon replied. "How about looking for a job at, say, a small-town restaurant, as kitchen help, out of public view?"

"Yeah, and she'd drive a pickup, the older the better," Charlie suggested.

"So what you're saying, is that she could be almost anywhere within four hundred miles. Nearly every city or town in this state is small, but this is a big state," Gordon pointed out.

"We've got to start somewhere," Charlie concluded, taking the Central ramp north on I-25, racing out to merge in with the mid-evening traffic. "Let's see what a woman thinks of this."

"Gina?"

•　　•　　•

Less than fifteen minutes later they pulled up in front of Gina and Nancy's town house in Albuquerque's Northeast Heights. The outside was generic, with drought-resistant flowers, gravel, and a few ornamental trees and shrubs. The ladies did, however, have a backyard with a tiny lawn and a grill. The four of them sometimes got together to barbecue steaks or burgers. Charlie and Gina had grown up together in Shiprock and their friendship had been rekindled after he left the Army.

As they stepped up onto the small porch, the light came on above them and Gina opened the door. "Hi, guys, come on inside. Nancy's still on the job, but she and I have talked a little about Lola Tso and these crimes and I'll give you my slant on her situation. As an attorney, I've had women clients who've been forced to go underground—usually as a result of domestic violence situations. There can be several effective options for a woman on the run."

They stepped inside the open-space design combo living room–kitchen, moving immediately toward the Mexican tile-topped breakfast bar. There were tall, leather upholstered chairs on both sides and a plate of cookies in the center.

"So, you've come up empty so far?" Gina asked, stepping over by the coffeepot on the counter. "Coffee, right?"

They both nodded, and she poured three mugs full.

"If I recall, Nancy said that Lola was a pretty bright girl," Charlie ventured, taking the offered cup, then reaching for a cookie.

"Yeah, and more. According to Nancy, Lola was a survivor. What Nancy couldn't figure out is what she was doing pawning jewelry stolen from a dead man—one who'd been killed and the victim of an active investigation. Not to mention grave robbing and the rest. Talk about raising flags to the authorities."

"We brought that up the other night and Al suggested that maybe Lola didn't know about that at the time," Gordon said, accepting the mug from Gina.

"Okay. Going with that assumption, then where did she get the necklace? From her boyfriend Jerry, who's part of Fasthorse's crew?" Charlie offered.

"Guys, Nancy told me that Lola was a thief, at least at the time she was hooking. The girl bragged more than once about stealing cash from a john's wallet. So why not grab a squash blossom necklace when nobody was looking?" Gina suggested. "A quick pawn for even quicker cash, then tearing up the ticket, never intending on redeeming the piece."

"No honor among thieves, that's a given. Clearly Lola didn't know this necklace would link her to theft and murder," Charlie said.

"Now she's stuck in the middle. That necklace points back from Buck's grave to Jerry, and from Jerry to Clarence Fasthorse," Gina said. "That suggests that one of Fasthorse's crew, Jerry or Clarence himself, killed the silversmith during the carjacking, then robbed the grave and snagged the jewelry. Holding on to that necklace was a mistake, and whoever had it is trying to save their ass."

"By killing Lola before she goes to the cops," Gordon said, shaking his head.

"Lola knows the truth now, in retrospect, because they're after her. That's why she's on the run, and why we came here to get your take on where she might be hiding," Charlie said. "Gordo, tell her our theory regarding where a really bright girl might lie low."

Gordon quickly described their logic of a smart fugitive trying to avoid doing anything predictable. "It's what I call the 'country girl in a pickup' theory," he said with a grin, grabbing another cookie.

"That makes sense. But you know how many small communities there are within just a hundred miles of here? Lola could be anywhere," Gina added.

Charlie shrugged. "That's the problem. If she figures that we, the cops, or Clarence Fasthorse have guessed her plan, she might just do the opposite. She did risk a visit with Mike the Pimp to pick up some extra cash."

"How long ago was this?" Gina asked.

"It was last night, late, and we just found out about it less than two hours ago," Gordon said.

"Better pass that along to Nancy and Detective DuPree. They have people scouring the metro trying to find Lola before the bad guys do," Gina advised.

"I'll make the call," Charlie said, standing and reaching for his phone as he walked across the room.

"Don't tell her where you got the information, bro," Gordon advised. "If we rat out Mike the Pimp he'll quit helping us. And Lola trusts him more than she does the cops."

"How does Nancy feel when you keep secrets from her?" Charlie asked, phone still in hand.

"Hates it. But I'm also bound by client privilege, so it's nothing new," Gina said.

"But Lola's not your client," Gordon reminded.

"But you guys are."

"Good point," Charlie said with a sigh. "I'll see how she reacts," he added, bringing up Nancy's number on the display.

Five minutes later, Charlie ended the call and turned to Gina and Gordon, who'd remained beside the coffeepot, watching and listening as they drank the final dregs.

"Nancy sounded pissed," Gordon said.

Gina shook her head. "No, when she's pissed, you don't hear any sounds at all. Trust me on this."

"She's going to call DuPree now, and, at least she won't have to lie," Charlie said.

"Think DuPree will figure it out?" Gordon asked.

Charlie shook his head. "He's going to track us down first. Hopefully, before he does that, we'll get in some sleep."

"You don't want to stay until Nancy gets off duty? She'll be home in an hour," Gina said, looking at the kitchen clock.

"Naw, we've got to work regular hours tomorrow and we need to stick close to the shop for a few days. We've been kicking at the ant den lately, and there's no telling how Fasthorse is going to react. He's already warned us off," Charlie reminded.

"Don't forget trying to kill us," Gordon said, grinning.

Gina looked at them with sad eyes, shook her head, then walked over and gave them both a big hug.

"What was that for?" Charlie asked. "Not that it wasn't nice."

"Dammit, guys, the way you get into trouble, I never know if I've just hugged you for the last time."

"We've got it under control, don't worry," Charlie said, winking as he backed toward the door. "Ready, Gordo?"

Gordon nodded. "Like he said, Gina. Under control."

Gina kept the porch light on as they walked over to the Charger.

Chapter Fourteen

Charlie woke up to a loud crash, and something heavy landed on the bed. Instantly awake, he sat up and turned on the lamp. The window had been broken, glass was everywhere, and there was a brick on the covers down by his feet.

"Crap," he grumbled, reaching for the pistol underneath the other pillow. He started to stand, thought about the glass, and looked down for his slippers beside the bed.

As he slipped on the slippers he heard another crash toward the side of the house, and his car alarm go off. Cursing again, Charlie grabbed his car keys from the nightstand and ran into the living room.

Through the thin curtains of the front window he could see the taillights of a car racing away down the street, engine roaring and tires burning rubber.

He thumbed the button on his key fob and the car alarm shut off. Cringing at what he might see next, Charlie unlocked the inside door leading into the garage, opened it up, and reached for the light switch.

The garage window had been shattered, and there was the Charger, a sitting duck in the middle. Cringing, he circled around the back end of the car and walked along the side, expecting to find the passenger window broken, or worse, body damage. Pane glass was everywhere, crunching beneath his feet, but as he checked, he couldn't find any dents or damage to the car at all. There was no sign of whatever had come through the window.

Reaching the hood, he crouched and looked across the surface, wondering if a graze had scored the finish. Nothing. Maybe he'd gotten lucky this time. But what had set off the car alarm?

Circling around to the driver's side, he found a brick on the concrete floor about a foot from the front tire, and a scuff on the sidewall where the brick had apparently bounced off the tire, jarring the Charger and setting off the alarm. Looking up, he found a big dent in the garage wall about chest high where the brick had struck after flying through the garage window. "Yes!" he yelled aloud.

Hearing the sound of the phone inside the house, Charlie hurried back into the kitchen and grabbed the cordless landline receiver off the wall.

"Charlie, some asshole just threw a brick through my front window, just missing my TV," Gordon announced. "Better watch out . . ."

"Too late, Gordon. At least I got lucky this time. They broke some glass and dented a wall, but they missed my Charger."

"You parked your ride outside?"

"No, the bastard took out my garage window. The good news is that he threw too high and missed the car completely."

"You got lucky, all right. That it?" Gordon asked.

Charlie shook his head. "No. They tossed the first brick through my bedroom window and it ended up on the bed. I almost took a brick in the leg."

"I should've known you'd be more worried about your car than your carcass, Charlie. You'd probably take a boulder in the chest to stop anyone from scratching your Dodge."

"True," Charlie admitted. "But what about your pickup? It okay?"

"Yeah. Thank God my garage has no windows."

"You sure that's all they did?" Charlie asked, walking into the bedroom, stepping around the glass and finding his cell phone.

"Yeah, I'm searching the place, phone in one hand, pistol in the other."

"Me too," Charlie replied. "You get a look at the rat bastards?"

"No, I just heard the sound of squealing tires and a racing engine. A pickup, based upon the noise. I never got a look. You?"

"Taillights—a dark sedan. That's it. We might as well call the cops and report this—for our insurance agents," Charlie suggested.

"Your agent's gonna hate you by now. What is this, the third time someone's trashed your house or car?" Gordon asked.

"Yeah, and my rates are already sky-high from last year. I may decide to foot the window repair bill on my own. You know who did this," Charlie added.

"Yeah, the Night Crew—Fasthorse's thugs. Thought they'd lie

low for a while. I'm not going to take this lying down," Gordon added softly.

"They need payback, but if we roust the restaurant and give his crew a beat down we could end up in jail, especially if some unconnected civilians join in. That would be bad for business—ours."

"Got that right," Gordon said. "How about a little tit for tat?"

"Good call. Maybe if something happens to our boy's blue SUV?" Charlie said, feeling a little better now.

Gordon chuckled. "You know, when dealing with animals, unless you discipline them immediately they don't learn the lesson. Right now, those suckers are probably crowing to each other about how they stuck it to us."

"Get dressed, Gordo, grab a brick, and I'll pick you up in a half hour."

"Naw, we'll take my truck. It's slightly less conspicuous than your purple hot rod."

Charlie sighed. "Let's gear up. We can call to report the crimes while we're on our way to commit one."

"You know we're going to catch hell when we die, trying to explain all this."

"Yeah, but worry about that when it comes. Hopefully, it won't be tonight," Charlie responded.

"God's ears," Gordon said, then ended the call.

They drove toward Clarence Fasthorse's home, knowing the restaurant was closed at this hour but hoping to pick up the GPS signal from the bug they'd placed in the man's SUV. Charlie had loaded the app on his cell phone, but still hadn't been able to get a signal when they drove past Clarence's house.

"Nothing. No SUV, no GPS, no road noise from the mike," Charlie reported, looking up from the phone display.

"Suppose they found the bug?" Gordon asked.

"That could have triggered the brick attack. Let's try the area around Rex's Auto. There are a lot of warehouses up Second Street from there," Charlie suggested, deciding to do a visual search as well just in case Gordon was right and they'd lost their advantage.

"Yeah, with Rex's Auto compromised they've got to have a new place where they take their stolen cars," Gordon pointed out. "Or, more likely, they already had an alternate stash location."

Charlie nodded. "Yeah, they've been pretty smart. So far, Clarence's only weak spot is his temper. He has to strike back and we can use that against him. Ultimately, I think he'll lead us to whoever killed Cordell Buck."

Gordon looked over, grinning. "I like it. We keep antagonizing the guy until he makes a fatal mistake. I'm getting close to Second Street, any hits on the GPS?"

"No. Wait, yes." Charlie examined the simple street map on the display. "The SUV isn't moving, and is between Second and First, about halfway down the block between the cross streets of Willow and Rascon. From the position of the dot I think it's an alley," Charlie reported. "We should be close enough to listen in now. I'm turning off the GPS and activating the bug."

Charlie looked up as Gordon turned north onto Second Street. "The next east-west street is Willow," Gordon announced.

There was a thud—the sound of a slamming car door—then Clarence's voice came in clearly over the monitor's speaker. "It's time to get out of here, Leroy. Head downtown to that truck stop off of Gold. We'll go in for coffee and make sure we're seen. I don't want to be anywhere near this place while that bastard is being punished."

"Right, boss," Leroy's voice came out loud and clear. There was the sound of a racing engine and the change in tone from the shifting of car gears.

Charlie looked at the blip on the display. It was moving now.

"I wonder what bastard he's talking about?" Gordon looked over at Charlie. "It can't be us."

Charlie shook his head, signaling with his hand for silence. He had a sinking feeling he already knew.

"Slow down. Don't do anything that'll get us pulled over. We're still too close to the warehouse," Clarence ordered. "I want eyewitnesses who can place us elsewhere while that weasel is being laid out."

"Don't worry, C.J.," Leroy replied. "They'll take their time punishing Biggs. And if it turns out he's really a cop, I guess that's just too bad."

"Damn. Biggs is Al," Gordon exclaimed, speeding up.

Several seconds of silence went by before they heard country-western music coming from the SUV.

"No need to follow Clarence now. We've got to bail out your brother," Gordon concluded. "Right?"

"Yeah, and we might need to go in hot." Charlie turned off

the monitor. "They have Al somewhere up that alley," Charlie said, pointing ahead. "There's a warehouse."

Gordon drove down the block so they could take a look. The building was a three-story brick-and-stone structure running the entire length of the block, lined with large windows on the second story. There were two sets of doors facing the streets, and Charlie read "For Rent or Lease" and a phone number on each as they passed.

Gordon made a right turn onto Rascon. The end of the warehouse had no exits or windows, just blank walls three stories high. Halfway along the wall he pulled over to the curb, parked, and turned off the engine.

They slipped out, pistols in their holsters just inside their jackets, then shut the doors quietly.

"I don't know how much time we have, bro," Gordon said, keeping his voice low. "From what Clarence and his driver said, it sounded like they were going to beat it out of Al."

"Unless he's handcuffed or drugged, that'll take some doing. Al has skills," Charlie said as they walked down the sidewalk toward the rear corner and the alley entrance. "He's going to do some damage of his own."

"Maybe they have a guy who can take him," Gordon said, coming up beside Charlie.

"I don't know if *I* could take Al, Gordo," Charlie whispered as they crossed the alley. He took a quick look behind them. Checking their six—covering their backs—was a practiced tactic from their Special Ops days.

"Really?" Gordon asked. "You think Al could take *me?*"

Charlie laughed, feeling the humor. "Hell, Gordon, it would take *both* Henry boys to lay you out. Jayne's the only one in the family who could really beat the crap out of you."

They kept walking, and Gordon looked puzzled as he glanced over his shoulder. "I thought Jayne was the debate club type."

"She is . . . was. The reason why Jayne can beat us up is because we can't stop laughing long enough to defend ourselves. It's a hoot. She yells and flails with both fists at once. One time she broke Al's nose with a lucky punch."

They stopped close to the building wall, out of view from the warehouse doors now, and Charlie took a look around the corner. "There's a wide loading dock with stairs at both ends and a big double bay overhead door in the center. Farther down is another overhead door, completely open, with a gentle up-ramp. Inside, there's a light on, not very bright, probably deep inside. There are no windows at street level. No vehicles are parked anywhere I could see, so they must have driven up the ramp and are inside the warehouse," Charlie concluded.

"They'll have someone watching the alley, you think?" Gordon asked. "Oh, and did you see any cameras?"

"Too dark. If they have a security guard watching monitors they'll see us coming, but I'm thinking we'll get to the door unnoticed. When was the last time guys didn't stop what they were supposed to be doing to watch a fight?" Charlie replied. "Let's walk down the alley along the back wall."

"If the security is with the others, they'll have to poke their heads out to see us," Gordon approved. "And once we're inside . . ."

"We take them out and free Al without shooting anyone."

"We're worth six of those punks in hand-to-hand—sooner or later they'll start shooting," Gordon reminded. "Or gang-tackle us."

"So we'll have to get the drop on them and take away their guns."

Gordon nodded. "Let's pray they're as stupid as their boss."

"I've got an idea," Charlie whispered.

"Hope it's a good one."

"Police!" Charlie yelled, holding out his wallet with his license photo showing as he stepped from behind a parked car. Beneath the fluorescent light fixture in the rear half of the warehouse garage was a loose circle of eight men. In the center of the audience were two bloodied men throwing punches.

The laser sight on his Beretta shifted back and forth slowly as the red dot landed on one man, then the next. That held their attention. The big Hispanic man exchanging blows with Al turned to look and Al took the cheap shot. He hammered his opponent with a fist to the side of his face. The guy sagged to the concrete floor, spitting out blood and saliva.

"Only one cop? There are eight of us," one of the punks muttered, reaching for a pistol at his belt.

"Count again, dickhead!" Gordon yelled, stepping out from behind a parked car, the laser beam from his sight flashing in the man's face.

"Don't shoot! It's okay, I'm cool," the man responded, blinking at the laser light in his eyes and raising his hands slowly.

Al took a stumbling step, paused to gather himself, then stood stiffly erect and reached over to grab the man's weapon. "On the floor, all of you assholes, or I'll blow you away."

The men reluctantly got down on their knees, not taking their eyes off Al.

"Over here, Biggs," Charlie ordered Al, watching Fasthorse's crew instead of his brother. Gordon had stepped back, weapon still out but now protected by an engine block.

"I'm going to point my sights at one man at a time, when that happens, that man will take out his weapon very slowly and slide it across the floor toward me," Charlie instructed clearly. "My fellow officers will have their weapons aimed at the rest of you, so don't do anything fatal."

"You're not cops, you're the pawnbroker guys!" one of the men said clearly. "You can't do this!"

"And yet here we are. Unless you're planning on taking a dirt nap tonight, you'd be wise to pull your head out of that dark place and follow our instructions," Gordon ordered.

The warehouse grew very quiet. Charlie aimed the laser point on the closest man. "Two fingers, only," Charlie ordered. The man complied, bringing out a small semiauto that looked like a .32.

"Set it on the floor, then slide it over toward me," Charlie ordered, aiming the laser beam at the guy's crotch. The man set the weapon on the concrete, then propelled it perhaps ten feet closer to Charlie across the floor.

"Okay, friends, now that you've seen how it's done . . ." Charlie added. "Next."

When he got to the fourth guy in the circle, an older man wearing greasy coveralls, there was a hitch. "I'm a mechanic, I don't have a gun. Really, sir, don't shoot me."

"Are you sure?" Charlie asked, directing the bright red beam at the man's pocket.

"It's my working knife. I'll show you," the man replied, his voice faltering slightly. He brought out a four-inch lock-back knife, holding it between fingers and thumbs. "My son gave it to me for my birthday."

"Okay, just set it down on the floor and scoot it over by the pistols," Charlie said, glancing over at Gordon, who nodded in agreement. This man just worked here.

The process continued until there were five semiautos of various sizes and calibers and a big revolver scattered along the floor between the group and Charlie. As he placed the dot on the chest of the last man on his knees, the guy Al had decked, groaned, rolled over, and tried to sit up.

"Stay, down, boy," the mechanic, who was closest, whispered harshly.

"Hey, why is it so quiet all of a sudden?" came a voice from a walkway overhead.

Charlie looked up just as a security guard noticed Al pointing his weapon at the groggy boxer. The guard drew his pistol.

"Gun!" Gordon yelled.

Al turned and looked up, then took a bullet to his shoulder, flinching but not going down.

Charlie fired high, forcing the armed guard to jump back.

Everyone jumped to their feet and scattered, running for the closest door or passage.

"I'll pin him down!" Charlie yelled, firing another gunshot up toward the walkway. Gordon grabbed hold of Al and pulled him outside. Charlie followed, taking one last shot in the direction of the guard.

"Get him to the pickup!" Charlie yelled, watching for trouble. Two of the men from inside were fleeing down the alley but in the opposite direction, and Charlie ignored them.

Al stuck his pistol in his belt and shook Gordon off, putting his hand on his wound to stem the blood. "Forget running off, I'm fine. Call DuPree! That warehouse is full of stolen shit."

"Go ahead, Gordon, I've got our six," Charlie replied, now shuffling quickly backward, like a basketball player on defense. So far, nobody had poked their heads out of the bay door yet.

Gordon ended the quick call by the time they reached his pickup. "Somebody's already sent a message to DuPree and he's on his way. Ambulance too. Hang on, Al," Gordon said.

Hearing the roar of a V-8, they turned and saw a sedan race out of the alley, swerve to the right, then accelerate down Rascon, heading east.

"I counted four of them in the car," Charlie said, watching the fading taillights as they stood on the sidewalk beside the truck.

"Nobody's sticking around, except maybe for the security guard and that mechanic. They call him Jack. He was just in the wrong place at the wrong time," Al pointed out.

"What the hell happened?" Charlie asked, still watching for trouble, weapon down by his side.

"How the hell should I know?" Al replied angrily. "We were

standing around beside the cars in there while four of the guys bragged about scaring the crap out of you two. Then Clarence got a call. He put away the phone, pulled a gun and told everyone I was a cop. Suddenly I was facing a roomful of firepower. I denied it, but Clarence said his source was a hundred percent reliable. He told Melvin, the big guy in his crew, to make sure I wasn't going to be a problem. Then he and Leroy took off in his SUV."

"We overheard Clarence talking about it when we came into the neighborhood. He said that Biggs was going to get a beat down," Gordon added, opening the pickup and reaching behind the seat for a first aid kit.

"How'd you . . . ? Never mind. You two play things your way, right?" Al said, watching as Gordon brought out a wound dressing. Charlie's pal had plenty of experience treating gunshot wounds while deployed.

"Yeah, and if we hadn't been coming to check out the warehouse, you'd be ground hamburger by now."

"Hey, I could have taken the guy." Al grimaced as Gordon tore away some of his shirt to expose a nasty wound.

"Tell that to your face. You're even uglier than usual tonight, bro," Charlie joked. He looked up toward Second Street, hearing approaching sirens.

"Yeah, well, enough bullshitting. We need to get our stories straight before APD arrives," Al said, flinching as Gordon applied the sterile, absorbent dressing.

"Hopefully, DuPree will get here first," Gordon said. "But let's put the weapons away just in case. If any other officers arrive first, they won't know who we are. We don't want to send the wrong signals."

"And I'm not carrying a badge or valid ID," Al pointed out.

"Great. Maybe we should just place our weapons on the hood, in plain sight—as much as I hate being disarmed . . ." Gordon suggested, wrapping the bandage in place with gauze, then taping the ends.

Charlie's phone rang. It was DuPree. Charlie spoke for less than thirty seconds, motioning them all into the truck while he spoke. Al climbed into the back, grunting and groaning.

"We're leaving, Gordon. Circle to Rio Grande Boulevard, then drive north to Rio Rancho—if you think you can hold off on further treatment another fifteen minutes, Al," Charlie reported, getting in beside his brother in the back.

"The bullet is long gone. Let's roll," Al responded. "DuPree wants me to avoid the attention?"

Charlie nodded as Gordon drove west, then turned north again on the next through street. "He'll call ahead and have someone there to treat you at the new hospital in Rio Rancho—actually the clinic wing, not the ER. Hopefully it won't make the news. Rio Rancho cops will cooperate, he insists. If the doctors say you can travel, DuPree wants us to take you out of the area, then lie low. Once you're settled, one of us will call him with the location and he'll arrange for twenty-four-hour protection."

"Al, does Fasthorse know exactly who you are, or just that you're a cop?" Gordon asked. "That'll play into where we—you—go."

"I don't really know. He never used my name, all he said was that I was an undercover cop," Al replied. "There's no way I'm going home to the Rez until I find out. I've got Nedra and the boys, not to mention Dad, Mom, and Jayne to worry about now."

"So we find a safe house here in the city. DuPree has to know, of course, but I'll insist he keep this from the rest of the undercover unit. If one of them leaked your identity we can't risk giving away your location as well," Charlie added.

"How much do you trust DuPree?"

"He's a pain in the ass, but he's a decent cop and smarter than he looks. He can keep a secret," Gordon said.

Charlie nodded. "Gordon's right. In the meantime, let's take care of that gunshot wound. You're going to need bandages, antibiotics, painkillers, and whatever else they can add to the bill."

Chapter Fifteen

They made good time, and twenty minutes later Al was being treated in a doctor's examination room in the clinic wing of the new hospital. A Rio Rancho cop was standing in the lobby guarding the door, and another uniform was outside the clinic, watching the parking lot.

Charlie put a dollar in the coffee machine, punched the right buttons, then waited as the device clanked, sighed, then emitted a hint of aromatic steam. Gordon, hot brew already in hand, took a sip and nodded his head. "Not bad, for machine coffee."

Charlie looked down at the machine as the brew trickled down into the foam cup. "Anything to keep my eyes open, bro."

"You think maybe it was Al who screwed up?" Gordon whispered.

"Wouldn't be the first time, but if he didn't, then the alternative is a bit scary. Who called Clarence and told him Al was an officer? Undercover work is filled with pressure, and there must be a lot of opportunities to go bad," Charlie suggested. "It could have been another cop."

"Okay, that's a possibility, but I doubt it was the same person who tipped off DuPree that something was going down. He was already on his way to the warehouse before I made the call," Gordon pointed out.

"Maybe it was one of the men at the warehouse not tied to the Night Crew? The mechanic?" Charlie suggested.

"At least the way it turned out, whoever tried to help out Al won't end up in the bull's-eye. It'll just be you and me—again."

Charlie nodded. "We can't put Ruth and Jake in any more danger, though. We need to stay in business—and look after our people."

"Okay, then how about you take care of your brother—get him to a safe place, and I'll take care of our quarters and FOB until he's tucked away?" Gordon offered. "We've also got three broken windows to deal with."

"So, I'll split with Al in your truck and you'll take care of the rest? You've got a key to my house."

"Okay." Gordon looked at his watch. "Nancy should be getting off her shift pretty soon. I think she'd give me a ride to your place."

"If not, you can take a cab," Charlie said, grinning.

"You know how far that is? I'll need to take out a loan. I'll call Nancy right now."

It was nearly two in the morning when Charlie took one last look at Al, who was asleep in the master bedroom of the upscale town house, then stepped outside onto the covered porch. The safe house in a gated compound had once belonged to a district attorney, now deceased, who'd willed his home to the city. The residence was set aside for visiting dignitaries and celebrities who needed security and anonymity.

The guards at the gate were retired APD officers, as was the private security firm responsible for this high-end housing development. Most of the residents were retired physicians, attorneys, and other businessmen and officials, including senior administrators from the big government-funded labs. Al had been impressed, though he knew he'd soon be returning to the Navajo Nation.

DuPree's captain had called ahead, clearing the way for Charlie and Al, who'd been eyed suspiciously by gate security nevertheless.

When he stopped at the gate on the way out, he had to wait for a quick once-over of the interior of the big pickup and the bed. After years of roadblocks and security outposts, he never gave it a second thought.

When Charlie arrived home he was happy to see the sheet of plywood over his garage window. He parked Gordon's pickup up close to the overhead door and climbed out, locking the truck with the key fob.

Once inside, Charlie checked on his car first, noting that the floor had been swept free of glass. In the bedroom, Gordon had duct taped heavy cardboard over the hole left by the broken pane and swept and vacuumed the carpet. He and Gordon had learned how to clean expertly and quickly as they'd advanced in rank in the Army, and Gordon was obsessive when it came to cleanliness.

The bed was unmade now, but Gordon had set out clean sheets, pillowcases, and two blankets, leaving them folded on the bare mattress. The bedspread—Charlie had only one—was probably in the hamper in the utility room.

Thinking he'd gotten the easier job getting Al hidden away, Charlie quickly made the bed and crawled in, hoping, at least for the rest of the night, he wasn't going to find any more bodies or bricks in his house. Reaching under the other pillow and feeling the cold comfort of his Beretta, he patted it good night and fell asleep almost immediately.

Charlie and Gordon arrived at FOB Pawn just as Jake and Ruth were bringing out the cash register trays from the office safe. It was ten minutes before the eight AM opening time posted on the front door and they were all in a bit of a hurry.

"Looks like even our bosses are on time this morning," Jake said to Ruth, who'd come out into the short hall just ahead of him.

"Hi, guys," Ruth said, turning to give them a smile before heading out into the display area. Gordon nodded, then turned to lock the heavy back door.

"Morning, Ruth, Jake," Charlie said cheerfully, walking behind them. "We were able to get our transportation straight again and arrange to have our respective windows replaced. Hopefully, everything will be back to normal for a while."

"There's always something weird going on with you two," Ruth said, stepping aside as Jake went behind the counter and headed toward the cash register closest to the entrance.

"You're smiling instead of grumbling this time, boss, so they must have trashed something besides your car," Jake concluded. "Maybe just a raging fire in the kitchen, or all your furniture ripped to shreds?"

Everyone laughed, knowing how Charlie loved the Charger. Gordon continued on toward the front entrance. He stopped at the door to take a look out through the small window.

"It all started with a brick. Well, three bricks," Gordon replied. "Tell them about the miracle in the garage, boss," he added, nodding to Charlie.

Charlie was brief, cutting out most of the warehouse incident. He also omitted mentioning Al's current situation except that he'd been barely shot.

"How does someone get barely shot?" Ruth asked just as the first customer walked inside, ringing the bell attached above the door. The middle-aged woman, wearing a pink UNM Lobos ball cap, looked over at Ruth, then quickly around the room. "Shot?"

"We're talking TV, Mrs. Radcliffe," Ruth added with a beautiful smile. "Did you happen to watch *Grimm* last night?"

Mrs. Radcliffe was one of their regulars, and she'd been bringing in pieces of estate jewelry to sell or pawn every week since the death of her mother-in-law. She shook her head sadly. "No, all those strange creatures were giving me nightmares so I changed channels. I'm watching *Survivor* now. This season it's between those former contestants from California who got voted off early."

"Sounds entertaining," Ruth replied. "So what treasure do you have to show me this morning?"

• • •

A few minutes before ten, Nancy came into the shop a few steps ahead of Detective DuPree. Gordon was writing up a ticket for a young man pawning an old-looking shotgun, so Charlie, who'd been patching a newly discovered bullet hole, walked over to greet the two officers.

"Good morning, Sergeant, Detective," Charlie said, carrying the bucket that contained the repair tools and supplies.

"Hello, Charlie," Nancy said, eyeing DuPree with raised eyebrows before giving Charlie a look. What about, he had no idea.

"Henry, Sweeney, we need to talk in private," DuPree announced.

"I'll finish up, Gordon," said Jake, who was coming up the aisle toward the front after taking a coffee break.

"Thanks, Jake, but we're almost done here. All we need is your signature, sir," Gordon said to the customer. "Here and here. Be right with you, officers," Gordon added, smiling at Nancy as she approached.

The young man, temporarily distracted by the tall, attractive woman, turned back abruptly to Gordon. "Uh, sorry. Sign where?"

"Follow me," Charlie said to DuPree, nodding toward the office.

A minute later, Gordon joined the others. Ruth, who'd been working in the back, left the office to help Jake out front.

"Hey, guys, what's going on?" Gordon asked immediately.

"Alfred Henry is now staying at your sister's place in Corrales," DuPree announced.

"The mayor overruled APD. He decided Al wasn't important

enough to stay at a city government guesthouse," Nancy added cynically.

"Politics," Gordon offered.

"Let me clarify that," DuPree interrupted. "The residence had already been set aside for presidential hopeful Senator Doull, who's scheduled to be here for the dedication of the Executive Convention Center."

"Which doesn't take place for two weeks," Nancy added.

"Politics," Charlie responded.

DuPree shrugged. "If it matters, tribal police officer Henry said he'd be happier staying with his sister than among the one percent. Reverse snobbery, maybe?"

Charlie cut in. "I'm not sure that's such a good idea. Jayne's live-in boyfriend, Rand Brewer, is a loser and maybe a druggie. Sometimes I worry about *her* safety. We don't talk much and I've only been over to her place a couple of times. Brewer hangs out with some rough-looking people."

"What does the guy do for a living?" Nancy asked.

"Supposedly he buys stuff then resells it online," Charlie replied.

"You mean, like stolen stuff?" Gordon got right to the point.

"Probably shoplifted sports jerseys, jackets, and caps, for instance," Charlie replied. "Jayne defends him, though, and she's pissed off with me because I asked too many questions last time I was there."

"The important thing is, will Al be safe in Corrales with her until he's fit enough to go back to the Navajo Nation?" DuPree asked.

"That depends. Is he getting protection from APD or the sheriff's department?" Charlie asked.

DuPree shook his head. "No, just increased patrols by the state police and the Corrales cops. According to what I heard, Officer Henry should be able to return to desk work within a week, maybe less. He's been pulled from his undercover assignment, naturally."

Gordon looked over at Charlie, who shook his head. "Bad vibes on this?" Gordon asked.

"Yeah. But it is what it is. Any *good* news today, officers?" Charlie asked hopefully.

"The warehouse contained three missing vehicles that were taken in carjackings within the past month. One, a damaged Escalade, was being stripped, apparently by the mechanic our people arrested. The parts were still on hand, however, in boxes. They included the catalytic converter and twenty-four-inch rims and skinny tires, which sell for a bundle, I guess," DuPree reported.

"A low-profile setup is expensive," Gordon confirmed.

DuPree nodded. "There were also items reported to have been inside the carjacked vehicles, such as leather jackets, cell phones, tools, even a couple of antique guns—old Civil War–era revolvers. Also, there were watches, expensive purses, and stuff like that."

"How about Indian jewelry? Any silver and turquoise pieces?" Nancy asked, looking at Charlie, who nodded.

"No jewelry at all, even though every one of the carjackings on record in the area had rings, necklaces, and other jewelry taken from the passengers. Speculation is that the gold items were melted down immediately and the other stuff sold at flea markets and such," DuPree said.

"What evidence is there linking the Night Crew to this, especially Clarence Fasthorse?" Charlie asked DuPree.

"We know Fasthorse was at that warehouse just prior to our arrival," Gordon pointed out.

"You saw him, then?" DuPree asked. "An eyewitness really helps the case. Al, of course, identified Fasthorse as being there, pulling the gun on him, and making the threats. Unfortunately, his story is contradicted by the mechanic and the warehouse security guard. Their story is that Al turned up, got in a fight with some other strangers in the alley, and that the fight moved into the warehouse garage. Then you two showed up, started shooting, and everyone split. They've stuck to their story, and Clarence has three people that say he was at some truck stop at the time."

"Unfortunately, we never saw him face-to-face, just his vehicle as it was leaving the area. We know it was his because the license plate matched the one he rides around in," Charlie answered. He didn't want to reveal the bug they'd placed, which was, of course, illegal.

DuPree looked over at Gordon, who nodded, but Charlie saw Nancy rolling her eyes. She didn't know about the bug, but Nancy was a smart cop and she knew them well.

"Neither the security guard nor the mechanic is talking much. They'll probably continue to keep quiet. The mechanic was moonlighting from his day job at an auto shop on Central Avenue, but refuses to say who was paying him to strip the cars. The guy is otherwise clean and has already posted bail. We spoke to the owner of the warehouse, and, supposedly, it's a legitimate facility. Most of the square footage of storage is used as a public school textbook depository, believe it or not," DuPree said.

"And Fasthorse?" Charlie asked.

"I went to his home and confronted him," DuPree answered. "He cooperated, even came to the station with me. When we arrived, his attorney was already there. Fasthorse denied everything, of course, and his lawyer challenged us to provide proof or let his client go. We had no choice. Until we get more than just Al's word—he couldn't wear a wire—we can't make an arrest that'll stick."

"So what's gonna happen now?" Gordon asked.

"My guess is that we've put Fasthorse out of business for the time being. He knows he's being watched, and we have officers out looking for the others in the Night Crew that Al has identified. Unfortunately, even if we track them down, we're still going to need more than Al's testimony," DuPree said.

"So we're not much closer to identifying Cordell Buck's killer than when this all started?" Gordon asked.

"Maybe, maybe not," Nancy said. "I heard from Lola."

Chapter Sixteen

All eyes shifted to her.

"Well, indirectly. A friend of hers—she wouldn't give her name—said Lola was staying with her and that Lola wanted to meet with me," Nancy said. "The woman said that Lola had some information regarding the necklace she pawned, why Cordell Buck was killed, and that if she could be guaranteed protection, she'd help out the police."

"That's great," Charlie said, noticing from DuPree's dropped jaw that this was the first he'd heard about this.

"When the hell did you get this call, Sergeant Medina?" DuPree erupted.

"About an hour ago. I thought I'd tell you all at once," Nancy replied calmly.

"So when is this meeting taking place?" Gordon asked.

Nancy shook her head. "Don't know. I'm waiting for a call back."

"Lola's friend. She's an old friend of hers?" Charlie asked.

"I see where you're going with this," Nancy said.

"I don't," DuPree said. "Enlighten me."

"What *do* they teach you at detective school?" Gordon asked. "If she's an old friend, others might know of that relationship too, including Lola's ex-boyfriend, Jerry. He might have passed that on to Clarence Fasthorse."

"And Clarence might have someone watching the woman's place, hoping Lola will turn up," DuPree acknowledged. "Our officers have been watching Lola's old apartment. No luck there."

"The longer this nameless woman waits to call me back, the more time Clarence will have to act—if our worst-case scenario is in effect," Nancy said.

"You get a number?" Charlie asked.

Nancy shrugged. "Yes, but it belonged to a fast-food place in the southwest part of the city. You think she'd go back there to call?"

"I can have an officer watch the restaurant, but who should they be watching for, someone who looks like Lola, or her faceless friend?" DuPree asked.

"If Lola decides to meet with you, that might be the place she'd choose, well away from the Old Town area where Fasthorse hangs out, and across the city from her old apartment," Gordon pointed out.

"Knowing that I'd likely have the call traced?" Nancy replied.

"Probably not, then," Charlie said. "The next call, if there is one, might come from a burner phone, made from the apartment or house where Lola is staying. Lola is smart, and will stay off the streets and out of sight."

"When she calls, make her give you an address so you can send officers to patrol the area, for her protection. Tell her you'll approach out of uniform and with a friend, in a private vehicle. She'll recognize you, Sergeant Medina. You okay with that?" DuPree asked.

"You look too much like a cop, Detective," Gordon pointed out. "What friend will be least threatening, Nancy?"

"Charlie's Navajo, so is Lola, but then, so are Jerry, Clarence, and a few others in the Night Crew," Nancy said. "So I'm thinking maybe the least intimidating of you guys—Gordon."

"Good idea. Gordon's a blue-eyed Anglo, small, charming with the ladies, and, of course, can kick ass better than most," Charlie pointed out.

"Better than most?" Gordon joked.

"Okay, better than everyone."

"Nobody's that tough," DuPree answered, shaking his head. "But Sweeney's a good choice. He'll likely be underestimated."

Nancy's phone rang just then. "Maybe we're about to put these theories to the test, boys. Stay quiet, I'm putting this on speaker."

"Nancy?" came a woman's voice.

Nancy nodded. "Yes, it's me again. Can I speak to Lola now?"

"No, she wants to meet you in person, like I said on my last call."

"She's doing the right thing. I can leave right now, what's the address?"

"Go to the Circle K just west of Eldorado High School. Park there and wait for my next call, a half hour from now."

Nancy checked her watch. "Give me more details. I want to send some officers into the area to watch for anyone who might be looking for Lola."

A half minute went by, accompanied by whispers too faint to make out. "No, just you and one other person. No uniforms. What car will you be driving?" the woman asked.

Nancy looked over at DuPree, who shrugged.

"My green Jeep Liberty—hardtop," Nancy answered.

"Call you again in thirty," the woman said. "Be there."

The call ended.

"Let's get started then. Nancy, you have your Jeep outside right now?" Charlie asked.

Nancy nodded. "Gordon, you're with me. You need to get something first?"

Gordon lifted his jacket to show her his Beretta. "Nope, all packed."

DuPree made a face. "You're with me, then, Charlie, in my vehicle. I see you're also armed. Good."

After a quick conversation with Jake and Ruth, the two teams set off for the convenience store, which was, according to Nancy, on Juan Tabo Avenue, the major street directly west of the big public high school in Albuquerque's Northeast Heights. From the north valley, the drive would take at least twenty minutes or more on a weekday close to noon.

Charlie and DuPree arrived first, driving down the street past the store while they looked for any parked vehicles where the caller, and perhaps Lola, might be watching.

"We're five minutes early," DuPree said, glancing east across two lanes of highway toward the high school. From this spot they could see tennis courts and a grass practice field.

"Look ahead, beyond the high school grounds to the east. There's a three-story apartment building with balconies facing this direction," Charlie observed, raising a pair of binoculars DuPree kept in the vehicle. "Someone is standing just inside a patio door on the second level," Charlie added. "It's a woman, blond."

"Need me to slow down?"

"Negative," Charlie advised. "I'm guessing that this is our caller. It's the only open door in a building that has at least thirty apartments facing west."

"There's nobody sitting in their car on the same side of the street as the Circle K, so let's go with your gut. I'm going to circle east and approach that building from the other side," DuPree replied.

Charlie's cell phone sounded. It was Gordon. "Putting you on speaker," Charlie advised.

"We're pulling into the convenience store lot now. Any idea on a location?" Gordon asked.

"Yeah, that pale pink apartment building across the street. A woman was standing on the balcony of a second-story apartment, south end, looking toward the Circle K. We're going down the street fronting the apartments and approach from the east side."

"Gotcha. Hang on, Charlie," Gordon said as Nancy said something to him.

About ten seconds went by, then Gordon spoke again, quickly. "Hurry it up, Charlie. Get to that apartment, the one you said. The woman, Didi, just called Nancy. Says they just spotted someone watching the building's parking lot. Lola thinks it might be Jerry Benally, her old boyfriend."

DuPree hit the gas, racing up to the apartment building. "Can't see anyone outside. We're going in through the front. Hurry and back us up," the detective said.

DuPree slowed, easing into the lot as quietly as possible, pulling right up in front of the no-parking slot by the main entrance.

Charlie was out before the car stopped rolling, looked left and right, then sprinted toward the double-door entrance. Inside he discovered a hall leading toward stairs at one end of the building, an elevator at the other. "Take the elevator," he called to DuPree, who was a few steps behind him.

Charlie ran down the hall, then opened the door to the stairwell. He took the stairs two at a time, reaching the top of the first flight just as he heard two rapid gunshots, then a third and fourth spaced a few seconds apart.

His weapon out now, Charlie took the next flight in three steps. He stopped, looking through the small window in the door before opening it up. Nobody.

He stepped out and immediately saw a middle-aged man in a Hawaiian print shirt standing in his apartment doorway, holding a cell phone. "Police!" Charlie lied with a harsh whisper. "Get back inside!"

Charlie raced to the open door of the end apartment, stopped by the jamb, and looked inside. One Indian man was leaning against the sofa, bleeding from his side, aiming a pistol toward a short hallway in the apartment. The door beyond was closed.

Hearing a noise inside to his right, Charlie dropped to one

knee, swung his Beretta around, and saw a bandaged Jerry Benally aiming a pistol at him.

Benally fired, striking the metal doorjamb and the wall at the end of the hall.

Charlie shot him in the center of his chest, then ducked back as the guy by the sofa snapped a round in his direction. Hearing running footsteps coming down the hall and hoping they belonged to DuPree, Charlie decided to try to save the wounded man for questioning.

"Police! Put down your weapon!" he yelled. Charlie paused, heard a curse, then decided to jump across the door opening to the far side.

Two bullets struck the wall where he'd just been standing. Looking in, pistol first, Charlie caught the surprise in the man's expression as the guy realized he'd missed.

Charlie had him flat-footed. "Put it down!" Charlie yelled again. Out of the corner of his eye, he saw that DuPree had arrived and was now at his left shoulder.

The idiot swung his pistol around, firing, the second of two bullets kicking up the carpet as DuPree fired a double tap into the shooter's torso.

Charlie stepped into the room, avoiding the two men now on the floor as he swept the room with his gaze. He heard a gasp behind the breakfast bar fifteen feet away and sidestepped along the far wall, weapon aimed toward the blind spot. Then he saw the blond woman, the same one who'd been looking out the balcony.

She lay flat on her back, and was trembling slightly, the tremors of death, an image Charlie knew well. There was blood everywhere, and her throat had been shredded by a bullet.

"Who's out there?" came a surprisingly familiar voice from a back room.

DuPree, crouched low, was covering Charlie, but looked over at him, puzzled.

"That you, Mike?" Charlie asked.

"Mike Schultz. You that Navajo guy, Charlie Henry?"

There was a footstep in the hall outside and a voice. "It's us, Charlie," Nancy whispered.

"What the hell?" Gordon asked, slipping in and looking down at the two dying men.

"Yeah, it's me, Charlie. Mike, where's Lola?" Charlie said, walking toward the hall, still reluctant to lower his weapon.

"Who the hell is Mike?" DuPree whispered to Gordon.

"She's gone," Mike replied. "I'm putting down my weapon and opening the door, okay? Don't let anyone shoot me."

Charlie looked back at his three companions. Nancy had come in and was kneeling down beside Lola's friend—the blonde. DuPree nodded, still covering the bedroom. Gordon had come around and was behind and to his right, weapon aimed.

"Okay, Mike. Slowly. We've got three weapons on you."

The door opened, and Mike the Pimp stepped out, hands up, dragging his right leg, which had a stream of blood flowing from the thigh down. "The bastards shot me. How about calling the EMTs before I bleed to death?" he asked, a weak grin on his face.

"First, where's Lola?"

"Gone. She managed to climb out the bedroom window and

drop to the grass while I was keeping these men back." He looked over at the woman by the counter. "Didi? She took the first bullet. Is she . . ."

"Dead," Nancy said, phone at her ear.

Charlie stepped toward Mike, steadied him with one arm, and looked through the doorway into the bedroom. The window was wide open. "Where'd she go?"

"The hell away from Albuquerque, I hope. Lola said that the necklace she pawned belonged to Cordell Buck. She'd ripped it off from Jerry's boss."

"Who was Jerry's boss?" DuPree asked.

"Clarence Fasthorse's mom, Sheila something," Mike said, his voice trailing off and his face going paler by the second. His strength gave way and he slid on his back down the wall and landed on his butt. "Get that Sheila bitch, and her son too," he added, his eyes closing.

"Sergeant Medina, keep this apartment clear until more officers arrive," DuPree ordered.

"Gordon, can you keep Schultz from bleeding out? I'm going to look for Lola," Charlie said, turning toward the door.

"Wait, Charlie! No, better yet, go and take Nancy with you. I'll protect the scene," DuPree said, motioning toward the door.

"Find me a towel or something," Gordon yelled as Charlie stepped out into the hall. Nancy was already ahead of him, running down the stairs.

Five minutes later, Charlie was two blocks away in a residential area, knocking on doors and asking anyone who answered if they'd seen a young Indian woman running or hurrying through the area within the past several minutes. Nancy had taken her Jeep and was circling the neighborhood, using her phone to set up a search grid with officers who were now entering the area.

Charlie's cell phone rang just as he was trotting across Montgomery Avenue toward a Smith's supermarket. He brought out the phone as he stepped onto the curb and looked at the display. It was Gordon.

"Bad news, Charlie," Gordon reported. "Mike doesn't have any car keys, which means he probably gave them to Lola. She could be miles away by now. DuPree is trying to find out from Mike's people at the Firehouse what kind of car that might be. It's not Schultz's Mercedes, that's all we know. It's still at the bar."

"Mike won't tell you?"

"Can't. He's out like a light. The EMTs are here working on him now. They think he'll make it, but it'll be awhile before he can talk. Nancy's leading the search for the vehicle, once we know what to look for," Gordon said.

"I might as well come back," Charlie said. "See you in five." He ended the call, then turned around for one more look. He waited for the light to change, then crossed back to the south toward the apartment building. When he arrived there were at least seven cop cars in the parking lot, emergency lights flashing, and maybe twenty tenants outside in a loose cluster.

It would probably take minutes to get in without an escort. He brought up his phone, touched Gordon's image, and waited. "Gordo, can you ask an officer to meet me down in the parking lot? Otherwise, once they see I'm packing they're going to hang on to me for sure."

As he continued across the parking lot, Charlie wondered what was going to happen once Sheila Ben heard about the death of two more of her crew—and Lola's escape. Suddenly it made sense that Clarence's mother was the brains behind the Night Crew— her son was just the front man and she was the one who handled the money. What Charlie didn't know, and needed to find out, was how Sheila ended up with Cordell Buck's favorite piece of jewelry. Once he found that out, instincts told him it would lead directly to whoever killed Buck, and why.

Chapter Seventeen

Two hours had passed and Charlie and Gordon walked into FOB Pawn, having been dropped off at the front entrance by an APD patrolman. Nancy was leading the countywide search for Lola, DuPree was still at the crime scene, and Mike the Pimp was undergoing medical treatment at Saint Mark's hospital under the protection of APD officers.

"You guys look like you've been through the wringer," Jake said, looking over from behind the front counter. "I'm glad you called. Ruth heard about a shooting in the Northeast Heights. The police were involved, and several people were killed. We were worried . . . is that blood on your shirt, Gordon?"

"Yeah," he said, looking down. "I've got a spare in the back. I'd better go clean up."

Ruth, hearing their voices, looked over through the office window, saw Gordon walking in her direction, and ran out of the office. "You're hurt?"

"Not to worry—it's not my blood," Gordon said, smiling.

She nodded, looking past him now at Charlie. "How about . . ."

"Charlie's okay too. I'll let him tell you all about it," Gordon added. She reached out, touched him on the shoulder briefly, then walked up to join Charlie and Jake.

"Hi, Ruth. We're all okay, including Nancy and Detective Du-Pree, but a friend of the woman we've been looking for was killed today along with her two attackers. We were just a few minutes too late to prevent that. Another friend of Lola's helped save her life, but ended up in the hospital. He should be okay."

"What about Lola? She's the person who started all this when she pawned the squash blossom," Jake asked.

"She's on the run again, unharmed, apparently, but probably scared as hell. Nancy and half the county are trying to find her, but who knows?" Charlie replied.

"So, you're back to square one trying to find out who really killed the Navajo silversmith?" Ruth asked.

"Yeah, and Lola claimed she knew. Unfortunately, she never told anyone else, apparently, before she split. At least we've ruled out more of the carjacker gang—process of elimination, I guess you could say," Charlie hedged, not wanting to talk about people he'd killed. "Unless it was one of those already deceased, it's either one of his remaining gang or Clarence Fasthorse himself."

"I can see how killing the person you robbed serves to get rid of the obvious eyewitness, but I'm still fuzzy why they dug up the grave to steal more jewelry off the body," Jake wondered. "You think it was the same people both times, don't you?"

Charlie nodded. "That's been a foregone conclusion, not just with me, but for the tribal police and the other agencies."

"Somebody must have really hated the silversmith to do this kind of thing to him. I read that his body was torched in his casket," Ruth added. "You and Gordon are taking on some really nasty people. But, after what they tried to do here to get the squash blossom necklace back, I guess it goes without saying."

"To me, it sounds like someone had an unpleasant history with the dead jewelry maker. He was stolen from, killed, stolen from again, then his body desecrated," Jake said.

Gordon, coming up wearing a fresh shirt, caught the last of their conversation. "Yeah, I was thinking about that, too."

"The original attack on him outside the casino was planned, right?" Jake asked.

"Yeah, and there lies the answer. Whoever chose him as the target is responsible for his death, even if they paid someone else to do the deed," Charlie concluded. "That suggests Clarence."

"Or his mom?" Gordon suggested. "She ended up with the squash blossom, right?"

"That's what Mike the Pimp said Lola told him," Charlie replied.

"Mike the Pimp? What a horrible nickname," Ruth retorted.

"That isn't a nickname, that's kinda his profession," Gordon said, smiling wickedly. "Well, one of them."

"Yeah, well, in spite of that, Mike was the one who saved Lola today," Charlie added.

"And maybe us," Gordon added.

The front doorbell sounded and they all just stood there, silent, as a woman in her early twenties wearing tight jeans and a crop top entered. With her was a spike-haired guy who looked about her age, dressed in an unbuttoned leather vest and tan cargo pants. They were carrying an electric guitar and something in a cardboard box.

The woman saw them staring at her. "What?"

"Um, sorry, come on in. We were . . ." Charlie began, knowing he couldn't mention their conversation topic.

"Expecting the UPS guy," Jake responded smoothly. "But hey, is that an SG Special you've got in your hands, sir?"

The young man, in his early twenties, narrowed his eyes, a little confused. "The guitar? It's a Gibson, supposed to be a classic. My grandpa bought it back in the sixties and played it for a while. It still works like new, according to my dad."

"Can I take a look?" Jake said, reaching his hands out toward the man, who seemed eager. The woman placed the box she was carrying onto the counter. "Got some old music records here too, and a Homer harmonica, or something like that. What price can we get for this junk if we sell it?"

Ruth came over and looked into the box. "It's a Hohner Chromonica, Jake! This is a nice collection. Let's set everything out on the counter so I can have a look. I'm Ruth," she added, smiling broadly.

Charlie and Gordon took advantage of the interruption to head back to the office.

"Hope those customers didn't steal that stuff. They didn't have a clue what it was," Gordon commented, grabbing his mug and reaching for the coffeepot.

"At least the kid had a credible history for the guitar. Jake will be able to sort that out, and Ruth is good with almost all the musical instruments and jewelry. If those youngsters shy away when it comes to showing a photo ID and having it copied, that'll be a good sign. We couldn't have better help than those two," Charlie confirmed.

"It's more like we're the help, not Jake and Ruth. They've been running this place without us the past few days. I wish we could have brought in Lola and given her the opportunity to rat out Clarence and his mommy," Gordon said. Sipping his coffee, he leaned back in his chair and closed his eyes.

Charlie brought out his cell phone to make a call and spotted a text message. "Something from Al," he announced.

Gordon sat up straight. "What's the news?"

"Jayne and Rand, her boyfriend, are driving Al up to Shiprock. He'll call me when he gets home. Once he's alone he wants the latest news. Says he's out of the loop now, but expects to start desk duty in a few days."

"Staying with his sister must have worn thin. It's been less than a day, Charlie," Gordon said, grinning.

"You met him. Al's a pain in the ass after about ten minutes, and Jayne has never gotten along with anyone in the family since eighth grade except for Dad. Besides that, Rand is a dick and probably up to something illegal. I told you about his Internet 'business.' He won't want a cop roaming around the house," Charlie admitted.

"So how'd you three kids get along growing up?"

"Mom and Dad laid down the rules, kept us busy, and held us responsible for our actions. We had to show respect for each other, but sometimes I think there was too much competition. My brother and I got into some serious fights, and not just arguments. Al got married right out of high school, skipped college, and went to the police academy. Less than six months later, along came a son. Instant family."

"You skipped college too. Your dad wanted you to become a lawyer, like him. Right?"

"Mom did too, but they couldn't exactly forbid me not to enlist, with the wars going on and all. They respected that and supported me all the way. Mom told me once that I looked better in a uniform than a suit, and that one lawyer in the family was enough," Charlie replied, pouring himself the last of the coffee.

"Jayne seems like a free spirit."

"Yeah, with a mind, maybe two, of her own. She's such a lousy judge of character though, trying to save one guy after another. They're always weak and loaded down with problems. She has an elementary certificate, like Mom, but never applied for a teaching job. She says she's not ready to work with kids yet. She'd rather work retail, so she does."

Gordon nodded. "I remember you posting her photo in our quarters. Suppose she'd go out with me after she dumps the current boyfriend?" He grinned.

Charlie shrugged. "I gave up trying to understand my sister about the time she turned thirteen. Despite your small stature, you'd be a real step-up from the guys she's been choosing. But I don't see her ever settling down."

"Small stature. Is that a short people joke?"

"What do you think, shorty?" Charlie said, laughing. "Enough of this. Maybe it's time we go and relieve our staff?" He nodded toward the front of the shop.

"That's not a bathroom joke, is it?"

"Not intentionally. I was suggesting we get to work."

"Yeah, well, please excuse my momentary lapse into twelve-year-old-boy-think. First let me brew up a fresh pot of coffee for Jake and Ruth," Gordon replied, reaching over and grabbing the empty pot.

Charlie and Gordon handled the customers the rest of the day. At closing time a police sergeant came by, acting on DuPree's behalf, and had them sign their written statements on the events at and around Lola's apartment. Once that was done, Charlie and Gordon locked up and went home.

Charlie had just sat down at his kitchen table with a lasagna TV dinner and a Mexican Coke when his cell phone rang. It was Al.

The conversation didn't take long. Al was home now with his wife Nedra and the kids, and Jayne and her boyfriend had decided to immediately return to Corrales, a nearly four-hour trip.

Charlie looked at his watch. They should be home by now as well, out of danger from Al's enemies. He didn't give a crap about Rand, but Jayne was still his little sister. He wished they got along better.

Charlie told Al about what had happened, and from the descriptions Charlie was able to provide was able to verify the identity of the Night Crew guy who'd been killed along with Jerry Benally. Al hadn't known that Sheila Ben was that deeply involved in the criminal operation, but he'd only been able to penetrate the gang long enough to know some faces and first names.

Finally Charlie began with his questions. "Now that you've had time to think about it, do you have any idea who and how you got made as an undercover cop?"

"Nobody in the regular crew or restaurant knew me from before. They all grew up around Albuquerque," Al said. "I'd like to think it wasn't any of the other officers on the undercover team. DuPree is trying to find out if any of the officers have connections or relatives connected to Fasthorse, Sheila, or the guys in the crew."

"How about someone you might have met before, maybe on the Rez, like the guy throwing punches at you?"

"If I came across him during an incident on the Rez, I certainly don't recall it. But I was a patrol officer for three years before making detective," Al replied.

Plus the time recently after being demoted, Charlie thought. "You spend any other time in Albuquerque, then, where one of them might have seen you?"

There was a pause. "Nedra and I brought the kids to the State Fair last year, and we've been to the Gathering of Nations event at the Pit twice now," Al said. "We spent the weekend each time."

There was a voice in the background. "Hang on a second, Charlie," Al said, talking to someone.

"Okay. Nedra is here, and she reminded me of a Law Enforcement Seminar I attended for a week last summer with about fifty other agency officers. It was held at UNM and we were put up in one of the dorms. I was with law enforcement people pretty much the whole time—no real police work took place except for meetings and training sessions," Al added.

Al's voice shifted slightly to that quick tone—the one that Charlie knew was a tell for his brother when he was hiding something. "No bar hopping, bro?" Charlie asked, trying to bring him out. It was a time when his brother was drinking heavily.

Al laughed, and there was a short pause. "Naw, we took in a few movies at one of the big theaters, but when it came to booze we brought enough with us in our luggage to last. Don't rat me out to the campus cops."

Charlie laughed back, wondering if Al was saying this for him or for Nedra. He also wondered if Nedra knew the tell—that Al was lying about something.

Charlie wasn't in the mood to start something with his brother, so he let it go. "If you think of anyone or anything that may have blown your cover, let me know, Al. I'm still keeping my nose in this. Gordon and I don't have any plans at the moment, but one way or the other, we're going to continue cranking up the heat until we figure out who knocked off the silversmith."

"Copy that, Charlie. Just be careful, okay?"

"You too, Al, and take care of yourself, Nedra, and the boys. Fasthorse and his people take everything personal, you know."

"Yeah. And thanks again for bailing me out, little brother."

"Sure," Charlie said. "Later."

"Later," Al replied, and ended the call.

Charlie set down the phone, took a deep swallow of Coke, then stirred up the lasagna in the plastic dish. It was cold, but he was hungry and another pass in the microwave would turn the lasagna into shoe leather. He dug in immediately, trying to figure out what to do next. He wasn't a cop, and he needed help from a fresh outlook. Maybe Dad.

Chapter Eighteen

The long, dry ridge known as Hogback loomed in the distance as Charlie slowed to make the right-hand turn off Highway 64. The private road led to his parents' home a few miles east of the Rez border. The drive from Albuquerque had been smooth and he'd made good time on the sections of newer highway off tribal land.

Jake and Ruth were holding down the fort and Gordon was keeping an eye on them while he made this quick run back to his own home grounds.

Charlie had woken in the morning with the thought that maybe his dad could help them come up with a strategy that would enable them to nail Clarence and his mother before any more harm was done.

His mom sounded excited—his last visit had been almost a year ago—but she ordered him to bring a suit and tie. They were attending some kind of tribal event that evening and they wanted to show him off.

Charlie had cringed at the thought, but Mom had finally agreed to introduce him only as their youngest son, nothing else. He'd only been back to the Rez twice since that god-awful parade, and though he knew the tribe had to have its heroes, he sure didn't feel like one. Doing your job didn't make you a hero. In his mind that was supposed to be reserved for someone who went way above and beyond what was expected of them—beyond bravery.

All he'd discovered while in the Army was that he was skilled at taking prisoners and destroying the enemy. The only thing he could be proud of, if such a thing really mattered, was that at least he hadn't personally killed anyone who wasn't trying to kill him back. If only he could forget about having to turn over his captives to civilians who'd turned around and done God-knows-what to them.

His mom and dad's retirement home was off the Rez, barely, and it wasn't where they'd actually raised their kids. Charlie had grown up in Shiprock up on the northern mesa, in one of those old brick apartments left over from when the days when the government maintained boarding schools for Navajo children from remote communities.

Dad was a lawyer and had been a tribal judge for over twenty years while Mom taught at the elementary school just up the hill from the family apartment. They'd eventually made enough to be able to buy a home, which meant it had to be off-Rez. Both were now retired and doing well, apparently.

As he approached the metal gate, it swung open, courtesy of an electric motor powered by a battery and solar panel atop a post. Dad had been installing it last visit and he'd helped.

The double garage was open, and as he drove into the graveled driveway, Dad rose up from the footstool beside the engine compartment of the old VW Bug he was working on and walked out onto the gravel.

"*Yáatééh*, Dad," Charlie greeted the equivalent of hello as he parked to the right of the garage, making sure he wouldn't block the drive. He stepped out and met his father halfway.

He and his dad, Alfred Senior, looked alike in facial features and stature, tall and slender, while Al Junior was shorter and barrel-chested, like so many Navajo men. Jayne and Mom were even smaller, almost delicate, and, fortunately, a lot better looking.

"Didn't take you that long, Charlie," his dad commented with a grin. "Looks like you made every light," he added, shaking his hand firmly. It was an old joke—there were less than six stoplights in the two hundred–plus mile drive once out of Albuquerque proper.

"Wind at my back, Dad," he responded. Both of them loved to drive, work on cars, and ride horses. Growing up in the community of Shiprock, the entire family had gone on trail rides up and down the San Juan River bosque on weekends. During summer, at least into high school, all three siblings rode at least an hour or two each day.

The horses were long gone now, a distant, pleasant memory when the Henrys had been the all-first American family. They'd worked hard, had good jobs, and were better off than most Navajos, or even most New Mexicans for that matter.

"Where's Mom?" Charlie asked, then heard a door slam inside the garage. Out came his mother, a hard-gentle woman who was as loving as she was firm with her children. Charlie blamed her razor-sharp eyes on her thirty years in an elementary school classroom. He and Al had never gotten away with anything for long, at least with Mom, but it was Dad who really watched out for Jayne. She was, no question about it, Dad's favorite, and had been completely spoiled until she reached puberty. After that, her father was truly the judge—at least when it came to boys dating his princess.

Mom's hug began a dozen feet away and was as warm as it was loving. "So glad you're here—and safe, Charlie. I just spoke to Al, who's healing well, and he said you've both been involved with some very dangerous people. He's a police officer, but I thought when you left the Army you were done with all that . . . violence."

"He has the right to defend himself, dear," his dad commented softly. "But let's move on. How about some coffee, son? Looks like you could use a jolt to open your eyes."

Charlie nodded. "And a cinnamon roll?" he asked hopefully, looking at his mom.

She smiled. "That's my Charlie."

An hour later, Charlie was back outside, sitting on the ground beside his father, who was static timing the old VW with a ten millimeter socket wrench, a small light that was alligator clamped to an electrical contact, and a big open-end wrench clenching the pulley nut.

"So you're looking to tie together all these incidents—the robbery, the shooting, the grave robbing, and the necklace—to this Night Crew?" his dad asked, turning the small distributor slightly until the light came on.

"What am I doing wrong, Dad? There seems to be some pieces missing," Charlie said, tightening the nut on the distributor with the ten mil wrench.

"You're right, it all has to tie together. I think what you need to find out here is why the first crime took place—the robbery and the killing of the silversmith," his dad replied, snapping the distributor cap back in place.

"Well, the Night Crew, Fasthorse's people, specialize in carjackings, mostly. You don't think this was just a robbery gone bad?"

His dad shook his head. "There's more to it, a deeper motive, I'm guessing. Actually, this gives me an idea. Clarence's mother, Sheila Mae Ben, used to manage one of the tribal casinos."

"Yes, sir. She's got an MBA or something. But she lost that job, right?"

"Officially, she resigned, but there's more to it than that, Charlie. Did you know I sit on the tribal casino advisory board?"

Charlie shook his head. "I knew you're on several tribal boards, but I didn't know about that one."

"The tribal president appointed me to that position about six months before Sheila was forced out. It was all kept confidential to avoid a tribal scandal."

"Why? Was she stealing from the casino?"

"There was never any suggestion of that. No, there was a potential scandal. Sheila was recorded having sex with a man on her office desk," his dad added.

"On? So, did the guy claim sexual harassment?"

"No, the man, a Navajo and also well known, didn't work for the tribe and had never applied for a casino job. There's more. This sexual encounter was recorded on an illegal, hidden camera and the recording was sent anonymously to the tribal president. A threat was made. Get rid of her or the recording would be posted on the Internet."

"She was set up?"

"Exactly. It was clearly a case of blackmail, and because of that, I voted against letting her go. But the majority of the board was worried the recording would end up on the Internet, so they voted in favor of damage control. We all knew she'd been framed, but there was a lot of pressure from the tribal president, who was coming up for reelection. The blackmailer won out. Sheila was given a choice—take a generous severance package and resign, or be shown the door. Either way, she had to go. The board agreed to do everything possible to keep this from going public, and Sheila was paid well to cooperate. She also knew that if word got out, her reputation would be ruined, even if she won in court."

Charlie nodded. "So she got screwed—twice—in exchange for a golden parachute. What happened to the man involved?"

"His face was blurred in the video, but everyone knew who it was. There was enough to see, especially from his unique silver buckle with the initials 'C.B.' He already had a reputation as a womanizer. Still, he faced no consequences whatsoever. No questions were ever asked."

"Ahh, now I see the silversmith connection. That explains why Mr. Cordell Buck is dead. Payback is a bitch. But I'm guessing he got more than the obvious for helping set up Sheila. After she was forced out, who got her job running the casino?"

"The silversmith's cousin and Sheila's assistant at the time,

Nolan Bitsillie. Nolan also happens to be one of the tribal president's biggest financial backers."

"Politics. What a surprise."

His dad sat there for a moment, staring into space. Charlie was familiar with the thousand-yard stare from his years of deployment, but these spaced-out moments from Alfred Senior always ended with profound conclusions.

Charlie waited patiently.

"You need to be careful this evening, son. She's going to be there."

"Sheila Mae Ben is a guest at this tribal thing we're going to tonight?" Charlie would have stayed away, had this been a few days ago, but it was pointless now that the woman and her son already knew who he was. Al had escaped, for now, and he really doubted any of the Night Crew that still remained would try to harm a retired tribal judge with his father's reputation.

Al Senior nodded. "Sheila's a big contributor to the tribal small business association, which provides members of the tribe with start-up loans. Despite her leaving the casino, I've heard she's done quite well in her private business operations, like that restaurant in Albuquerque she operates with her son."

"That ties in with one of the reasons I wanted to talk to you," Charlie said, proceeding to summarize what he and Gordon had learned the past week or so, leaving out their illegal activities. Charlie had always been pragmatic, but his father was a stickler when it came to breaking the law. It was important he didn't know anything that might put him in a compromising position.

When he was finished, his dad shrugged. "Clearly there's a lot you left out—like how you know all this. I'm not going to ask you about that, but the fact is that if you hadn't been there at the right time, your sister-in-law Nedra would be a widow. I don't agree with all your methods and decisions, especially the violence, but I respect what you've done and are trying to accomplish in the name of justice. You've got my support. So what are your plans tonight— with that woman there? It's clear she knows who you are and what you're trying to do."

"Al's not coming, right?"

His dad shook his head. "The tribal department wants him to keep a low profile. He's staying at home."

"With a loaded weapon handy, I hope."

"Back to my question, son. What are your plans?"

"I think I need to keep it neutral—pretend nothing is wrong, be social, not say or do anything that'll put either of us on the spot."

"Observe, scout it out, learn about your enemy. Sounds like a good strategy."

"Any idea if Clarence will be there? He suffers from poor judgment in these matters," Charlie replied, knowing he'd be leaving his Beretta in his Charger and be defenseless except for his hand-to-hand skills and the lockback knife in his right front pocket.

"I've never seen him with her at tribal functions."

"They spend a lot of time together in Albuquerque. His mom has a lot of influence over him and she apparently finances their illegal operations."

"Then maybe his legitimate work keeps him from attending. You said he runs the restaurant, right?"

"Yes, sir. If he has any common sense at all, he'll be keeping a low profile, like Al," Charlie added, looking up as his mother came out from the house, accompanied by the wonderful scent of fry bread.

"You two need to come in and clean up. Then we can have a snack. Dinner doesn't begin until seven, and I know how you two love to eat."

That evening, when they took their seats for dinner in one of the community college's meeting rooms, Charlie spotted Sheila Ben immediately. The woman was seated several tables over with three middle-aged Navajo couples—tribal honchos, he imagined.

He'd never seen her up close under normal lighting, just a photo, but the woman was exceptional looking. There was a silver streak in her ebony hair, and she had high cheekbones, full lips, and a face reminiscent of Irene Bedard, one of the few Native American actresses he recalled. In that respect Sheila didn't look that Navajo, her face was too long. Of course, Navajo women weren't all the same, either. Or maybe she had Plains Indian blood in her.

Cordell Buck had undoubtedly been a willing volunteer for the desk job that got her fired. There were a lot of attractive Navajo and Native American women Charlie had met over the years, but this lady, even in her early fifties, was beautiful.

They'd made eye contact for a moment when he initially glanced in that direction, and except for a slight furrowing of her brow, there'd been no reaction. Experienced at maintaining subtle surveillance for hours at a time while on an urban operation, Charlie positioned himself so he could keep watch out of the corner of his eye. Something told him Sheila would be keeping an eye on his behavior as well.

Dinner came quickly, the five-star equivalent of Navajo tacos, green chile stew instead of mutton stew—*thank God*—and lighter-than-air fry bread with honey and plenty of butter. It was almost as good as what Mom made, Charlie decided.

The meal reminded him of where he was—the Dinítah, Navajo country. Charlie hadn't been around that many members of his tribe at the same time since the parade down Highway 64, Shiprock's main street. Until tonight he'd never seen that many men in his tribe wearing suits either.

Charlie had grown up among bolo ties, flannel, Levi jackets, sweatshirts, jeans, cowboy hats, and boots. Even his dad, the judge, dressed casual unless his job or meeting required it. His mom wore more traditional clothes, a many-pleated, long skirt and velvet blouse with a multistranded liquid silver necklace instead of the heavy squash blossoms that seemed to be in great abundance tonight.

That brought his thoughts back to how his latest quest all started, and he took another glance in the direction of Sheila. She had on a black dress with a little cleavage enhanced by a single strand of white pearls—something more suitable for Albu-querque society than Rez dress. Judging from the attention she was getting from the men—and women—at her table, she was get-ting her share of admiration and envy.

Why a woman with her assets and obvious intelligence had turned to a life of crime was beyond him, but, then, he knew little about her.

As they were finishing dessert, there were speeches, three or four, Charlie lost count because they all seemed pretty much the same. He wasn't tuned into the subjects, but tried to make it look like he was listening. His dad and mom made a show of it, but he knew them well enough to see they were bored as well. They kept smiling back and forth, and for all he knew, they were playing footsie under the table. He focused on watching the guests.

Finally the speeches were replaced with live music—guitars, drums, and even a violin—fiddle around here. Country music worked for Indians as well as for cowboys, and his parents got up to dance.

He was thinking of finishing off his mother's flan when he smelled perfume. Charlie turned and watched as Sheila Ben sat down next to him.

Chapter Nineteen

"Good evening, Charlie. I thought I'd take this opportunity to come by and introduce myself. We obviously know about each other, but we've never officially met."

Sheila was no traditionalist, and fortunately wasn't holding a weapon or cutlery at the moment, so he shook her hand. Her grip was strong, but she wasn't flirting, just trying to convey a message.

"Ma'am," he responded, trying not to smile at the contrast between her relaxed composure and the reality of their relationship. He'd never been face-to-face with such an attractive criminal and possible killer, yet here she was.

"Love your family restaurant," he said, not eager to discuss anything meaningful. "Your son runs a tight ship."

"Most of the time. Lately, though, we've had a few setbacks."

"Nothing consequential, I hope. Your waitstaff and chef are certainly without equal. I look forward to dining there again soon."

"I thought you'd moved on and were now dining at another

local restaurant. The Firehouse Tavern, I believe. Word is that you've recently cultivated a friendship with the man who runs the place. It turns out we have mutual interests."

Clearly she was referring to Mike Schultz, letting him know her connection to the attempt on Lola Tso. Sheila also knew that he and Gordon had been involved in that incident. He looked into her eyes, realizing they were more hazel than brown, trying to see where she was going with this next. She held his gaze, her face hardening slightly.

"Then I guess I have to pay you a return visit before too long, Mrs. Ben."

"We'll try to make it an experience you'll remember the rest of your life," she said, her voice becoming hard.

"And you as well," he replied.

The song abruptly ended and dancers began to return to their tables. Out of the corner of his eye, he could see his parents approaching.

Sheila stood, then reached out and touched his shoulder. "You're a killer. Don't you dare hurt my son," she ordered in a whisper.

"That's up to you, isn't it?" Charlie responded, looking her straight in the eyes.

"If you hurt him, I'll hunt down and kill your entire family," she whispered harshly. Her nails dug into his shoulder for a second, then she turned and walked away gracefully, head held high, as if she'd just shared a few congenial minutes with an old friend.

"That was Sheila Ben. You know her?" his mom asked as they arrived at the table.

Charlie looked at his father, who shook his head just slightly.

"Her son and I have met. He runs a restaurant near Old Town," Charlie replied off-handedly. "The Piñon Mesa Steakhouse."

His mother smiled. "I don't like her, but I'm not really sure why. She seems a little too . . . duplicitous."

"I agree," Al Senior replied. "What did she have to say, Charlie?"

"Just discussing business," he replied, hoping to have a chance later to talk this over while Mom wasn't around. Dad was very protective of Mom—all the kids were—and there was no sense in giving his mother information that could put her in danger.

"Just business, my behind," his mother responded immediately. "You and your brother have been involved in something over in Albuquerque ever since that silversmith got killed near the tribal casino. This woman has a shady past and she's making way too much money from that restaurant of hers. I can put two and two together. There are a lot of Navajos involved in what's been going on in the criminal world lately, and she's part of that, isn't she?"

Charlie looked at his father, who shrugged. "She's smarter than the both of us, son. I haven't said a word."

"I was a teacher for thirty years, Al. I'm a great detective too, and I know when someone's trying to keep a secret. When Charlie shows up for the first time in months, the day after Al gets shot in Albuquerque doing something he can't talk about, I know something's not right. Now tell me, you two, unless you want me to go beat it out of Sheila. She's a few years younger, but I think I can take her."

His mom grinned right then, and Charlie grinned back. He already knew how strong his mother really was, at least in mind and spirit. But he also didn't want to overanalyze that grin—he already knew how dangerous the other members of his family could be. Mom too?

Not wanting to ruin the dinner with the threat of a middle-aged chick fight either, he decided it was time to tell her—and Dad, what had just transpired.

"Hey, Gordon, you still up?" Charlie asked, talking into the cell phone on the console as he drove north on Highway 291, still in the town of Shiprock—barely. He'd left his parents' home twenty minutes ago and was headed for Al's house, which was located in a tribal housing development northwest of what passed for downtown.

"No, this is his answering machine. What's going on in Indian country? Your father any help?" Gordon replied.

Charlie could hear a television set in the background, and what sounded like a football game. His pal recorded several games a week, then watched them late at night.

He told Gordon the news about Sheila and the casino sex-tape frame-up, then finished up with tonight's encounter with the woman. By then, he was easing up the street toward his brother's boxy home at the end of the block.

"She's got balls, letting you know that she knows we know, then ending with a threat against your family. Sounds like us," Gordon said, "well, except for that family retribution part."

"Sorry. Guess we'll have to stay even higher up on our toes. At least she's worried, and aware of what we can do," Charlie added, pulling up to the curb in front of Al's home.

"She'll either go on the defensive or strike hard and fast."

"If Clarence has any say about it, they'll try one last hit—hoping to take us all out, you, me, Al, and Lola," Charlie concluded.

"Ah, but remember what your father said about the casino job. There's probably at least one more target on her list."

"You're right. The guy who took her place—Buck's relative, Nolan Bitsillie. He's got protection at the casino, and probably, since Cordell was taken out, a bodyguard or two. I imagine he also has casino security at his disposal wherever he goes," Charlie said.

"You gonna warn him?"

"Unless he's stupid, he's already watching his back, but maybe it wouldn't hurt to talk to him. It's late, but the casino is open all night. Maybe I can catch up to him."

"Okay, good luck. Stay safe, Charlie."

"Always." Charlie ended the call, and looked over at the house. The driveway was empty, so Al's pickup was probably in the single-car garage. According to their mom, Nedra and the boys had been sent to stay at her dad's house just this afternoon, so it was impossible to know if anyone was inside. No lights were on either. Al was avoiding attention.

His phone rang. It was Al.

"It's me. You ready to take a ride?" Charlie asked.

The casino was located on Navajo Nation land between Shiprock and Farmington, the largest city in the Four Corners, and the drive normally took less than twenty minutes. Charlie and Al, however, weren't going there directly. Al, at Charlie's urging, called the casino office on the way and arranged to meet Bitsillie, the manager, at a truck stop café across the highway from the casino.

"Bitsillie was eager to talk when I told him I had news about the death of his cousin Cordell," Al commented, sitting forward in the bucket seat just a little, favoring his injury.

"And you didn't lie—you *were* part of the investigation into his death," Charlie responded, checking his rearview mirror for the third time in five minutes. Despite the late hour, there was a lot of traffic on the road and he'd have a hard time spotting a tail.

"Yeah, but if he calls my boss I'm screwed. I was yanked from the case the moment I got shot."

"No pain, no gain," Charlie replied, then gave his brother a big grin. "But now we know the motive, and that should help, right, Sherlock?"

"Yeah, I guess so. It's damn strange, though, coming from our dad. A cop is supposed to sleuth this out. We got lucky."

"You make your own luck, Al. Hard work and all that shit. If you can get a shortcut every once in a while, take it."

"I'll just be glad when this is all over. We still need hard evidence to arrest Clarence, Sheila, or whoever did the deed," Al said, awkwardly bringing out his department weapon with his uninjured left hand and checking the magazine. "And I'm not much help shooting lefty if we run into the Night Crew."

"Their numbers have declined, I'd imagine. I've got your back tonight," Charlie assured.

"That'll do. Wish your buddy Gordon was here, though."

"He's saved my ass too many times to count, Al. There's no

better backup, that's for sure," Charlie admitted. "Someday I'll have to tell you some of those stories."

"Maybe later. Here we are." Al nodded toward the turn as he placed his weapon back into his holster.

The casino was so brightly lit it could be seen for miles, but the area glow also made it impossible to miss the truck stop. Charlie slowed, signaled, then made the right turn into the asphalt parking lot surrounding the fuel pumps and drove to a slot in front of the café. About ten eighteen wheelers and a few smaller rigs were parked in rows about a hundred yards across the lot. No one was visible in or around the trucks. The drivers were either in the sack, having a late dinner or early breakfast, or across the highway losing money.

Al looked around as Charlie parked in a slot about fifty feet from the entrance to the café. "No other cars around, but we're five minutes early," Al said, checking his watch, then yawning loudly. "I hate working graveyard shifts. Must be the traditional Navajo in me."

"Night can be your friend. I spent most of my service time on night operations. Of course we had eyes in the dark. Technology made us harder to locate and take out," Charlie reminded.

"What's it like, going from firefights to running a business?"

Charlie shook his head. "Haven't seen much difference lately."

"You've got a point," Al replied, then checked the Dodge's side mirror. "Here we go. White Cadillac crossing the highway and coming in this direction. It's either a high roller coming over for gas, or Nolan Bitsillie."

The car drove into the lot, turned around, and backed into a parking space, leaving an open slot between them. The driver, wearing a black jacket with the casino logo, looked at them carefully for a moment, then motioned with his head for them to approach.

"Bitsillie is paranoid, Al. He probably has a good idea why his cousin was killed and that he could be next. His driver looks meaner that a rabid coyote," Charlie commented.

"He may not want to go inside to talk, especially with other ears listening," Al pointed out. "Let's go over. Just keep your hand away from your weapon. If either he or his bodyguard gets jumpy they're going to race out of here, even if it means running you down."

"You first, you're the cop."

Al climbed out, then came around the front of the Charger, into the light beneath the café sign, smiling all the way. He nodded to the driver, then lifted his jacket to show the badge clipped to his belt.

Charlie got out next, followed by the driver, who eyed him carefully, pulling back his jacket enough to reveal a big handgun at his waist.

"I'm Officer Henry with the tribal police, and this is my brother, Charlie, who has a personal interest in this case. Is Mr. Bitsillie your passenger?"

"That's right," the driver acknowledged, looking over for a second at an old pickup that was just turning into the parking lot. "I've heard a lot about you Henry boys. I'm Fred Nakai, former sergeant in the Gallup PD. Thanks for your service, soldier," he said, reaching out to shake Charlie's hand.

Al accepted the offered hand next, shaking it quickly. "We need to talk with your boss, Nakai. Inside, or out here?"

"Let's go inside," a voice called from the other side of the Caddy. A tall Navajo in his mid-forties with slicked back hair, wearing an expensive-looking black suit and tie, came around the front of the car toward them. "I don't like standing here in the open, boys."

Charlie and Nakai both turned at the sound of a vehicle coming into view from behind the nearest row of parked trucks. The black four-door Crown Victoria sedan moved toward the street, then suddenly swung around in a skidding turn and raced back across the lot.

"Down!" Charlie yelled. Nakai reached for Bitsillie, pushing him down just as a burst of gunfire erupted from the open windows of the Crown Vic. The car slid to a stop, with at least two shooters firing rapidly at the casino manager and Nakai, who was trying to stay between the vehicle and his client.

Charlie had his weapon out in a heartbeat. Lying prone, he fired several rounds into the big sedan, aiming at the windows. Al, somewhere behind him, also began to return fire.

The Crown Vic accelerated and raced toward the street, weaving, apparently out of control. The car struck a stop sign, bounced off the curb, then angled into the highway, crossing both lanes. It swerved erratically another fifty feet, then suddenly exploded with a blast that deafened Charlie and shattered the window of the café behind him. A brilliant plume of flame shot up from the inferno and chunks of metal and glass arched across the sky. One of the Crown Vic's doors skidded across the parking lot, spinning around like a pinwheel before it stopped, smoking and on fire, beneath a light pole.

"Call it in," Charlie yelled, scrambling to his feet and running over to where Nakai and Bitsillie lay on the asphalt.

Blood was flowing from at least two wounds in Nakai's left leg, and one in his left bicep. He groaned, rolled off Bitsillie, then leaned over the casino manager.

"Shit!" he cursed. "Call the EMTs."

Charlie could see Bitsillie clearly. He'd taken more than one hit in the torso, and bloody bubbles were forming around his upper chest. But that was the good news. His face was a mess, and it would take a skilled mortician to avoid a closed casket at this man's funeral.

"Al, you hit?" Charlie yelled.

"No," Al mumbled, stumbling over. "Just twisted my ankle. Bitsillie?" he said, stepping close.

Nakai was shaking his head. "Never should have gotten out of the fucking car."

Charlie's eyes were on the parking lot now, ignoring the fireworks display coming from the black sedan. He could see drivers climbing out of their rigs, yelling back and forth. The old pickup was gone, having slipped away in the confusion.

He looked over at Al and pointed toward the sedan, which was roaring like a blowtorch. "We got in some hits, but no way our bullets did that. That blast didn't come from the fuel tank either, at least not the first one. I've seen it before."

Al looked at him curiously. "Don't tell me the shooters decided to blow themselves up. This isn't Afghanistan."

"No, it isn't, and if suicide was on their mind, why not just drive right up to us and push the button?"

"The dark red pickup. It's gone. I saw a woman looking over just before the shooting started," Nakai broke in. "This can't just be a coincidence—it was all too well timed."

"You think you could identify the woman?" Al asked.

"Probably not enough to make an arrest. All I recall is that she had black hair," Nakai replied.

"Good-looking?" Charlie suggested, already with someone in mind.

Nakai nodded. "Come to think of it, yeah. I got that impression."

"You know what I'm thinking, brother?" Charlie said, looking over at Al. "We were followed, and we led that bitch and her people right to her next target."

"Yeah. I have no doubt now that Sheila Ben was behind this."

Charlie nodded. "With the loss in manpower, she's now getting personally involved. After that necklace screwup, she's also making sure nobody in her crew is going to be in a position to point fingers."

"What the hell you two talking about?" Nakai asked, then groaned loudly.

"Tell you later, Fred. Al, get the first aid kit out of my glove compartment," Charlie ordered, looking down at Nakai's leg. "This is one life we can save tonight."

Chapter Twenty

Al knew most of the responding officers—a mix of county deputies and tribal cops and one of the county fireman, so he did the
talking.

Charlie stayed with Nakai until the EMTs loaded the bodyguard up and took him away, getting what description he could of
the woman's image Fred had seen briefly. It could have been Sheila,
but it would be up to the local investigators to get an ID from a
photo array or whatever.

The burning sedan had been extinguished quickly once the
firefighters had arrived, and now the locals were checking the
wreckage and trying to locate the scattered debris, which littered
the highway, the parking lot, and had even been blown across the
highway onto casino property.

Inside the café, which was semi-open air due to the blown-out
window, Charlie wrote his statement as a Navajo cop sat across
from him. Al was still outside, talking to one of his supervisors.

Sensing he was being watched, Charlie looked toward the door and saw his mom and dad standing just inside. "I'm okay. I'll be done here in a few minutes and then we can talk."

The tribal officer turned to look, saw Charlie's father, then stood. "Judge. Mrs. Henry," he said respectfully, waving his hand toward an empty table. "Have a seat, if you'd like."

"Thank you, Sergeant Begaye, I think we'd rather stand," Al Senior replied, looking at Charlie's mom, who nodded.

The officer turned back, saw that Charlie had stopped writing, then looked down at the paper. Charlie slid it over and the officer read it for a while. "Very detailed. You never got a good look at the woman in the old pickup, then?"

Charlie shook his head. "Just the vehicle and two shapes inside, the driver and passenger. Mr. Nakai gave me these details of the woman. When he's interviewed at the hospital, maybe you can match this up with what he later recalls."

"Then we're done. Thank you, Mr. Henry, once again. You may leave unless my supervisor outside has some other questions for you. He's the detective talking to your brother."

Charlie stood, suddenly tired, and noticed the blood on his sleeves and hands. So much for shaking hands, something most Navajos weren't too fond of anyway.

Sergeant Begaye had seen his reaction. "There's a restroom where you can wash up a bit," he said, pointing across the room.

The manager of the café, who'd seen a sudden increase in business despite having to clean up broken glass, stood as Charlie walked in that direction. "Extra towels and soap in there, Mr. Henry. Grab a cup of coffee on the way out, okay?"

Charlie nodded at the gesture. By the time morning came around, everyone in the Four Corners would have heard all about last night. He could see the headlines now. *Tribal casino manager murdered in Navajo Nation shootout. Tribal cop and war hero brother kill suspected gunmen in fiery blast.* So much for trying to live a normal life.

Of course there was no way he and Al's pistol shots had caused that explosion, and before long the forensics would find that the vehicle was a mobile bomb. Of course, then Homeland Security, FBI, and the State Police might get involved.

Maybe, though, the explosives used could be traced. At least Al was in a position to recommend which direction to look.

He'd already made a quick call to Gordon and his pal was doubly alert. If Sheila and Clarence were resorting to explosives now, how much more of the stuff did they have, and who was advising them on bomb construction?

Charlie left his parents' home right after eight the next morning and pulled into a parking slot in the alley behind FOB Pawn just before lunch. When he walked in through the back, Ruth was in the office entering records into the system.

"Charlie, glad you're back—and safe!" she said, turning around and standing as he entered the office. For a second she seemed like she was about to hug him, but finally reached out and touched his arm.

"Gordon told me about it. The news got it all wrong," Ruth said.

"It'll take awhile for the facts to come out. You and Jake haven't had any problems, I hope?"

"Gordon's watched over us like a momma pit bull."

"Are you calling me a bitch?" Gordon said, stepping into the office.

Ruth laughed.

"See you're back in one piece," Gordon said, giving Charlie a punch on the shoulder. "Your brother too."

Charlie nodded. "We still need to step up our security," he said, looking at Ruth. "You might want to consider taking a few days off."

"No, I feel safer here than alone in my apartment. And from what Gordon's been saying, neither Jake nor I are likely targets from this crazy lady and her son. It's not like they're going to come in the front door . . ." she began, then stopped abruptly, looking up at Charlie, clearly remembering that had already happened once.

"Not likely," Charlie assured. "That didn't work out for them last time. Just keep an eye on the monitors for anything odd outside in the alley or out front, and don't take any chances." He turned and saw Jake standing there.

"I got that, boss," Jake said, nodding. "Good to see you back at work and . . . intact."

Gordon turned to the big ex-wrestler. "Why don't you and Ruth take lunch now? Charlie and I will hold down the fort. Okay with that, partner?"

"Good idea. Anyone out front?" Charlie asked.

"Nope," Jake responded, "but there was a kid about nineteen eyeing that Xbox at the far end of the display, and I'm guessing he's going to come back and make an offer. I quoted him sixty bucks, and he said he had to go find an ATM. I told him we'd hold on to it for a couple of hours—after that, it was on the market again."

"Thanks, Jake."

"Where we going?" Jake asked Ruth.

"Frank and Linda's? Their sandwich bar?" Ruth suggested, referring to the mom-and-pop grocery with the sit-down deli area as she grabbed her purse.

"Works for me," Jake responded. "You two stay out of trouble," he said to Charlie and Gordon, pointing to each of them.

"Yessir," Gordon responded, saluting.

As soon as Jake and Ruth were gone, Gordon took a look out front, saw no one in the shop, and nodded toward the computer. "Your brother sent a copy of some surveillance footage taken from the truck stop and casino cameras."

"Show me." Charlie nodded toward the monitor.

Gordon sat down, and with a few clicks of the mouse an image appeared of the parking area in front of the truck stop café. In the background were the outlines of parked big rigs. After a few seconds Charlie pulled up in the Charger. The rest of the video from this angle showed the arrival of Bitsillie's car—closest to the camera now—the Crown Vic pulling up to the right of the screen, and all the rest. At the end of the segment the sedan exited the viewing field, and briefly, after that, a bright flash came from that same direction, lighting up the area.

"There's a different angle from the fuel pumps you'll wanna

see," Gordon said, clicking on another file. This time, they could see the old pickup pulling in, then parking. As the sedan with the shooters came into the lot, the pickup slipped out behind it, moving toward the street. There was little to see except the gun flashes coming from two different weapons, then the black sedan pulled out, bounced off the stop sign, swerved out into the highway, then raced off, weaving. Immediately there was a big explosion originating from the trunk of the vehicle, and it veered across the highway in flames. A second explosion, probably from the fuel tank, finished it off.

"Clearly, our pistol slugs didn't cause either explosion," Charlie said. "Tribal authorities have called in federal explosives experts to check out the wreckage."

"Any idea about the shooters?"

"Last I heard they were still looking for enough remains to ID. No luck yet. You mentioned casino cameras?" Charlie asked.

"Next video. They have better cameras, but the distance and lighting are problematic. Take a look."

This video presented the entire incident from a distance of several hundred yards, and all they could really see were the involved vehicles from the opposite direction.

Neither of them spoke for a few moments, then Gordon asked, "You think the wounded bodyguard—Nakai, will be able to ID Sheila Ben as the woman in the pickup?"

"When I brought it up, he didn't think so. Did you get any word on the plates from the two vehicles? I noticed the angle and lighting were good enough in the second camera video for them to show up."

"Al mentioned in his cover letter that the plates were stolen, so, no, it doesn't help much."

The bell in the front of the store rang, and both of them glanced over as a young man in a denim jacket came into the shop. "I'll handle that," Charlie said. "Time to get back into the groove."

Another customer came in a few minutes later, so Gordon joined him out front. Before long, there were several people in the shop, three waiting around with stuff in boxes. They kept an eye on these people at first, despite the fact that two were women in their late fifties and the third a man who looked like he hadn't gotten off the sofa in the past thirty years except to grab another beer. If they were working with the Night Crew, Sheila and her son had gotten to the brine at the bottom of the barrel.

About the time the last of that bunch cleared the shop, Jake and Ruth returned, coming in the front, laughing and clearly having a good time. Charlie was pleased—they'd been pretty grim when he'd left for the Rez the other day. Hopefully, the business wasn't going to be involved in what was still to come for him, Gordon, and probably Al.

Neither one of them had had lunch, so Charlie and Gordon left their two employees and walked down to Frank and Linda's. The grocery-deli combo was a long, narrow room, with shelves stacked high in two narrow rows on either side of a wider central aisle. From where they sat at a small bistro table, munching burritos and Cokes, they could see the length of the store, right out the front door onto the sidewalk.

Halfway through his second burrito, Charlie saw a familiar

face. It was Detective DuPree, who spotted him at about the same time. Charlie waved him down the aisle.

Gordon looked over and saw who it was. "Hey, DuPree, join us for lunch while we catch up on current events."

DuPree strode to their table with a puzzled expression on his ruddy face, then looked over at the deli counter. "Why not? I'm going to be here for a while." He located the chubby Italian owner, who was wearing a long white apron and cap. "What's good today, Frank?" he asked.

Charlie looked over at Gordon, who shrugged. They listened to the two men talk, quickly learning that DuPree's father, a long-time law enforcement officer, had known Frank and Linda for years when the deputy had patrolled this part of the county.

A few minutes later, DuPree, armed with a bowl of Frito pie, joined them at the small table. "It's time to share information, boys. You first, Henry."

"Basically, I believe that Sheila Ben is behind the death of Cordell Buck, that she arranged for the attempt on Lola Tso and the shooting of Nolan Bitsillie last night, and then proceeded to blow her hired gunmen to pieces to make sure they couldn't identify their employer. This is based upon all we've learned so far, culminating in last night's events."

DuPree nodded. "That's one of the theories sent my way via the tribal police chief and the investigating officers, including your brother. I understand Sheila wanting to retrieve the squash blossom necklace—which probably tied her to Buck's death—but why did she kill the silversmith in the first place? And why Bitsillie? Was it because the man got her job at the casino?"

"More like how he got the job. She was fired a couple of years ago for doing the nasty on her casino office desk with Cordell Buck," Charlie explained. "Actually, she was bought off with a handsome severance check."

"Unusual. Who ratted her out?" DuPree asked.

"It was filmed on a concealed camera—probably planted there by Cordell Buck's cousin—Nolan Bitsillie. The video was sent to the tribal president anonymously, and he handed it over to the tribal board who oversees casino operations, wanting them to make it all go away. None of this was ever made public, though. Sheila was just paid off and quietly removed."

"And Bitsillie got the job. Nice setup. But if this is such a secret, how did you find out, Charlie?" DuPree asked.

"My father, a former judge, is on that same tribal board. He saw the video and was sworn to secrecy. But once Al and I became targets, he decided we needed to know the details. He helped me put it all together."

"We're talking revenge here, payback major league," DuPree replied, nodding. "Seems like a little overkill, though. Robbing Cordell Buck, I get that, but killing him, then robbing his grave? Is Sheila nuts?"

Charlie thought about it for a moment. He was no shrink, but he'd been around people that could be sent over the edge with just one tiny push. "Maybe there's something we don't know about yet that triggered the killing itself. And why wait over two years before gunning him down?"

"Blackmail?" Gordon suggested. "How about if Buck had approached Sheila recently, trying to squeeze some money out of her?

He obviously plays the tribal casinos. Maybe he's been on a losing streak."

"Okay, he could have been threatening to make her humiliation from the casino incident public unless she paid him to keep quiet," DuPree concluded. "But wouldn't that revelation also put Buck in the spotlight?"

"So? He'd probably get more high-fives than criticism from men," Charlie suggested. "Besides, Buck was a silversmith, while Sheila owns a family restaurant. It could really hurt her image—him probably not at all. Or maybe Buck had found out about the Night Crew and he threatened to expose Clarence."

"Okay, motive notwithstanding, if Sheila really did off the men who set her up, how do we catch her?" Gordon asked. "Are we getting any actual evidence from all of this?"

"What about the old pickup, the dead shooters, Sheila's whereabouts, the explosives, stuff like that?" Charlie asked DuPree.

"The lab boys are all over it, including the FBI crime lab. Several agencies are working on the evidence, including a detailed analysis of the surveillance tapes. The best witness concerning the woman in the pickup—Nakai—is under guard at the Shiprock Medical Center. He's set to be interviewed by the feds either this morning or afternoon," DuPree explained.

"Sheila went too far this time," Charlie said. "The woman is a piece of work—good-looking, but cold as hell. She came up to me earlier in the evening . . ."

"What? You holding out on me, Charlie?" DuPree asked, leaning forward. "I want details."

Charlie explained how the not-so-subtle threats against his family came out when the subject of Clarence's safety came up.

"Her son is her weak spot," Gordon suggested.

"Yeah, but you two better stay away from her and Clarence. Word's come down just this morning that the feds have been working the auto theft ring from the Mexican end of the pipeline, looking for an informant. Unfortunately, we still don't have enough to arrest all the players. Until we do, we don't want anyone else hurt, like your family, Charlie," DuPree said, this time softening his tone.

"Agreed. But we can keep looking for the other women involved, right?" Charlie asked.

Gordon looked at Charlie curiously for a second. "You still have no idea where Lola is?" he added, switching to DuPree.

The detective shook his head. "Not at this time. There are photos and BOLOs all over the Southwest, and we now have a description of the vehicle she fled in. She's got to turn up somewhere. That shot-up bar owner, Schultz, still insists he has no idea where she was headed."

"So you have no problem with us going in a different direction," Charlie concluded.

DuPree looked at him through narrowed eyes. "Why do I think you're up to something, Henry?"

"Me?" Charlie asked.

"Him?" Gordon echoed.

"Never mind. Just stay away from Clarence and Sheila, okay?" DuPree stood. "And let me know what, if anything, you learn that'll help the case."

"If you'll do the same," Charlie responded, holding out his hand.

DuPree took it reluctantly, then shook. "Okay. Deal." He turned to Frank, who was working behind the counter. "Good to see you again, pal. Say hello to your father for me?"

"Will do, and to your pop as well," the proprietor replied.

DuPree was barely out the door when Gordon looked over. "This detail slipped by DuPree, but I picked up on it. On the way back to the shop, you gonna tell me what other woman we're going to be looking for?"

Charlie stood. "Do you happen to remember a red Mustang?"

During the short walk back to FOB Pawn, Charlie got Nancy on the phone. "Nancy, remember Melinda Foy, the woman who regularly pays Clarence Fasthorse a visit? We never really checked her out because I figured she was incidental to the investigation."

"The sometimes hooker and catering server? Maybe she's just an off-the-books housekeeper now keeping a regular work schedule," Nancy suggested.

"Not based upon the way she dresses while on the job. I'm guessing she's having an affair with him, or maybe even selling herself again. Whenever she shows up Clarence has already turned on the romantic music."

"And you hear this music all the way from the street? Or are you into window peeping now?" Nancy asked. "Never mind, do I really want to know?"

"Not really. Anyway, can you get us a name and address? We'd like to speak with her about Fasthorse and his mother. We've been warned off Clarence and Sheila."

"Yeah, DuPree told me how the feds are working the car theft angle into Mexico. Nice for them to finally tell the local cops. Also, I heard about last night. Glad you and Al dodged the bullet again. Well, bullets and bombs."

"Thanks. When I catch up to you again I'd like to discuss Sheila Ben and her possible motivation for all this. DuPree knows about that now, we just spoke with him, but I'd like a woman's viewpoint and theories."

"Of course. I'm not on duty at the moment, but give me the Mustang's plate number again and I'll get back to you in a few minutes. Talk to you later."

They were in the shop office when Nancy returned the call. "Putting you on speaker," Charlie declared, getting Gordon's attention.

"Melinda Beth Foy is divorced and her two prostitution busts followed that breakup. There's nothing new in the three years since, though, so she's either being very careful, or gave up hooking. As for her most recent gigs, she's listed as an exotic dancer."

"Stripper," Gordon said.

"You ever hear of her from your time in vice, Nancy?"

"No, I'd already been transferred to traffic by then. If you talk to her, what's your angle, anyway? You think she's ever seen you in connection with Fasthorse or his mother?"

"Unless she's been shown my photo, no. If she'd been in the restaurant the one time we went inside, I would have noticed her," Charlie said.

"I saw her photo. She's attractive," Nancy replied.

"True enough. We were just hoping to learn something more

about Clarence and his family that she may have picked up during their . . . pillow talk, if that's what you call it," Charlie said.

"Sounds iffy. What you really want to do is piss off Clarence again, right?" Nancy replied. "Mess with his private life?"

"That would be a side benefit, I suppose. But no, from our admittedly limited monitoring of their relationship, I'm thinking Melinda depends on Clarence for some of her income. If we offered to trade some information she might be able to provide in exchange for our silence in her relationship with Clarence . . ."

"Blackmail, you mean," Nancy interrupted.

"Naw, we wouldn't really give her up. But that might motivate Melinda into providing us with some insight on Clarence and what he's thinking right now. She might even be able to provide details that could confirm once and for all if it was Sheila, not Clarence, who murdered Cordell Buck and Nolan Bitsillie. We're still not clear on who exactly shot the silversmith, though we think we know what motivated the hits."

"With all that's been going on the past few days, what if Melinda isn't hooking up with Clarence anymore?" Nancy countered. "When was the last time you saw them together?"

"Been awhile. But we need to do something. It's annoying having the answers, or thinking you have the answers, and not being able to follow through."

"Now you know what it feels like to be a cop," Nancy replied.

Charlie looked over at Gordon, who shrugged. "She's right."

"Damn right I'm right. Just make sure you two don't get shot by an angry boyfriend, Clarence or otherwise. All of the locals are on stand-down with the Night Crew investigation now that the feds have taken over."

"I thought the murder of Cordell Buck was still part of this," Charlie responded. "The main focus, actually."

"Those in charge, I suppose, believe they need to make a move on the carjacking and theft ring while there's still someone left to arrest. You two have whittled the procurement side of their illegal operation down a bit," Nancy reminded. "There's a good chance the feds can make a case with Clarence. His mom, I'm not so sure. I get the feeling she's never been on the scene at any of the Night Crew carjackings."

"And that's where we come in. I'll keep you informed, Nancy, and we'll honestly try to stay away from Clarence. I'm more interested in taking down Sheila. She's either the one who killed Buck and the casino owner, or the person who ordered it. Those two set her up to lose her job and that clearly pissed her off." Charlie quickly told her about the sex video.

Nancy thought about it awhile before responding. "That's a motive, all right. Too bad she turned violent instead of fighting it out in the courts and suing their asses."

"The lady isn't right in the head, and she's gone way too far with this. Several people have died because of her, three or more have been shot, and the only witness we know about who has a chance of tying her directly to the deaths is a target on the run. It's time to bring this to an end."

"You're right, Charlie, and there's not going to be a happy ending even when justice is done. You and Gordon do what you can, and if you need my help call my cell. And here's Melinda's address." Nancy read it out before ending the call.

After leaving word with Jake and Ruth to be on their guard, Charlie and Gordon left in Gordon's pickup.

Melinda lived in an apartment over by the university, according to the address, but if she'd kept to the schedule they'd mapped out days before, she could still be at Clarence's home.

"Do you suppose, after all that's been going on lately, that Clarence has rescheduled his sex life, or that Melinda's given up on him?" Gordon asked as they approached the neighborhood where Fasthorse lived. He and Charlie were both wearing caps and sunglasses.

"It's not too far out of the way to check and see. She may be fitting *him* into her schedule, not the other way around," Charlie answered.

Gordon turned the corner and approached Fasthorse's residence. They cruised by, Gordon keeping his eyes on the road and Charlie surveying the area.

"Mustang in the driveway," Charlie announced.

"Moving on. Shall we get into position to follow her home?"

Charlie nodded. "Or wherever she goes next. The good news is that she's still in contact with Clarence, so she might be up on the latest events."

They circled and parked close to the corner of an intersecting street so they could see the front door of Fasthorse's home. They'd know if anyone came out and be able to change directions if necessary.

After about fifteen minutes, Charlie, taking his turn with the binoculars, saw the door open. "Melinda's leaving, and there's some-one at the door, showing her out. Not Clarence. It's a woman."

"Clarence's mom?"

"Can't tell. The door closed immediately. Melinda's heading toward the gate."

Gordon started the engine. "Think Clarence had an audience?"

"More likely, Sheila walked over and interrupted the activity."

"You know, they could have been playing cards or having a conversation," Gordon offered hopefully. "Discussing business?"

Charlie nodded. "Who knows?"

"Either way, for now we're following Melinda." Gordon sighed, easing out into the street, a block behind the red Mustang.

Gordon hung back, keeping the car within sight and using other vehicles to screen himself whenever possible. They'd only gone a mile or so, however, when it was clear Gordon had lost her.

"What happened? Did she see us?" Gordon shook his head. "All of a sudden, she's gone."

"Probably went down one of those alleys after the last turn."

"Want me to head for her apartment?" Gordon asked.

"Naw, let's circle first and see if we can spot her parked car. Maybe Sheila advised her to avoid being followed by the cops—or us. Look who she's in bed with," Charlie added. At this point it was likely that Melinda knew Clarence was involved in illegal activities. Depending on how deeply she was committed to him, she might even know about Lola.

"You really think her ditching us could have been beginner's luck?"

Charlie shrugged. "Could be you're losing your touch," he said, grinning.

"Hey, we weren't trained to follow cars in a city. Our job was hunting down the bad guys on foot, in the desert, the villages, the mountains. We also had drones."

Charlie looked at his watch. "Nancy will be coming on duty pretty soon. If we can't find Melinda, I'll give the sergeant a call and see if she can help us out."

"Good idea. For now, I'll circle the area and concentrate on places she might shop."

"Hey, I've just got an idea," Charlie said after a few minutes.

"That's new."

"No, really. If she's an 'entertainer' then she must book gigs. We could hire her to dance or something, like for your birthday. We won't have to approach her as investigators or make her suspicious, at least not at first," Charlie explained.

"One major problem. I've been to some birthday and bachelor parties, and the girls always bring a companion—like security. Assuming we can even discover how to book her, how do we get around that?" Gordon replied.

"Yeah, it wouldn't work. How about we just park at her place, wait her out, then come up to her on the sidewalk or street corner. Nonthreatening, of course," Charlie suggested.

"What if she parks that Mustang in a garage," Gordon countered.

"Only one way to find out."

"Right. What's that address again?"

• • •

They were parked within view of the apartment complex listed for Melinda Foy when Charlie's cell phone rang. He looked down and saw it was a private number. "It's Nancy," Charlie announced.

"You didn't hear it from me, but the feds are about to arrest Clarence Fasthorse and some of his crew at the Piñon Mesa Steakhouse in ten minutes, give or take. I'm helping provide APD backup."

Charlie looked over at Gordon. "She hung up."

Gordon started the truck engine. "We gotta see this."

"We're less than ten minutes away. I hope we can get there in time."

"Suppose Sheila is also on the naughty list?" Gordon speculated. "If I recall, we've never seen her at the steakhouse until evening. Of course, we've never followed her around, either."

"Sheila has probably insulated herself, unless the feds have been monitoring her conversations or have found a money trail," Charlie pointed out.

"Guess we'll see," Gordon said, speeding up to make a traffic light as they headed toward the Old Town area.

Chapter Twenty-one

Gordon pulled into the restaurant parking lot via the main entrance and was motioned to a stop by an APD police officer in a dark blue uniform. There were four police cruisers at the entrances and exits to the lot, including the rear of the building, and each vehicle had two officers beside them.

Charlie saw Nancy and another officer blocking one of the lot entrances. It was clear, with all the commotion, that the arrest operation was already underway.

"What's going on?" Gordon asked innocently from his open window as the APD officer approached the pickup.

"Law enforcement officers are conducting an operation inside the restaurant, sir, so you'll need to park away from the building and remain patient for a while." He stepped over and saw Charlie up close.

"Officer Roseberg," Charlie greeted. "I'm Charlie Henry. We

met when you were working on the kidnapping several months ago. You were riding with Detective DuPree that night."

"Sergeant Medina's friends. I thought you two looked familiar," Roseberg said, relaxing a bit, then turning back to watch the restaurant as he spoke. "From what I've heard, you guys have been pretty busy the past week or so. The robbery attempt and shooting at your shop, getting run off the road. It goes on and on. You two are leading charmed lives."

"Hopefully we won't require all that charm for too much longer," Gordon replied. "How long have the feds been inside?"

"So you *did* know about this."

"Let's just say we had a feeling," Charlie replied. "Naturally we wanted to watch. Mind if we get out of the pickup?"

"Just as long as you stick close to me," the officer replied, still focusing his attention on the restaurant.

Charlie and Gordon walked around to the front of the pickup and watched as two men in suits came out the front entrance of the Piñon Mesa Steakhouse, followed by three more in blue FBI jackets leading Clarence and two other prisoners in handcuffs.

Charlie noted that Sheila wasn't with them. "How many individuals were facing arrest here?" he asked.

"Four men—Clarence Fasthorse and three accomplices in the vehicle theft ring. Mexican authorities are supposed to be rounding up several subjects at their end right now."

"No females here, maybe a girlfriend or relative of Fasthorse?" Gordon asked.

"Not according to our briefing," Roseberg replied. "I understand the target's mother is co-owner of the restaurant, though."

A call came through on the officer's radio and he acknowledged the contact. "Time for me to escort the transport, guys. Just stand back until we clear out, okay?"

"Copy that," Charlie replied as the officer hurried to his vehicle. Some distance away, Clarence and the others were placed into unmarked vehicles.

A minute later, as the Bureau vehicles passed by, Clarence glanced out the window and saw them. He looked away, without expression, as the feds turned into the street.

Gordon turned to Charlie. "I was hoping Clarence would have reacted a little more, seeing us standing here. Maybe give us the stink eye."

"Disappointed?"

"A little. Hey, do you suppose the remaining warrant was for Clarence's bodyguard, Leroy Williams?"

"Probably. I didn't see him with the others, and none of the witnesses to the carjackings reported seeing a black guy among the crew. Of course, they were masked, so maybe . . ." Charlie paused to consider it.

"Well, he certainly knew what was going on, being at Clarence's side most of the time. But then again, we don't know where Clarence was at when the crimes were committed either. He gave the orders, though," Gordon acknowledged.

"Or was Sheila's mouthpiece. Apparently the feds had enough on him to make the arrest," Charlie replied. "Let's go have lunch inside and see who they missed."

"You just want to see if hot momma is in there," Gordon teased.

"I don't see any red Mustangs in the lot, so you must be talking about Sheila. If she's inside, remember to watch my back if she picks up a steak knife."

"Gotcha," Gordon responded. "But first I'd better park the pickup in an official slot. Don't want to get a ticket."

When they reached the entrance, there was an older male employee standing there, placing a neatly hand-lettered sign that read CLOSED UNTIL 9 AM TOMORROW—PARDON THE INCONVENIENCE.

Charlie tried to look past him, but the interior featured subdued lighting and he couldn't tell who was still inside.

"You think they'll impound his car?" Gordon asked, nodding toward the blue SUV, which was parked in a staff slot.

Recalling the bug they'd place underneath, Charlie shrugged. "Hope if they do they won't find the bug. That could hurt the fed's case. No warrant for that."

"If they don't haul it away, let's come back and remove it," Gordon replied.

"Then we'd better stick around. I'm guessing that as soon as the customers still inside leave, the staff that wasn't arrested will be cleaning and locking up."

"True. But let's stay out of sight in case Sheila shows up. If she sees us, she's gonna call . . . not the cops," Gordon realized. "And if any of her crew are left and have managed to stay off the suspect list, they're probably waiting for the opportunity to disappear."

"You're right, we don't want her to panic and drop out of sight before we can nail her for the murder . . . murders," Charlie said. "If we set Sheila off, we may never get answers on who did what.

We've got to see who she contacts, where she goes, and what she does."

"I get it. Let's hunker down in my truck."

After about a half hour had passed, Leroy appeared, having apparently come out the back door of the restaurant. He climbed into the blue SUV and drove around front.

Charlie got the receiver out of the glove compartment and activated the bug. "It still works," he announced, hearing the engine sounds as the SUV idled outside the main entrance.

Out came Sheila, who quickly climbed into the backseat. "Take me home, Leroy. My attorney is already downtown working to get Clarence released on bail."

"Hopefully he'll be home in a few hours, ma'am," Leroy replied. "Want me to go down there just in case?"

"No, I need your protection in case those pawnshop bastards come snooping around. Thank God there are only two of them," Sheila replied as Leroy drove toward the street.

"There's also the older brother—the cop," Leroy responded.

"He's only got one good arm—and he's apparently gone into hiding now," Sheila said.

Gordon started the engine, but held back as they listened closely.

"Any idea where Matt is? The feds had a warrant for him too," Leroy said. "They were asking all the staff."

"He's en route to El Paso, delivering one of the Toyota Tundras taken last month. I gave him a call on my burner phone once the feds were gone. He's going to disappear for a while," Sheila said.

"Keep using phones that can't be traced. They're going to be monitoring our calls and e-mails from now on," Leroy mentioned. "Maybe they've already hidden some bugs in the restaurant and your and Clarence's homes. We won't know how they found out about the operations unless this goes to court."

"Don't worry about any electronic surveillance. That's being taken care of," Sheila replied. "My house is being swept right now."

"Good."

There was silence for a while, so Gordon found a gap in traffic, pulled out into the street, and headed by the best route to the street where Sheila lived.

Charlie spoke. "If this Matt character is on the run, who's still out there besides Sheila and Leroy? The guy doing the sweep? Who could that be?"

Gordon shrugged. "Maybe there's a live-in bodyguard or some assistant we haven't seen yet. I don't remember seeing a second car at her place. But then, she has a three-car garage and we've been watching Clarence's house, not hers."

"Looks like that's about to change," Charlie replied.

They were parked two blocks away from Sheila's home. The SUV was apparently in her garage now, so they'd kept well back. Leroy was probably keeping watch. Charlie suspected the man was a lot more dangerous than any of the Night Crew.

His phone rang and Charlie looked down, recognizing Nancy's private cell. "What's up, Sergeant Medina? Clarence spill his guts yet?"

"How'd you know I was calling about that?"

"He did?" Charlie replied, putting the call on speaker so Gordon could listen in. "Spill his guts?"

"No, that would be wishful thinking. The feds can't get anything from Clarence—he's lawyered up. Detective DuPree was hoping you might be able to loosen his tongue a little if you sat in on the next interview."

"You mean get his blood pressure up."

"Not the way I'd put it, exactly, but DuPree does know how you tend to set people off. Can you come down to the station now?"

"Actually, we've staked out a certain lady's house, hoping we can come up with a plan or learn something new that'll add to today's jail population," Charlie responded, looking over at Gordon, who was using the binoculars. "We know she was behind the silversmith's murder, but knowing and being able to prove it are two different things. The feds don't have enough on her yet, or she'd be in jail by now." Gordon nodded.

"I know. By the way, we have a team here watching you, Gordon, and the residence."

Gordon checked the rearview mirror. "The cable van that arrived about ten minutes ago?"

"Yes, Gordon. But if you don't mind sticking it out alone for a while, I can come by and give Charlie a ride downtown. You'll have to circle the block on foot, Charlie, so I can pick you up out of sight of the subject's windows."

Gordon shrugged. "I've got it here," he said. "Go do what you can, Charlie."

"Worth a try," Charlie affirmed. "You still in your squad car, Nancy?"

"No, it's a faded gold Ford sedan, unmarked. See you in five?" she replied.

"Copy," Charlie said, then ended the call.

"I'll call when I'm done, Gordon, and have somebody drop me by here again. With the bug we still have an advantage over the surveillance team when the SUV is used again. It would be good to know when Sheila and company leave," Charlie pointed out.

"If they take the SUV."

"Right. Stay safe, they're going to be gunning for us," Charlie added, getting out of the pickup. "If you have to leave, text me."

"Yes, Mother. Later."

Charlie walked off without looking back. Today might end up being even more interesting than he'd expected, especially with Sheila on the warpath. The weight of the Beretta on his hip was particularly comforting at the moment.

When he reached the far corner and started down the sidewalk, parallel to the street where Fasthorse and his mother lived, he glanced up at the residence closest to him. It was also two stories tall with an upper-story patio leading out from what looked like a bedroom. This structure had iron railings and a tile roof, and was probably constructed by the same builder as Sheila's home. It looked virtually identical.

Charlie heard a vehicle approaching from behind and glanced back. It was Nancy. The gold Ford pulled up to the curb just ahead and he walked over. Nancy was seated on the passenger side in street clothes, as was the young man behind the wheel. "Good timing, Charlie. Hop in," she called out. "This is Officer Spears."

•   •   •

The downtown station was about five minutes away, a few miles farther south. The sedan stopped only briefly at the security booth before entering the underground garage beneath the multistory APD headquarters.

Charlie had only been in the building once before to give a statement on an incident that had occurred last year. As he climbed out of the car into the cool concrete structure, he wondered if this was the same route prisoners were taken when brought in.

"The detective is waiting outside an interview room," Nancy announced as they walked toward the closest elevator and stairwell. Officer Spears followed a few steps behind, and hadn't said much more than hello. He looked barely twenty-one with the shaved head of a newbie, though his relaxed expression suggested he'd been on the force for a while. Since he was in plainclothes and driving an unmarked car, it suggested to Charlie that he worked undercover. Perhaps he'd been on the same team with Al.

They took the stairs and Spears led the way, Nancy beside him.

Once they were at ground level, Spears said good-bye and took off down the hall. They had to stop at a visitor's desk, where Charlie signed in, traded his firearm for a visitor's badge, then followed Nancy into the elevator. "We're going to the sixth floor, where there's a cell block, prisoner library, and two interview rooms," she announced.

"I hope I never know my way around this place," Charlie mumbled.

"Before we go into the interview room, take off your visitor's badge and put it into your pocket. Wear this instead."

Nancy hooked her gold shield over his belt.

"DuPree's idea?"

"No, mine. If Fasthorse thinks you've been working undercover all this time, it'll beef up your authority."

"Makes sense. But I should let DuPree do most of the talking, right?"

"He'll probably brief you before going into the interview," Nancy replied.

They stepped out onto the sixth floor. There was a wide hall devoid of decoration except for a recessed fire extinguisher cabinet and painted lettering on the walls. Arrows indicated the direction of a library, holding cells, and interview rooms. A guard in gray uniform with a Taser, baton, and handcuffs at his waist nodded to both of them. "Detective DuPree is waiting at interview room A."

"What's the prisoner library for?" Charlie asked as they walked down the hall. They passed a thick Plexiglas window that revealed a room containing several seated prisoners in orange jumpsuits. "Gives them something to do?"

"That's the idea. It's limited to inmates charged with nonviolent crimes who stay out of trouble. The prisoners can read, even play a few games, but they can't send or receive e-mail or get on social media. All they can do is take notes with pencil and paper. It's kind of like an old-school library without the books. It's all done on desktop computers. The keyboards are anchored down," she explained.

They turned the corner and arrived at a door marked with an A. Nancy knocked, and Detective DuPree came out into the hall.

"Glad you could make it, Henry," DuPree said, shaking his hand. "As soon as the prisoner arrives we'll let him stew awhile before going in. What's with the shield?" He looked at Charlie's belt.

Charlie took off his visitor's badge while Nancy explained her idea.

"Sounds good. Keep the bastard guessing," DuPree acknowledged, then put his finger to his lips as they heard footsteps.

A corrections officer was leading Clarence, in handcuffs, down the hall toward them, and, at the same time, another officer, a sturdy-looking black man, was coming from the direction of the library. There were two inmates in front of the officer, one of them a Hispanic male carrying a yellow legal pad.

The officer leading Clarence stopped by the interview room door, waiting for the other inmates and the corrections officer to pass. Charlie watched as the other inmates approached. The Anglo prisoner was watching Nancy, the Hispanic guy ignoring them all, which to Charlie seemed odd. Nancy was a very attractive woman.

This prisoner, as he approached, subtlety switched the legal pad to his left hand, clutching his pencil firmly in his right, almost making a fist.

Chapter Twenty-two

Charlie stepped forward to block the move, thinking Nancy might be the target. The prisoner lunged at Clarence instead, jabbing him in the stomach. As Clarence doubled over the man grabbed his hair with his left hand and plunged the bloody pencil into Clarence's face with a right uppercut. Charlie had his hands on the attacker by then and yanked him back.

Chaos followed as DuPree and Nancy both jumped in to pin the man. Charlie already had him facedown on his knees, but the assailant fought back, punching and kicking, cursing in Spanish. Clarence's guard tried to protect his injured prisoner, who was thrashing on the floor, hands over his bloody face as he screamed.

"Down on the floor," the black guard yelled at the other inmate, who'd already dropped back and was holding his hands up to show he wasn't part of this.

"Taser this guy," DuPree shouted, still struggling with the Hispanic prisoner.

The black guard unholstered his yellow Taser and aimed it at the attacker, who continued to yell and struggle despite the fact that Nancy had his right arm wrenched around at an impossible angle.

"Now!" DuPree said, jumping back, along with Nancy and Charlie. The darts hit the man in the butt, and he screamed and jerked convulsively. Then he smashed his head against the wall. There was a dull crunch. His body stiffened and all movement stopped within a few seconds.

"Turn it off!" Nancy ordered, looking down at Clarence's attacker, who was unconscious now, or worse, and bleeding from the mouth. Corrections officers ran up from both directions, then stopped, looking down at the chaos.

"Get a medical team up here ASAP!" DuPree ordered, looking over at Clarence.

The guard who'd escorted Clarence stood, shaking his head slowly. "That isn't going to help. I think he's dead."

Clarence wasn't moving now, sprawled on the tile like a carelessly discarded rag doll. His arms were splayed out from his body and his hands smeared in blood and gore. The flow of blood was trickling slowly from his punctured gut and around the pencil, still imbedded in the center of his right eye socket.

"What the hell was that all about?" Charlie asked Detective DuPree a half hour later as the officer entered the bullpen cubical.

"The screw-ups run from here all the way down to Mexico, Charlie," DuPree answered bitterly, flopping down in his desk chair and spinning around to face him. "Apparently the Mexican federal police arrested the help but not the bosses in this vehicle theft ring. One of their leaders obviously managed to get word to one of their men here in lock-up."

"The inmate with the pencil—now dead from a broken neck," Charlie concluded.

"Yeah, he was Hector Archibeque, here legally but recently busted for, surprise—auto theft. Apparently Archibeque's lawyer spoke to his client about five hours ago."

"Telling him to take out Fasthorse? Your timing is off, DuPree. Clarence hadn't even been busted then."

"No, and here's why. The Mexican police jumped the gun and made their move early, hours before the feds here arrested what's left of the Night Crew. Word never reached Clarence that this was going down, obviously, but it certainly got to Archibeque's attorney," DuPree explained.

"Archibeque was told to silence Clarence before he could cut a deal and identify his major contacts in Mexico," Charlie said, nodding.

"That's what the feds think. Me too. The only good news is that we've plugged the pipeline at this end, at least until the Mexican gangs get someone else to provide them with stolen pickups and SUVs."

"So what's going to happen to Sheila Ben?" Nancy asked.

"Well, unless we can nail her for the death of Buck and the casino manager, she's probably going to dodge any serious charges on the Night Crew carjackings and the local incidents. Clarence was her representative, and everything was done through him," DuPree responded. "I doubt the Mexicans know she was involved, or she'd already be on the run or dead. But here's something interesting I got from the feds, who've already started to look at Clarence's financial records."

"Not Sheila's?" Charlie asked.

"No. Apparently they haven't got that far yet," DuPree responded. "What they did find, however, was a financial connection from the restaurant account to Cordell Buck that existed until just before his death. The silversmith had been getting a thousand dollars a month from Piñon Mesa Inc. since April."

"I find it hard to believe Clarence would be doing business with the man. It sounds more like blackmail payoffs to me," Charlie reasoned. "That also provides the motive for Sheila now wanting him dead."

"That's what I think, too," DuPree replied, "though the entries were listed for 'wholesale jewelry.'"

"That's still a pretty steep price for wholesale turquoise and silver," Nancy noted. "Is there any actual merchandise to back up those entries?"

"Don't know," DuPree answered. "But I'd like to be there when the feds interview Sheila, just to see her reaction when this detail comes up."

Charlie shook his head. "The feds may never get the chance. That lady is a loose cannon, and once she finds out Clarence is dead, I've got a feeling she's going to blow. Revenge is her trademark."

"Think she'll be going after the Mexicans who arranged the hit on Clarence?" Nancy asked.

"I doubt she has the manpower right now. I'm thinking she's

going to strike closer to home," Charlie said, "and fast, before the authorities can get anything solid on her."

"Closer to home . . . like you and your family?" Nancy asked. "She made that threat back in Shiprock the other night, right?"

Charlie nodded. "That's my guess. I'm too dangerous to attack again, and Al, his family, and my parents are in hiding. That leaves my sister, Jayne. She's local and within easy reach of whatever forces Sheila still has available. That makes her the most vulnerable."

"That's all we need," DuPree grumbled. "Who am I dealing with here? Is your sister anything like you and your brother?"

Charlie shrugged. "She's hardworking, but stubborn."

"In other words, yes," DuPree replied. "But is she as dangerous? Any police or military background?"

"Just the opposite. I doubt she even owns a weapon. Besides, Jayne tends to be naive about strangers unless she's standing up for family. Right now she's got a loser boyfriend and he's a bit of a liability. She's stuck by him, though," Charlie added. "Jayne's not the kind to run from trouble. If I gave her an airplane ticket and told her to get lost, she'd hand it right back."

"Okay, so that means she's going to need some protection. I think you mentioned that she lives in Corrales, right?" Nancy asked.

"Yeah. I should give Jayne a call and warn her to stay home and away from strangers until I get over there," Charlie said, standing.

"I've got officers watching the Ben house. Nobody's left there yet or I'd have gotten a call," DuPree commented. "Your sister's probably still safe."

"Gordon's watching too," Charlie said. "So I'll make the call and come up with a plan. Know anyone who can help out?" He looked at Nancy, then DuPree.

"More than ever, Sheila's the obvious suspect in the Cordell Buck homicide case," DuPree answered, nodding. "You want to be in on this, Medina?" he asked Nancy.

"Of course. You need to call your sister, Charlie. Now."

Charlie managed a smile, then touched Jayne's image on his phone.

Charlie came up from behind Jake's SUV and climbed in the passenger side, joining Gordon, who lowered his binoculars and eyed him closely.

"So Clarence is really dead."

Charlie nodded. "I saw the attack coming but tried to protect the wrong target."

"Wrong? Nancy's a real friend. I understand your instincts," Gordon added. "It happens, and it isn't as if Fasthorse was undeserving. Besides, like you said over the phone, it will probably push Sheila over the edge."

"Yeah, but maybe in the direction of my family. I think she'll make a move on Jayne. Sheila is smart and clearly knows something about my family. Dad was a judge on the panel that sent her packing, and Mom taught in the local schools. A few clicks on the Internet, a call to one of her sources, and she'll also discover where Jayne lives—if she doesn't know already."

"You've called Jayne and she knows the risks?"

Charlie nodded. "There's going to be a state police officer in the area for the next few hours, and Jayne has his cell phone number. Before I tell you the plan we've come up with, anything new on Mrs. Ben and her companions?"

"I've got the bug turned on right now, but unless they come into the garage or decide to leave, we have no way of listening in. I hope the battery holds out," Gordon said, looking over with his binoculars again. "No sign of activity, though someone has looked out the living room window a few times. So tell me about your plan."

It was close to 5:00 PM, and Charlie was getting hungry when a voice came out clearly over the bug monitor. It was Sheila.

"I'm going through all kinds of shit, but with my son gone I've got to hold it together. Payback is a guarantee now, but these pawnshop assholes know what's coming and will be ready. I've got to hold back and keep them looking over their shoulders, awake at night, wondering if they're going to be alive in the morning. Then, in a month, or three months, when they think maybe they can finally relax—boom!"

"Boom?" Gordon mouthed, raising his eyebrows. Neither of them had so much as breathed once Sheila started speaking.

Charlie shook his head, rolling his eyes, still listening intently.

"We need to keep a very low profile," Sheila said next, and there was the sound of a car door opening. "Tonight, Leroy and I will take care of the restaurant, calm our staff down, and conduct business as usual. We may have to run off some reporters once word gets out regarding my son, but we'll tough it out. I've got good people working at Piñon Mesa, and, if anything, business will probably pick up a bit."

"The boss would smile at that thought," came Leroy's booming voice.

Charlie looked over at Gordon. "Does that sound . . ."

"Rehearsed, and contrived. Either somebody's gone mechanical or they're acting this out for us," Gordon replied. "We're being played."

"Badly. They found the bug," Charlie agreed. "The third person, the one Sheila was talking to when she mentioned Leroy, must have swept the vehicles too."

There was the sound of machinery and Charlie looked down the street. Gordon was watching again with the binoculars.

"The garage door is opening, here comes the SUV . . . no, it's a white Nissan cargo van."

Charlie looked at him with furrowed eyebrows. "Sheila behind the wheel?"

Gordon shrugged. "Looks like. The windows are tinted, but I can make out a dark-haired woman—not Leroy, that's for sure. Take a look."

Charlie took the binoculars and focused on the commercial-style vehicle backing through the opening gate. "Wonder where she's going? Making a business run?"

"Let's follow." Gordon started the engine. "DuPree's team has the house covered, and we're not going to get anything useful from the bug anymore."

Charlie's phone rang. "Hello," he said, putting Nancy on speaker.

"That's Sheila in the van, right?" Nancy asked.

"I think. We're going to see where she's headed."

"My thoughts, exactly. But didn't you lose the last person you tried to tail?"

"Blabbermouth," Gordon said.

"Yeah, are we getting any help from other units?" Charlie asked, ignoring Gordon, who was creeping down the street as the Nissan turned left at the next corner.

"DuPree is on the ball and is going to acquire use of the APD fixed wing aircraft, which is above the Paseo Del Norte construction project beside the interstate. Just keep the vehicle in sight a few more minutes. I'll give you a number and you can contact the aircraft directly. I'll also call the state police officer in Corrales and put him on alert."

"Copy. And thank DuPree."

"Copy." She ended the call.

"About time. Eye in the sky. Almost as good as a drone," Gordon said, grinning, but keeping his eyes on the prize.

The drive took them north and east, and again, along the way, they lost her. Charlie called the cell phone of the spotter in the light plane somewhere overhead.

"You sure? West on Alameda?" Charlie said, loud enough for Gordon to hear, who turned north and sped up Fourth Street.

"Unless she turns back south on Rio Grande, she's heading across the river to either Rio Rancho or the village of Corrales," Gordon advised.

Charlie stayed on the line and listened. After about five minutes, he got another report from the spotter plane.

"She pulled over at a convenience store on Alameda Boulevard, a few blocks east of the bridge," Charlie reported, "and Corrales."

Gordon nodded. "Then we'll get to the river first. Wanna take a position ahead of her and guess at her destination?"

"Yeah, if she's headed for Jayne's house, we can be ready before she arrives," Charlie responded.

"Let us know if and when the van crosses the bridge. We think she's eventually headed for Corrales," Charlie said to the observer overhead.

He held the phone to his ear as Gordon reached Alameda Avenue from Rio Grande, then was forced to stop and wait at the stoplight. They were already a mile down Corrales Road when the spotter spoke again.

"Thanks," Charlie said, then told Gordon. "She's heading this way. Drive past the lane leading to Jayne's house, then do a one-eighty and park beside the road so we can keep watch. It's just ahead—Peach Tree Lane."

"Got it," Gordon replied. "What about the cop?" Gordon asked, pointing at the black-and-white state police car sitting just off the shoulder of the highway.

"I've got his number. I'll ask him to drive on into Corrales. We don't want to scare Sheila off right now," Charlie reminded, reaching for his phone again.

A few minutes later, they were parked beside the road beneath some huge cottonwood trees with branches that draped over half the highway.

"Here she comes," Gordon announced. "This might just be a

recon, you know. The woman would have to be stupid to try a hit in daylight."

"Or crazy," Charlie said, looking down at the Beretta he had in his lap. "When I called Jayne, I told her and Rand to stay away from the doors and windows until we showed up. But if Sheila gets out and makes a move toward the house or pulls a weapon . . ."

"We take her down," Gordon answered. "You better hit the floor before she sees you," he added, turning so he wasn't looking at the approaching white Nissan as he pretended to talk on his cell phone.

It was a recon, apparently, because the Nissan drove slowly down the graveled lane, which led to eight homes on one-acre lots, turned around at the end of the dead-end street, then came back out and headed south in the direction of Albuquerque.

Gordon started the engine and Charlie, who'd ducked again, sat upright. "Time to put the plan in motion? I'm anxious to see why you think I can pass for Jayne's loser boyfriend."

Charlie laughed. "Jayne says Rand is a changed man, so maybe I'm wrong about that."

"I guess that depends on what Rand's changed into, I guess. Is he compact and fit like me, or bulky and flabby, like, say, yourself?" Gordon teased.

Charlie looked over at his best friend. "I'd arm wrestle you for the championship, but I'd probably break your arm, as small and delicate as you are."

"If that's your way of backing out, I understand. Now let's go deal with your sister and her boy toy," Gordon said, turning down the lane.

Charlie was halfway up the flagstone walk when Jayne opened the door. She was the looker in the family, with her mom's high cheekbones, eyes, and slender build, and had her legions of suitors even back in middle school. If it hadn't been for him, and Al, and mostly Dad . . .

Jayne rushed out toward him, and before Charlie knew what was going on she had her arms around him, hugging him tightly.

"Charlie. It's so good to see you. I've been so worried about you and Al. He said you saved his life," she whispered, her words all coming out at once. He hugged her back, then lifted her off the ground for a second.

"Good to see you too, shorty. For a second there, I didn't know if you were going to hit or hug me," Charlie replied. It had been a long time since he and Jayne had exchanged anything besides criticism.

He held her at arm's length, looking at the smile on her face and her sparkling eyes. She was happy, healthy, and in a good mood.

Charlie looked over at Rand, a short Anglo with a wrestler's build and pale blue eyes. He was standing in the doorway, hesitation in his expression. Their last encounter hadn't been friendly. Rand looked kind of odd, and Charlie realized that was because the man now had neatly groomed, short blond hair and was wearing a shirt with a collar and tan slacks instead of calf-length shorts. It was almost a transformation. Today Rand looked more like a choir boy than a punk East Central drug dealer, his last incarnation.

Gordon came up behind Charlie. "Uh, bro, let's take this inside. We need to stay on schedule."

"Hi, Gordon," Jayne said, grinning and reaching over and giving him a quick, one-armed hug. "Come on in and tell me how you and my big brother are going to save our butts."

Nancy arrived about five minutes later driving her own vehicle, the Jeep. She was wearing a long black wig and dressed in civilian clothes except for her service weapon. In one hand she carried a rifle case.

After quick introductions Nancy and Jayne hurried into one of the bedrooms of the old adobe house. The three men stood around for a moment, then Charlie spoke softly. "Rand, I barely recognized you. You treating my sister right?"

Rand was nervous, clearly, but not nearly so much as the last time he and Charlie had spoken. "I understand how protective you and Al are of your sister and I appreciate how Jayne has helped me turn my life around. I'm not bullshitting you either," he added, his voice gaining confidence as he looked up at Charlie, who was almost a foot taller and sixty pounds heavier.

"You got a real job now?"

"Yes, for the last six months. I'm in a training program at Verizon, working full time in a local store, and have already applied for a management position. I've been passing all my drug tests and I won't be going down that path again. Jayne is my partner, inspiration, and harshest critic. I'm not going to let her down."

Charlie held out his hand to shake. "Good to hear. Just treat my sister and yourself as if your life depended upon it."

Rand looked at him curiously, nodded, then shook his hand.

"Speaking of your life depending on it," Gordon spoke, "if I'm supposed to be passing for you, Rand, I'll need to borrow one of your shirts and a pair of those killer slacks. Our hair length and color are close enough, and I can slump down a little to match your height."

Rand smiled and Charlie chuckled. If anything, Rand was an inch taller. "Okay, as soon as the ladies come out of the bedroom," Rand said. "I've already laid out something that should fit you. The good news is that I wear my shirt tail out when around the house, so it'll be easier to hide your pistol."

"While we're waiting, let's go over your part in this," Charlie said.

"Okay. Jayne and I drive Sergeant Medina's Jeep north out of Corrales instead of south so we won't pass by anyone coming over from Albuquerque who might be looking for us. We continue on to the town of Bernalillo, head east, then return to Albuquerque via the interstate. We go straight to your friend Gina's town house. We stay there with Gina until we get the all-clear from you."

"Exactly, and don't go or stop anywhere else or contact anyone except for Gina, Sergeant Medina, or me until we say you're out of danger," Charlie said. "Got that?"

"Yes. What about Al's family and your parents?" Rand asked.

"They know the danger and are going to be somewhere else until this is over," Charlie answered.

Just then, Nancy and Jayne came out of the bedroom. Nancy had applied heavy, darker makeup to give her Jayne's skin tones, which would work at a distance or in low light. Jayne's long black hair was tucked into a cap and she was wearing glasses and a bulky sweatshirt and skirt.

"Didn't know you had a skirt," Rand commented immediately. "You look so . . ."

"Sixties," Gordon suggested. "And you, Nancy, look more like Jayne than she does at the moment."

"Okay, now go and put on your Rand disguise, Gordon," Charlie said, motioning toward the bedroom. Rand led the way.

Nancy walked to the window and closed the curtains halfway before stepping to the side and taking a look down the road. "It'll be dark soon."

Jayne came over and touched Charlie's arm gently. "Sorry I was so . . . resentful last time you were here. It was like you thought I was a fool or something."

Charlie shrugged. "What can I say, Jayne? I'm the kind of guy who insists on taking a position when it comes to people I care about. Either way, it looks like you're on a good path right now," he said, nodding toward the bedroom door. "Do you remember that President Reagan quote Dad used to repeat when we were in high school—every time we caught him checking up on us?"

Jayne laughed. "Trust, but verify. You know he was right?"

"Ronald Reagan?"

"No, smartass, Dad. And yes, I'm not closing my eyes around anyone in my life—until they're family. And even then . . ."

The bedroom door opened, and Rand came out wearing a hoodie, jeans, and cross trainers. Gordon followed, dressed in a red knit work shirt with a company label and tan slacks. He wore his own brown deck shoes. Charlie noted the bulge of the Beretta at his waist beneath the shirt.

Nancy stepped over and looked Gordon up and down. "For a man, you'll do."

They all laughed, then Nancy turned, shook Jayne's hand, then gave her the keys to the Jeep. "You kids get going and stay safe. If you get lost in Albuquerque, the GPS on the dash will lead you straight to Gina."

"Be careful, guys," Jayne said, smiling at Gordon, then Charlie before reaching out and touching him lightly above his heart.

"Always. Same to you two," he added, walking toward the door.

Thirty seconds later the Jeep was heading toward Corrales Road.

Nancy turned to Charlie and Gordon. "It's six PM and we don't know how much time we have. Let's settle on a tactical plan, break out the hardware, then get Big Brother out of sight before the entertainment arrives."

Nancy flipped on the porch light, turned the TV to the local news, then went into the kitchen. "There's a pizza in the freezer, so that'll be dinner tonight. You keep watch, Gordon, and, Charlie, grab the shotgun from the case then get into the bathroom."

"Can't I hide in the closet?" Charlie joked. He walked into the bedroom and opened the gun case, lifting out the weapon. It was fully loaded with buckshot, but he took the extra bandoleer of shells with him as he crossed the hall and stepped into the bathroom.

Here he could remain with the light on, sitting at least, and be instantly ready. The window above the tub was frosted, with a dark shower curtain that further concealed his presence.

Charlie checked out the shotgun. It was a short, tactical semi-auto model good for providing close-in firepower without penetrating thin walls and hitting his own people. He'd looked over the adobe walls when first arriving and was very familiar with the ballistic protection the thick mud and straw offered. Most of the civilian structures he'd encountered in Iraq and Afghanistan were made of mud and stone. These walls were thick enough to stop or slow down anything smaller than a fifty cal.

The doors and the windows were the exception, and Nancy didn't want any rounds to reach one of the neighborhood homes. They all realized that if they were right, when Sheila finally walked through that door she'd be coming to kill someone. She and Clarence had a violent history, at least in the past few months. If Sheila had been the one who pulled the trigger on Cordell Buck and set off the bomb that killed the men hired to take out Bitsillie, there was no reason to expect anything different tonight.

Charlie sat there, waiting and listening to the low conversation taking place outside in the living room and kitchen. Gordon and Nancy were trying to decide when Sheila would arrive tonight—if at all. If the woman was planning on biding her time, how long would Jayne have to hide out?

He heard footsteps. "Yo, Charlie. Want some pizza?" Gordon whispered.

Looking around at the shower, the sink, the tiny medicine cabinet, then the porcelain throne he was seated upon, he decided that in spite of all this, he'd had dinner in a lot less appropriate places. There were no deceased people or animals within sight, and besides, the tiny room looked spotless. It even smelled like lavender.

"Sure," he said. "Just give me a minute to wash my hands."

A half hour later, sitting in the dark and already cursing the slow but consistent *drip, drip* coming from the mineral-encrusted shower head, he heard the low rumble of a vehicle and the crunch of tires in gravel.

"Vehicle outside," Nancy called. "White Nissan cargo van wearing a FedEx sign."

Charlie opened the bathroom door halfway, then reached over and picked up the shotgun he'd leaned against the sink. After verifying he'd already chambered a shell, Charlie inched out so he could see down the hall into the living room. When the front door opened, he'd be able to see whoever came into the small foyer. "Copy," he whispered, his hands shaking just a little.

"Same here," Gordon said. "Remember. Make her come inside before you expose yourself," he added softly.

"Copy," Nancy responded.

Once he'd lowered the shotgun barrel to a forty-five-degree angle, Charlie's hands stopped shaking. He'd always been nervous and on edge before and after a mission when the tension had no real outlet, but never during the actual event. His training was that good—and he'd always been too busy to get emotional during a firefight. He looked down at the relatively unfamiliar weapon to make sure the safety was off. His gut told him that shots would be fired within a few minutes, and at this range with the buckshot all he had to do was point and squeeze the trigger.

Chapter Twenty-three

There was a firm double knock on the front door. "FedEx. I have a package for Ms. Henry," an unfamiliar woman's voice called out clearly.

That's not Sheila Mae Ben, Charlie realized instantly. *Then who the hell was it? Really FedEx?*

"Coming," Nancy replied, then nodded to Gordon, who was crouched behind the sofa, looking out at armrest level. Then she glanced over at Charlie, who was angled so all she could see was the shotgun, his right arm and shoulder, and half of his face. Her pistol was still holstered, on her right hip but within reach.

"Can you get the door for me, please? My hands are full," the woman outside asked.

"Just a second," Nancy said, her voice as casual as possible as she reached for the knob, her right side protected somewhat by the door.

A young woman wearing a cap, dark blue shirt, and matching pants stepped in, holding a labeled cardboard box against her chest. Her hands supported the box from beneath—and she was carrying something in her hand.

Charlie saw the hidden gun at the same time he recognized the woman's face. Her long black hair was tucked up into the cap, but it was Melinda Foy!

"Gun!" Gordon yelled, rising to his knees as Nancy reached for her weapon.

Melinda dropped the box to one side and fired two shots into Nancy's torso at nearly point-blank range, the long-barreled, silenced .22 emitting mere pops. Almost at the same time, Melinda grunted, staggering from the impact from the buckshot from Charlie's shotgun. Grimacing in pain and bouncing off the open door, she still managed to shift her aim and squeeze off two more rounds down the hall.

Charlie was in the middle of a sidestep across the hall, but felt the heat of a bullet ripping skin on his neck. He fired another load of double 'ought, his ears still ringing from the roar from his first shot. He overcompensated this time, not wanting to hit Nancy, and it was a clean miss, punching a big hole in the open door. Melinda was already stepping back onto the porch, out of his view.

Gordon had to aim around Nancy, but fired twice. "Shit, I missed. She ducked around the corner."

Nancy took a big side-step, realizing she was in the way, meanwhile fumbling with her hand at the center of her chest where the bullets had struck. Her pistol was still in the holster.

"Check out Nancy," Charlie yelled, running down the hall toward the door.

He reached the entrance, took a quick look out, and saw nothing but a shattered flowerpot on the porch rail. Turning his head, he looked down the sidewalk, which paralleled the front wall of the house and led to the driveway. Looking back over his shoulder at the rest of the yard, all he could see were a few shrubs too small to hide anyone.

"She's headed around back!" Charlie realized, suddenly noticing that the gate to the back of the yard, on the other side of the driveway, was now open. He ran down the wall to the gate. Crouching low, he stopped and took a quick look around the corner into the backyard. In the distance he heard a mechanical sound—the click of the latch on another gate—and saw a moving black shape.

Charlie ran along the sidewall of the house, zigzagging in case she was crouching low in the dark, setting a trap. He heard a door slam, whipped around his shotgun, and saw Gordon bolting out the back through the kitchen door.

"There she goes." Gordon pointed. "She's headed for the *bosque!*" he added, meeting Charlie at the backyard gate.

"How's Nancy?" Charlie uttered, covering Gordon as he stepped out ahead of him into the alley.

"Her vest stopped both rounds. She's out of breath and pissed," Gordon called as he raced down the road at the fleeing woman, who was barely visible in the moonlight. "She's calling for backup."

Charlie caught up to him, his long strides nearly matching his friend's quicker but shorter steps. "I think she's slowing down. I know I hit her with the buckshot."

"The impact knocked her back so she's gotta be wearing a vest. If you'd had an M-4 . . ."

Charlie nodded. "It would have dropped her. From this point on, we take head shots."

"Why didn't she just race to her van and take off?" Gordon asked between deep breaths.

"Couldn't leave without finishing the job, I guess," Charlie speculated.

"Good help is hard to find." Gordon gasped, picking up the pace. "I admire her work ethic."

They were closing in, less than a hundred feet away, when the fleeing woman swerved and jumped off the ditch road down into the *bosque*, the wooded flood plain bordering the Rio Grande.

"*She's* been the killer all along," Charlie reminded, slowing to a trot as he reached into his jacket pocket for the clamp-on flashlight for the shotgun barrel.

Gordon had a laser sight on his Beretta, but it wouldn't provide any search capability. Charlie saw him fumble for the LED flashlight in his pocket, nearly drop it, then shove it back inside before they slid down the fifteen-foot embankment at the spot where Melinda had dropped.

They were in a soldier's environment now, and the would-be assassin was in unfamiliar terrain carrying an underpowered weapon. Charlie knew he and Gordon had the advantage now.

"I'm the bait. I search, you shoot," he whispered. "She'll need to get close, so expect to be stalked."

"Copy."

From that moment on, they moved silently, staying within each

other's sight. They paused often, listening and watching for movement, signaling with practiced gestures. There was almost a full
moon out, and that would help.

As they got farther into the willows, cottonwoods, and brush,
they had to orient themselves by the moon and the faint outline
of the Sandia Mountains to the east. Charlie crouched low, listening, but hearing nothing. She was in there somewhere, beside
some brush, behind a tree, maybe below a fallen cottonwood, waiting. But he and Gordon could out-wait almost anyone. Once, he
and Gordon had worked with a Marine sniper team. They'd remained almost immobile for over six hours waiting for an insurgent
sniper to finally poke his head up for a look—and be neutralized.

Charlie was completely still, controlling his own breathing rate
and listening for anything out of the ordinary. He'd presented himself as a target, now all he had to do was wait for Melinda to make
her move. After about fifteen minutes he heard the faint crunch
of dry leaves at ten o'clock, just to his left and ahead. Gordon was
to his right, but Charlie knew there was no way his buddy would
shoot him by mistake. They'd worked together so long they always
knew where the other was.

It was time to illuminate the target. Raising his shotgun, Charlie aimed and turned on the light. A ball cap and the woman's
head appeared for a split second at the edge of a tree trunk, thirty
feet away.

He fired just as Gordon did and bits of tree bark exploded from
the tree. But Melinda had ducked down and was already on the
move again. He'd been a bit slow and she'd seen him raising his
weapon.

Quickly he and Gordon backed up, covering their previous positions, watching their flanks. Sometimes the best offense was a good, active defense, and they usually succeeded when they stuck it out and remained patient. They waited, guessing that she'd be circling, stalking them now that she thought she knew where they would be.

Charlie unhooked the flashlight, set down the shotgun, and drew his Beretta. If it ended up close and personal, he wanted a more familiar weapon, one he aimed instinctively. It offered better penetration than the buckshot, held more rounds, and he also didn't like the idea of having his head so close to a flashlight beam. Melinda knew his setup now, so it was time to make a change.

It seemed like an eternity before he heard someone take a breath. He recognized the wet rattle from a throat or chest wound. The woman was hurting, running out of time, and that forced her into action. But it also made her even more dangerous. She was close, to his right, and though he'd put his back to a tree, there was a chance she'd already seen him.

Charlie extended his left hand and turned on the light. There she was, fifteen feet away, blood on her neck, pistol steadied in a two-hand grip. He sidestepped just as her weapon flashed. His left arm suddenly stung, and he realized he'd been hit. The flashlight slipped from his hand.

Gordon shot her twice in the side, just under the raised arm and above the protective vest. She collapsed, her legs giving away.

"Dude, you hit?" Gordon asked, his flashlight out and directed at the target on the ground as he approached, weapon aimed.

"Not much," Charlie replied as he holstered his pistol and picked up the flashlight with his right hand.

He aimed the beam at his forearm and discovered blood dripping down from the torn sleeve of his jacket. "Glad she was packing a .22 instead of a .45. I could have lost my arm."

"Or worse. Looks like she's not going to be getting up," Gordon announced. His eyes never left the target. "Let me secure her weapon, then take a closer look at your injury."

Fifteen minutes later, under the glare of floodlights and several law enforcement vehicles, Charlie sat in the back of the EMT vehicle as a bandage was placed over the deep scratch in his neck. Nancy was standing there, grimacing as she turned her torso from side to side slowly.

"I haven't hurt this much since last year's cop-fireman softball game," she grumbled.

The EMT turned to check out his work, and Charlie stood. "Get hit by a line drive?" Charlie asked.

"No, I was the catcher and a dumb-ass fireman threw the bat after striking out. The bat bounced up and popped me in the ribs," Nancy replied. "Chest protector didn't help that much."

"Shoulda stomped him with your cleats," Gordon offered, looking over from where he was standing.

"What cleats? I had on pink Nikes."

Charlie laughed. "We ready to go?" he looked over at the faux FedEx vehicle parked on the ditch road about twenty feet away.

"Yeah, any longer and the cat will be out of the bag," Nancy answered. "DuPree told me a minute ago that Sheila had been picked up at her home by Leroy Williams about the time Melinda arrived at Jayne's house. They went to the restaurant, spoke to a few employees, then Leroy dropped her at home and took off. Williams was followed to his apartment and officers are watching the place. At least we won't be running into him at her house. You sure you're good to go, Charlie?"

His left arm was pretty much useless, but the EMT had bandaged it carefully and he was able to raise it to chest level. "The hit was a through and through, just two small holes and a two-inch tunnel. She missed hitting any major veins and arteries. I'm going to be fine, isn't that right?" Charlie said, looking at the young medic.

"Most likely. But the doctors will probably recommend you spend the night in the hospital, Mr. Henry," the EMT answered skeptically.

"My neck hurts more than my arm," Charlie replied. "But thanks for the first aid and the aspirin."

The medic smiled, and began packing away his gear as Charlie, Gordon, and Nancy walked over to Melinda's cargo van.

"You've got bruised ribs. Want me to drive for a while?" Gordon offered as they reached the vehicle.

"Thanks, but I'll manage," Nancy responded, opening the driver's door. She'd already removed the wig, wiped off most of the heavy makeup, and tucked her hair into the cap worn by the late Melinda Foy. Her blouse was now beneath a dark blue APD raid jacket that would pass for a FedEx blue uniform shirt at a distance.

"I'm riding shotgun," Charlie announced, holding up the weapon.

Nancy shrugged. "Then remind me to stop before we reach the neighborhood. If she's looking out and happens to see I have a passenger . . ."

"You're right. No sense in wasting time making another stop," Charlie said. He stepped over to the side door, which Gordon had already opened.

"You first, wounded one," Gordon ordered, stepping aside.

Minutes later, they were across the river, heading south down Fourth Street, when Nancy got a call. "Putting it on speaker, Detective DuPree," she announced, setting the phone on the center console so all three of them could hear.

"I have some interesting news, which could explain some of what's been going down lately. I'm looking at a restricted access file on Melinda Foy compiled by the FBI office in Las Vegas—Nevada, not New Mexico."

"Why was the Bureau interested in Melinda Foy?" Charlie asked. "Is she a car thief too?"

"Worse than that. Melinda's maiden name is Giordano—and her father is Tony Giordano, a Vegas hood connected to several homicides and assorted acts of violence. Her mother was a showgirl at one of the casinos, but the FBI thinks that Melinda followed her father's career path instead."

"Wait, you're saying Melinda does wet work for the mob?" Gordon interrupted. "No wonder she was so . . . controlled."

"She's rumored to have made her first hit before she was eligible to vote. But law enforcement has never been able to get enough evidence to even make an arrest for any of that. Her record is clean—except for those Albuquerque prostitution busts," DuPree added. "Her mom and dad dropped out of sight around then. The Bureau thinks they're in Central America somewhere, maybe Costa Rica."

"What happened to Melinda's husband, Mr. Foy?"

"The man moved to Alaska after the divorce and has since remarried. The divorce wasn't contested and there was no settlement."

"Do you think he knew what his wife did during her formative years?" Gordon asked.

"I doubt it," DuPree replied. "He's apparently still alive."

"Good point," Nancy said. "Clearly, Melinda was working for Sheila now that Clarence is out of the picture."

"If my theory counts for anything, I'm thinking Ms. Foy has been working for Sheila a lot longer, doing her wet work," Gordon said.

"Like killing Cordell Buck?" Nancy asked.

"And taking out Bitsillie's killers the other night with the bomb," Charlie concluded. "That woman in the pickup might not have been Sheila."

"There's more. Here's something that may explain how Al was made," DuPree responded. "According to the file here, Melinda worked briefly for a company that caters university workshops, events, and ceremonies. Sergeant Medina mentioned the other day that Al Henry attended a law enforcement seminar at UNM last year."

"And Melinda was one of the servers. Damn, she must have finally seen my brother around Clarence or his crew and recognized him as a cop," Charlie said, shaking his head. "Knowing Al, he probably hit on her, and that stuck in her head."

"Makes sense," Nancy said. "We need to get someone to conduct a search of Melinda's apartment. Maybe we can find something tying her to Clarence and his mom."

"The feds are already there. Let me get back to you on that," said DuPree. "We also need to scoop up anything that might link her to the murders. By the way, I received a tip via the Bureau about the same time I got access to Melinda's Vegas file. An inside informant wanted to warn us that Melinda was planning to retaliate against the Henry family on behalf of Sheila Ben," he added.

"By then she was already shooting at us," Charlie replied. "Too little, too late."

"Any idea who this slow-motion informant might be?" Gordon asked.

"Not at all, and when I asked, I got the runaround," DuPree responded. "We may never know."

"We're getting close to the Ben residence now, Detective," Nancy announced, turning up the street.

"I see you. I'm in the sedan one block south of the residence."

"If we can get inside, you need to move in with your units and seal off the block," Nancy said, looking over and Charlie and Gordon, who both nodded.

"I've got plenty of backup in the area, but hold off for now. You need to wait for a warrant," DuPree warned.

"Not if we get an invitation," Charlie said.

DuPree groaned.

"Trust us, bro," Gordon piped in.

"Bro?" DuPree nearly gagged.

"It'll work. Need to go now, Detective," Nancy added, reaching over and ending the call. She pulled into the driveway and stopped in front of the tall metal gate. She honked the horn lightly.

"Stay out of sight, guys, I'm supposed to be alone," Nancy warned, looking toward the house.

Several seconds went by. "She's looking out the window," Nancy whispered through sealed lips. "All she can see is my outline, and I'm trying to look shorter."

"Gordon knows how to do that," Charlie whispered.

"Careful, one-armed man. I've got a gun," Gordon replied.

"Boys. Stay on task," Nancy mumbled.

Another half minute passed. "Get ready. The gates are opening."

From where he sat on the floor in the back, Charlie could barely see the top of the garage roof as Nancy eased the Nissan forward.

"She bought it!" Nancy whispered. "Sheila's opening the garage door. A light came on in there. Scrunch up against the driver's side panel and stay down until I give the word."

Charlie heard a faint mechanical buzz, saw the overhead door, then, as Nancy drove into the garage, noticed rows of large white cabinets along the passenger-side wall of the double garage interior. "No Mustang or SUV," Nancy whispered. "Just a big green Mercedes to my left."

"Just?" Gordon whispered.

"She's closing the garage door," Charlie whispered, watching and listening as the overhead door cycled back down. He reached up and grabbed the handle to the rear compartment sliding side door, ready to move.

"Quiet!" Nancy uttered. "I'm turning on my lapel camera now."

Only a few seconds went by before Charlie heard Sheila's voice.

"What the hell are you doing here, Melinda? I told you to dump the Nissan before you come back for the rest of your money. Don't tell me Henry's sister wasn't home."

Nancy waited silently, her arms crossed to hide the pistol below her left arm.

"Roll down that fucking window and answer me!" Sheila yelled. Charlie heard footsteps on the concrete floor as the woman walked out into the garage.

"Now!" Nancy whispered harshly, throwing her door open.

Charlie slid open the back door, covered by Gordon, who had his pistol out and up.

"Shit!" Sheila yelled, bolting around the front end of the Mercedes, racing for the open door leading into the house.

"Halt! Police officer!" Nancy ordered. She was out of the van a second before Charlie, moving down the passenger side of the Mercedes, chasing after Sheila.

"Gun!" Nancy yelled, ducked down below the high-end sedan.

Two gunshots echoed into the garage, accompanied by shattering glass.

Charlie circled around the back of the Mercedes as Gordon moved forward and took a position by the bullet-pocked windshield of the German car. Nancy was crouched below the hood, already on her handheld, calling for DuPree's team to close in.

Charlie edged along the interior wall of the garage, approaching the door leading into the house from an angle, pistol aimed at the opening. He was relying on the Beretta now—a shotgun was no weapon for someone who could only use one arm effectively.

"Cover me," Nancy replied, slipping around the front end of the Mercedes, pistol aimed at the interior. "Laundry room just inside," she called out, advancing to the opening. "I hear running."

"Can't see anyone beyond," Gordon said.

Charlie noted two shell casings on the floor, established that Sheila was using a self-loader 9 mm pistol, then moved to the door. He looked inside before signaling Nancy with a nod.

She inched forward, low, and worked her way through the tiny laundry room to the next doorway, which led into a much larger space.

Charlie followed, taking a position on the opposite side of the doorway. Taking a quick look inside, he realized this was one of those updated houses with the kitchen and living room all in one. There was a wall to his right lined with big stainless steel appliances interrupted by counter space and a double sink. This area was separated from the rest of the room by one of those islands topped with some kind of stone, probably granite. Beyond, he could see a big interior space with couches and chairs, and a set of French doors leading to a patio or backyard. The doors were closed. He pointed toward them and Nancy shook her head.

"Could she be hiding behind that island thing?" Charlie whispered.

"Guess I'll find out," she whispered back. "You guys give me some cover."

Gordon came up behind and tapped her on the shoulder, then took a position where he could watch beyond Charlie's field of view. Charlie covered the right side of the room.

Nancy moved into the room quickly, at a crouch, stopping at the near end of the island. She looked to either side, shook her head, then raced toward a big wooden table and chairs in a dining nook. As she moved, she kept her weapon aimed at the blind spot at the far end of the island. She took a position at the interior corner of the nook and nodded toward Gordon. He slipped in and looped around the kitchen side of the island, covering the patio door area. Charlie followed, stopping at the close end of the island.

From where he was now, Charlie could survey the entire space. Along the front of the house was a long, wide hallway, with the main entrance door halfway down on the left. Across from that entrance were stairs leading up. Way over to his right at the back of the building was another hallway, but from his angle he couldn't see what lay beyond.

"Charlie, stay here and cover the stairs and the hall to your right in case she tries to come up behind us or circle around and make for the patio," Nancy whispered. "Gordon and I will head down the hall on my side and clear the ground floor."

"Copy." Charlie nodded, aiming his Beretta at the hall to his right. Once they were around the far corner, he could safely risk shooting in that direction, if necessary.

Gordon and Nancy worked their way down the street-side hall, bypassing the stairs leading up for the moment. They disappeared around the far corner of the passage. Now Charlie had both directions to cover, looking back and forth, but keeping his weapon aimed at the hall to his right.

A few minutes later, Nancy came into view from the patio-side hall, having circled the ground floor.

She hurried over to join him. "Like I thought, the hall goes all the way around," she whispered. "We cleared the ground-floor rooms and couldn't find any sign of her. I just passed a duplicate set of stairs leading up, and Gordon is watching them now. There isn't any sign of a basement and she didn't go out any windows, so she's got to be up on the second floor somewhere—unless there's also an attic."

Charlie nodded as they moved toward the set of stairs opposite the front entrance. "We'll have to root her out," he said softly. "She'll either open fire while we're coming up, or try to slip down the back stairs."

"And meet up with Gordon," Nancy replied. "You want to wait for SWAT?"

"And give her more time to up-gun or set up a trap? I'm guessing she's going to shoot it out," Charlie responded. "I'd like to take her alive, if possible, and maybe have the chance to get a few more answers. The feds would probably appreciate that as well. But it's your call. Either way, I've got your back."

"Then let's roll, Charlie. We've taken enough crap from this bitch."

"You still recording this?" He grinned, taking a covering position so she could move up the steps. There was a landing halfway up, then the stairs reversed direction.

"Hell no," she whispered harshly, looking down at the small camera just to make sure it really was turned off.

Nancy kept her service pistol aimed up the stairwell as she took a quick look. Satisfied, she inched up the steps, hugging the wall, pistol directed toward the top. Charlie followed, covering any potential hiding place. She was almost to the first landing when something heavy rolled and thumped down the stairs, landing right in front of her on the platform.

"Grenade!" Charlie yelled.

"Get down," Nancy pushed him back, then dove down onto the device.

Cursing, Charlie flattened as best he could, covering his head with his arms.

A few seconds went by before there was a muffled bang, then a quick gunshot from somewhere higher up, on the opposite side of the house. Charlie flinched, then looked up at Nancy. She raised up onto her elbows and stared down at the grenade with eyes as big as a horse's. There was a gray smudge on the front of her jacket. She sat up quickly and patted at the smudge, which was smoking slightly.

Charlie stood, looked at the round M-67 grenade, then cursed. "Pin's out, no spoon. It's a practice grenade, a damned diversion."

Then he remembered the gunshot. He raced past Nancy, then stopped at the open doorway at the top of the stairs and peeked around the corner. Ahead was a narrow passage that led to a central hallway that branched toward opposite ends of the house. The other stairwell was somewhere to his right or left, branching off a room or landing down that hall.

Charlie moved quickly forward, and at the junction looked left. There were two closed doors facing the hall on either side, which ended at a wall. Checking to the right down that passage, he saw another set of doors, on opposite sides of the hall, like before. The first door on his left was open. *That must lead to the other set of stairs*, he deduced, advancing carefully.

He could hear someone breathing through that open doorway, so he proceeded as quietly as possible. The floor was oak, highly polished, but didn't creak at all despite his weight. Reaching the doorjamb, he crouched low and glanced inside. There was another open door on the opposite wall, and beyond a small landing and the other set of stairs leading down. Just inside the room from that entrance he saw a smear of blood on the hardwood floor. It formed a faint, darkening red trail that led around the foot of the bed, which was positioned along the right-hand wall. It didn't take any brain power to deduce that Sheila had been shot and was now hiding behind the bed. The bed was high off the floor, and he could see some of the bare floor beneath it.

A dangerous idea suddenly came into his head, and it might just work. After a quick check on the position of the dresser mirror, seeing it wouldn't ruin his plan, Charlie came into the room, walked up within ten feet of the bed, then turned away, his back toward where he thought Sheila was hiding. From her position on the floor beside the bed, she could easily see his feet—facing away from the bed.

Keeping his feet and legs still, he turned around as much as he could from waist up, looking back toward the bed, with his pistol up, over his left shoulder, aiming backward. It was awkward, but if she was watching . . . Taking a deep breath, he decided to go for it.

"Gordon! Where'd she go?" he said clearly.

Sheila rose to her knees, intending on shooting him in the back, then realized she'd been tricked. "Oh shit!" she gasped just as Charlie fired, striking her in the gun-hand shoulder. Sheila screamed in pain, dropping her pistol onto the bed.

Charlie spun around, holstered his Beretta, then grabbed the pistol as the woman slumped back against the wall, writhing in pain.

"What the hell?" Gordon yelled, stepping into the room, weapon up.

"Huh?" Charlie responded, his ears ringing and his eyes watering from the gun blast so close to his head. "I can't hear you."

Trying to shake off the momentary hearing loss, Charlie stepped back and placed Sheila's pistol on a sturdy oak dresser, never taking his eyes completely off the woman beside the bed.

"Yeah, gunfire indoors makes a hell of a racket." Gordon saw Sheila gripping her bloody shoulder. "What's this? Hit her in the shoulder? You were less than ten feet away. You're the one who's losing his touch, Charlie."

Gordon put his pistol back in his holster and walked around the bed to have a closer look at Sheila, who was curled up in the fetal position now. "Hey, I was the one who shot her first," Gordon complained.

Charlie heard that. "Glad I'm not the only one who can't shoot straight at the moment. I wanted her alive," Charlie said. He heard footsteps behind him and saw Nancy come into the room. She looked a little disoriented as she approached, fumbling twice before she could secure her pistol in its holster.

Nancy saw Sheila lying there on the floor, and managed a smile. "Damaged, but alive. Good."

Charlie stepped over, wrapped his arms around Nancy gently and pulled her close. "I can't believe what you did for me down there. Or maybe I can."

"Gina would have killed me if I'd have let you die," Nancy whispered. "Besides, I'm still the only one wearing a vest."

"What did I miss?" Gordon asked, his eyes still on Sheila, who was cussing in Navajo, one hand on her bloody shoulder, the other on her thigh.

Nancy cleared her throat, gave Charlie a kiss on the cheek, then stepped out of his hug and reached for the radio at her waist. "This is Sergeant Medina. The building is clear and the subject is down with multiple gunshot wounds. Send EMTs to the second floor."

"Already on it!" called DuPree, who was running noisily up the stairs. The detective came into view, weapon out, then saw Sheila, who'd managed to sit up, her back to the wall. Gordon looked over his shoulder as two armed officers came up the other set of stairs.

"That your dummy grenade, Charlie?" DuPree grumbled, nodding toward the staircase.

"Naw, it's Sheila's," Charlie said softly, reaching out and giving Nancy's hand a squeeze. "Thanks again."

Chapter Twenty-four

It was two in the morning and Charlie and Gordon were seated in Detective DuPree's cubical at the downtown station. In walked Nancy with Lola Tso, who was wearing baggy jeans, unlaced black high-top athletic shoes, a blue jersey with the number twelve, and a gray hoodie. With no makeup and her black hair cut shorter than Gordon's, she'd pass for a boy until someone got really close.

Charlie and Gordon stood.

"*Yáaťééh*," Charlie greeted in Navajo. "Good to see you again, Ms. Tso," he added, offering her his chair.

Lola smiled and sat down, her head lowered. "Thank you, Mr. Henry."

Nancy remained standing beside DuPree's desk so Gordon stepped out, grabbed a chair from the empty cubical, and brought it over. "Sergeant?" he said.

"You and Charlie take the chairs. I'm too tired to sit," she responded, then glanced across the big office, which was almost empty this time of day.

"Nancy told me all you two have done to protect me, going after Sheila and Clarence, and I wanted to thank you both. I never intended for any of this to happen," Lola said softly, her voice a little shaky. "So many have been hurt. Still, I'm anxious to learn the rest of the story."

"Together we can fill in all the gaps, I hope," Nancy said. "Here comes Detective DuPree, he's been meeting with federal law enforcement officers."

After brief introductions, Lola finally began to describe what she'd gone through. "As you already know, I was taking college classes and dating Jerry; Jerry Benally. After a few weeks together he took me to meet his boss, Clarence Fasthorse, at the Piñon Mesa Steakhouse. It was about eight thirty at night, and Clarence's mother was there too. Sheila was half owner, but Clarence was the manager, Jerry told me. I was very polite, but Sheila was rude, disrespecting me, and Jerry too, like we didn't even belong at the same table with them."

"How'd you feel about that?" Nancy asked.

"I kept my cool, but as soon as I had the chance I asked Jerry to take me home, saying I had an early class. I didn't, it was a Friday. Nobody cared, so we left."

"On the way to my apartment Jerry and I had a big argument. I told him that if they disrespected me they were disrespecting him too. How could he work for someone who treated their people like that?"

"What did Jerry say he did? What was his job?" DuPree asked.

"That he was a buyer, bringing in supplies and filling orders for Clarence. But he never said exactly what it was, really. It sounded like bullshit to me, and I guess I suggested that he was one of those gophers who ran errands and stuff," Lola said.

"He got pissed, said I was wrong, and that Clarence was celebrating his mom's birthday next week and that he was invited. He'd bring me along and see that I was treated right this time. He explained that Mrs. Ben—that's what he called her—was having a few business problems and that she'd taken it out on me—a stranger," Lola explained.

DuPree shrugged. "Okay, so it was at this subsequent party that you managed to come into possession of the turquoise squash blossom—the one that triggered the shootout at FOB Pawn."

"No need to be polite, Detective. I slipped away from the party, went into the bitch's bedroom, and found the necklace in a big jewelry cabinet. I had it in my purse when I left. It was Sheila's fault. She'd started dissing me from the minute I came into her house, whispering to me even before I took off my jacket that I was a slut and that she didn't want to see me in her house again after tonight. She said she'd been checking up on me, and she had a reputation to protect."

"So the next morning you brought the squash blossom into our shop and pawned it," Charlie concluded.

Lola nodded. "How was I supposed to know that she'd had her people steal it from that silversmith's grave, like some kind of trophy?"

"Her people?" DuPree asked.

"Yeah, the same men that were carjacking people on the Rez

and around the Four Corners," Lola answered. "Jerry was part of that. By then he'd told me what he really did."

"Why was it a trophy?" Gordon pressed. "That particular piece of jewelry."

"Because the dead guy, Buck, had really screwed her over on some job sometime in the past. Then, a few months ago, he'd begun to blackmail her after he'd had a losing streak at one of the casinos. It was about something that happened between them a few years ago—connected to that job she lost. I never found out the details. Sheila had Buck killed after that, you know."

"Who told you about the murder?" Charlie asked. "Jerry?"

"Yeah. He'd been the driver for some woman named Melinda the night it happened. He'd dropped her off outside the tribal casino where Buck was gambling. Later that night, Melinda weaseled her way into Buck's car, then shot him and dumped his body in a ditch. Jerry picked her up after that and brought her back to the city while some others got rid of Buck's car."

"Why would Jerry tell you he helped kill someone?" Nancy asked.

Lola shrugged. "He was really into me. I guess he wanted to show me how important he was."

"How'd Sheila find out who took the squash blossom?" DuPree asked.

"I was the only outsider at her party, and everyone else was afraid of her. She called Jerry and told him to get it back by the end of the day, or she'd sic Melinda on me—then him," Lola said, looking from DuPree to Nancy.

"So Jerry called you?" Charlie offered.

"Yeah, but I had my cell phone off because I was in class, so I had to text him back. I told him the necklace was at your shop and I would try and get it back that afternoon. I didn't tell him I'd already thrown away the damn claim ticket. But by then, I was getting worried. Jerry said he had to get the necklace back, one way or the other, and that I should get lost for a few days and not tell anyone where I was, just in case. Sheila was pissed and when she was pissed she got violent. I knew that already, so I just drove around, parking sometimes, waiting for his call that he had it back. By that time, I'd heard about the shooting at your shop, so I knew I was screwed. I had to drop out of sight."

DuPree looked over at Nancy, who nodded, then to Charlie and Gordon. "That confirms the final motive for Buck's death—and is consistent with the expensive jewelry purchases the restaurant was supposedly making. You guys have any questions?"

"Did you slip up and call Jerry later for some reason? He came looking for you at that woman's apartment. Her name was . . . Didi?" Gordon prodded.

"No. Jerry must have remembered me saying her name at one time or the other. Didi Bonner was my friend when we were both working the streets. She got shot trying to hide me," Lola said, tears forming in her eyes.

"Now that's over and you're safe," Nancy assured. "Are we done here, Detective?" she asked DuPree.

DuPree nodded. "For now. However, I'll need everyone to come in tomorrow morning to sign their statements. Needless to say, don't any of you leave town. Do you have a safe place to stay tonight, Ms. Tso?"

She nodded. "Yes, and I'll have someone watching over me," she responded. "I'll be very safe."

Charlie looked over at Nancy, who mouthed the word "Mike."

Lola noticed the action and smiled. "It's Mike Schultz. I think you've all met him."

DuPree rolled his eyes. "Mike the . . ." then stopped, seeing Nancy shake her head.

"Yeah, we know the guy," Gordon said with a weary smile.

Charlie woke up and looked over at the clock. It was six in the morning and someone was in the kitchen, running water and clinking dishes. But this was his place and he'd come home alone.

Reaching under his pillow, he brought out his backup Beretta, slipped off the covers, and stepped silently onto the carpet. He listened closely, barely breathing, and could swear he heard the coffeepot perking.

Step by silent step he worked his way down the hall, feeling his way along the hardwood floors barefooted. Ahead, there was a light on in the kitchen.

He was halfway across the living room when he heard a familiar deep voice coming from the kitchen.

"You buy good coffee, Charlie, but where do you keep your sugar?"

Lowering the pistol to his side, Charlie stepped into the doorway. "Leroy Williams?"

The broad-shouldered black man was wearing a dark suit, no tie, and was sitting at the kitchen table, coffee mug in hand.

"You can call me Tyler Jackson from now on, Mr. Henry. I'm with the FBI." He slid a gold shield across the table.

Charlie shook his head, looked down at the badge, then thumbed the safety on the Beretta and placed it on the table. "So you're a Full-Blooded Indian."

Jackson laughed. "Yeah, I hear that whenever I work on tribal land. I thought I'd drop by and answer whatever questions might still be bugging you this morning. In exchange for the coffee, of course."

"I guess I should be a little pissed at you right now," Charlie said, then walked over and poured himself a mug. He leaned back against the counter, watching the agent as he smelled the aroma of Italian roast.

Charlie took a sip of coffee. "You tried to help my brother. I'm guessing you were the one who called DuPree and told him about the guys planning on working over Al at the warehouse."

Jackson nodded. "Had to text my handler and hope he could relay the info fast enough. Didn't know you were listening in at the time."

"How long did you know there was a bug in Clarence's SUV?"

"I didn't, not until Melinda discovered it yesterday afternoon. That's when Sheila decided to produce that little *revenge is best served cold* conversation, hoping you were listening in," Jackson added.

"Yeah, we picked up on that. Sounded too rehearsed," Charlie replied.

"Sorry. Her script, not mine."

"So what happened to the bug? We never quite got around to removing it," Charlie pointed out.

Jackson smiled. "Melissa got rid of it before she left the last time. By the way, don't tell anyone in law enforcement about that. It could hurt the prosecution."

"No problem," Charlie replied. He thought about it for a moment. "You were undercover all this time trying to break up the vehicle theft operation?"

The agent nodded. "Unfortunately, my work had to be kept from the locals until this morning. My supervisors were afraid the Night Crew might have a law enforcement informant. The good thing is that I was Clarence's security so I didn't have to take part in any actual carjackings. I got to spend time with him and Sheila during their planning, however. The hard part was learning the names and identities of their Mexican buyers. Most of that information was gathered at the southern end of the pipeline."

"I understand there were some Mexican honchos that escaped the roundup," Charlie said, taking a seat across the table from Tyler. "What made your people finally decide to move in and make the arrests?"

"You and your buddy Gordon. You two had whittled away so many of the New Mexico operatives that the operation was about to shut down anyway. The Mexican people were upset, already looking for new sources of product. Our people had to get what they could."

"New Mexico was running low on car thieves?" Charlie asked with a smile.

"Right. Imagine that."

"Did anyone, Clarence or Sheila, ever say anything about killing Cordell Buck?" Charlie asked, wondering just how close the undercover agent had been.

"Not a damned thing. I didn't know about the connection or why they wanted that squash blossom back until I was briefed by Detective DuPree a few hours ago. Sorry."

"Still, I'm betting you were the one who tried to warn us about Melinda Foy last night," Charlie said, sure of the answer already.

"Yeah, but I wasn't able to get free to text until I dropped off Sheila at her home. Until that moment I'd ruled out Melinda completely. Clarence only spoke of her in sexual terms so I never considered her a threat or had her background traced."

Charlie nodded. "Same with us. But at least we figured out someone was making a move and who the likely target was. That gave us enough lead time to set the trap."

Jackson leaned back in the chair, stretched, then yawned. "You guys are great at psyching people out. You should consider law enforcement. But not the Bureau, okay?" Jackson stood, placed his mug in the sink, and reached out to shake Charlie's hand. "Time to go. Thanks for the coffee."

"Thanks for breaking in and making a pot," Charlie replied. "And for filling in the gaps."

"Hey, if you ever need a lock picked . . ." Jackson answered with a grin, reaching into his pocket and bringing out his card.

"Who knows, maybe someday," Charlie said, taking the business card. "Mind if I tell Gordon about you?"

Jackson shook his head. "Just him, okay? I may be working this area again one of these days." The Bureau agent stepped into the living room, then stopped and turned around. "Want me to lock up on the way out?"

Charlie laughed, shrugged, and stood there sipping his coffee as the agent left.

He looked at the clock above the fireplace. "Damn, six thirty already." Walking back into the bedroom, Charlie picked up his cell phone from the nightstand and called Gordon.

The phone rang six times. "Hey, guy, now that you're awake, how about joining me for breakfast at the Range in, say, forty-five minutes? I'm buying. You'll never guess who I ran into this morning in my kitchen."